Praise

"*Jazzed* suffuses the eroticism of Highsmith and the intensity of Ellroy in an ingenious gender-swapped take on the Leopold & Loeb case. In her lovers/killers, Will Reinhardt and Dolly Raab, Jill Dearman creates an unforgettable duo brimming with murderous passion and lusting for revenge on the society which won't accept them."
STEVEN POWELL, AUTHOR OF *LOVE ME FIERCE IN DANGER: THE LIFE OF JAMES ELLROY*

"Like some brilliant amalgamation of Patricia Highsmith's best work, Mary McCarthy's *The Group* and the Jazz Age tabloid-crime musical *Chicago*, *Jazzed* is a frenetic, scary, erotic, funny and darkly moving thrill ride with two mismatched anti-heroines who completely break the mold of their time and place—the elite Jewish intelligentsia of Roaring Twenties New York City. I thrilled to the twisted love affair and power struggle between Dolly and Wilhemina and how their unambiguous evildoing intersected with the intense sexism, homophobia and anti-Semitism of the world they were born into. Rife with authentic period detail and sizzling with complex and obsessive psychological realism, *Jazzed* will rivet you right through to its haunting final pages."
TIM MURPHY, AUTHOR OF *CHRISTODORA*

"I galloped through this dazzling, incandescent, thrill ride of a novel. Dearman deftly creates a wild, sexy, and poignant world of Jazz Age Sapphic love, sisterhood, prohibition, booze, freedom, Harlem rent parties, Barnard classrooms, and wealthy Jewish homes. When awkward Wilhelmina meets up with a former Brearley classmate, the vivacious Dolly, they improvise on clarinet and piano and spark one of the greatest love stories I've ever read, and what begins as a passionate flirtation turns into a dangerous obsession. Dolly is obsessed with danger, crime stories, and the thrill of becoming a criminal herself; Will is obsessed with Dolly and will do anything for her. As their love deepens and they try to carve out a public life for themselves, their mistakes multiply, and they become reckless. What will happen to our complicated, riveting lovers? Equal parts thriller, lesbian pulp sex romp, and literary queer history, Dearman's novel will leave you panting for more."
CARLEY MOORE, AUTHOR OF *THE NOT WIVES*

Praise

"*Jazzed* suffuses the eroticism of Highsmith and the intensity of Ellroy in an ingenious gender-swapped take on the Leopold & Loeb case. In her lovers/killers, Will Reinhardt and Dolly Raab, Jill Dearman creates an unforgettable duo brimming with murderous passion and lusting for revenge on the society which won't accept them."

STEVEN POWELL, AUTHOR OF *LOVE ME FIERCE IN DANGER: THE LIFE OF JAMES ELLROY*

"Like some brilliant amalgamation of Patricia Highsmith's best work, Mary McCarthy's *The Group* and the Jazz Age tabloid-crime musical *Chicago*, *Jazzed* is a frenetic, scary, erotic, funny and darkly moving thrill ride with two mismatched anti-heroines who completely break the mold of their time and place—the elite Jewish intelligentsia of Roaring Twenties New York City. I thrilled to the twisted love affair and power struggle between Dolly and Wilhemina and how their unambiguous evildoing intersected with the intense sexism, homophobia and anti-Semitism of the world they were born into. Rife with authentic period detail and sizzling with complex and obsessive psychological realism, *Jazzed* will rivet you right through to its haunting final pages."

TIM MURPHY, AUTHOR OF *CHRISTODORA*

"I galloped through this dazzling, incandescent, thrill ride of a novel. Dearman deftly creates a wild, sexy, and poignant world of Jazz Age Sapphic love, sisterhood, prohibition, booze, freedom, Harlem rent parties, Barnard classrooms, and wealthy Jewish homes. When awkward Wilhelmina meets up with a former Brearley classmate, the vivacious Dolly, they improvise on clarinet and piano and spark one of the greatest love stories I've ever read, and what begins as a passionate flirtation turns into a dangerous obsession. Dolly is obsessed with danger, crime stories, and the thrill of becoming a criminal herself; Will is obsessed with Dolly and will do anything for her. As their love deepens and they try to carve out a public life for themselves, their mistakes multiply, and they become reckless. What will happen to our complicated, riveting lovers? Equal parts thrillor, lesbian pulp sex rump, and literary queer history, Dearman's novel will leave you panting for more."

CARLEY MOORE, AUTHOR OF *THE NOT WIVES*

About the Author

Jill Dearman is the author of *Bang the Keys: Four Steps to a Lifelong Writing Practice*; *The Great Bravura*, a novel; *Feminism: The March Toward Equal Rights for Women*, as well as *Queer Astrology for Men* and *Queer Astrology for Women*. She is a part-time professor of writing at New York University, a writing coach, editor, and astrologist.

www.jilldearman.com

JAZZED

JILL DEARMAN

Cover design by Jessica Bell
Interior design by Amie McCracken
Musical note by Fahmi Dwilaksono

A catalogue record for this book is available from the National Library of Australia

For my father, Hal Dearman

Author's Note

Jazzed was inspired by a true crime: the Leopold and Loeb murder case. I have swapped the genders from male to female, and altered the setting from Chicago to New York City. The year of the crime remains the same:1924, as does their Jewish religion. Many historical facts, including a multitude of specifics from news coverage, trial transcripts, psychiatric reports and more have been woven in to *Jazzed*, albeit with names changed. Notably though, I have altered the speech by the true defense attorney (Clarence Darrow) to mirror the particular prejudices against queer women that existed then, and still. Like Nathan "Babe" Leopold and Richard "Dickie" Loeb, Wilhelmina "Will" Reinhardt and Dorothy "Dolly" Raab are precocious teenage geniuses, who hide their sexual relationship from their university and their extremely wealthy families. The young women are also musical prodigies, whereas the young men were focused on law. As in the true story, Will is also an ornithologist, though I have added in her passion for another science of great relevance to the era (and to the present): quantum physics. The final chapters that wrap up Will and Dolly's fates are fictional.

Prologue

Marion Davies. Oh! Marion Davies! Impish blonde curls and upturned nose. What would it be like to run away with a screen starlet? Two fancy-free young women. We'd laugh and hold hands under the table on a luxury ship bound for Europe. Sometime after the rare roast beef and Lady Baltimore cake, we'd retire to our cabin with a full flask. "Oh Will," Marion would whisper. "My Will." Not Wilhelmina, but my own moniker: Will.

Will sat upright, ready to consume every frame of *Little Old New York* and commit each image of Marion to memory. During the comedic short that preceded the main attraction, she looked up at the screen as if immersed by the clowning about. Secretly, she visualized Marion staring into her eyes with longing. No matter the fans and hangers-on who surrounded them, they managed to always exist in their own private world. All they needed was a look, a coded phrase, a surreptitious touch. Will had waited a week for her sister to take her to this screening. And now she was here!

It was during the newsreel reportage of two fly-boys performing a historic mid-air refueling on their biplane, setting an endurance record of thirty-seven hours, that Will first heard the intrusive shuffling. A portly codger in a dark topcoat lowered himself into the seat beside her. How dare he? The Gotham West Cinema must have been half empty. If only she'd placed her book upon the seat, as some women do their handbags. *Nietzsche Contra Wagner*, in

9

the original German. Even in darkness, with only the illumination of the flickering light of the screen, Will could recognize a true Aryan: his light eyes and blond-white hair when he removed his hat. Nietzsche's tirade against Wagner's anti-semitism could have served as a barrier and talisman to ward off this invasive pest.

Will cringed through the first reel of the feature, crossing and uncrossing her legs, hoping she'd kick him into another seat, but he would only nod and smile when she stole glances at him. Now Will could swear the vulture was *purposely* pressing his leg into hers, despite how much room he had. She inched her hips closer to the farthest edge of her seat, careful not to nudge Estelle.

Her sister did not notice. She was too busy whispering to Sanford, her fiancé, completely oblivious to the strange man edging toward her younger sister. They'd made a "friendly" offer to "take her out for some fun." "Join us on our date." Really it was Estelle's way of implying that Will could not find her own companion. She knew nothing of Will's real life, who she *really* was.

Since their lifeless courtship began the year before, they had judged her every move as odd, making it impossible for Will to relax. Yet, with cruel irony, ever since Momma died six months ago, during Will's senior year in high school, Estelle loved to play substitute mother. Unfortunately, Estelle possessed as much maternal instinct as a Kauai wolf spider—notorious for their habit of eating their young.

Will held her breath as the old man lifted his folded-up coat from his lap and placed it purposefully over his left arm. Now, she no longer saw his hand but could feel its reptilian chill on her knee through the lightweight wool of her dress. The creeping nausea in the pit of her stomach alerted her, second by second, to the sensation of his meaty fingers slithering down toward her hemline. This is why girls should wear pants! She hated the unnatural feeling of holding her legs daintily together. But Estelle had insisted she appear ladylike for their night out with her fiancé.

What good was Estelle to her now—or Sanford? If Will alerted them to the mauling, Estelle might make a scene, exposing her to more embarrassment. Or she might doubt the veracity of her claim—even worse! She always held Will suspect. She'd never forget the look on Estelle's face when Will had been playing dress-up with some of Pop's clothes. Will couldn't have been more than ten, Estelle, fifteen. The look on Estelle's face as Will drew a fake mustache on her lip, using Momma's eyebrow pencil. It was as if Will had gunned down the neighbors! Will explained it away as research for a theatrical production, but Estelle snorted and left the room, bidding her to change out of the garish disguise immediately. Estelle refused to believe anything but the worst about her little sister. Will felt trapped on all sides.

Then an idea came to her.

"May I borrow your fan?"

Estelle smiled and opened her pocketbook. As Will flipped open the garish rose-covered bamboo contraption, she saw her sister turn to Sanford and whisper something. She heard her mention her name, "Wilhelmina." Estelle was probably so thrilled by any feminine behavior on Will's part that she simply had to froth at the mouth about it. Meanwhile, after a few cursory swipes of the thing to back up her claim of being overheated, Will managed to lower the fan down to her knee and slide it under the slippery fingers of the old man. She'd been playing dead mouse and now felt ready to escape the cat's paw. With one thrust upward of the fan she managed to spatula his fingers off of her.

Success. Will exhaled silently but held the fan in place through the whole second reel and well into the third to guard against further intrusions. The cinema-going experience could have been a complete delight if Will had only been allowed to experience it alone. She could cross her legs like a man, smoke as many cigarettes as she liked, and lose herself in the pictures and story.

Marion.

Marion filled the screen, costumed in male garb and wearing a Dutch-boy bob in an attempt to impersonate her brother who'd been lost at sea. A burst of ardor made Will sit upright and not give a damn about Estelle or the cretin beside her. She watched as an angry mob hounded Marion, intent on punishing her for ringing a bell and stopping a boxing match mid-fight. How she would love to chase down Marion, pull her off the cobblestone path into a maze of alleyways, and tell her, "It's all right. You're safe with me!"

Will could not believe what she saw next: furious men tied Marion roughly to the whipping post. Will could feel an excitement building in her as the hulking boxer sadistically applied the lash. The on-screen crowd cheered with bloodthirst as they watched Marion's public humiliation. After each lash came close-ups of her pained face. Will wanted to comfort her, rescue her, but also relished in her punishment. The poor lass cried for the whipping to end, but to no avail. At last, her shirt torn to shreds, she released a final cry for mercy: "I'm a girl!" The crowd gasped as the fighter pulled her blouse down to inspect the goods.

The sight of the girl now untied, holding her torn garment against her bosom, weeping as her bare shoulders trembled made Will swoon. In her excitement, the fan must have dropped to the floor, for next thing she knew the old man was bending down and offering it to her. She grabbed it roughly, shot him a sneer and when he tried to lean in closer to her, elbowed him away. She did not want *any* distraction from the screen. Will imagined holding the shaking Marion close to her, whisking her away from the mob on horseback, and then laying her down on a soft blanket of blood-root wildflowers. Will would then remove the tattered shreds of clothing from her abused body, gently but purposefully, never breaking eye contact with the grateful girl. She couldn't wait to get home and slip into bed with these images in mind.

When the film ended, Will excused herself to the restroom, just to get a minute away from Estelle and Sanford. After rinsing her hands, she held the door for an older lady.

"Thank you, dear."

Will nodded and gave her plenty of time to exit. As Will stepped out of the bathroom she knocked right into that horrible old man who'd touched her.

"Oh!" Will said, sliding backwards against the wall.

But he moved his body closer and looked her straight in the face. "Enjoy the picture?"

"Excuse me please," she muttered.

Will could see Estelle and Sanford through the glass of the cinema entrance. She wished only to get to them.

"Excuse me," she repeated and escaped into the new crowd of moviegoers, angry tears rising up in her.

Part I
The Lovers' Pact

Chapter One
Will

Will

lean lines, geometrics, and sharp angles marked the foyer that led to the sitting room. The Raab home was designed to dazzle. Gorgeously decorated in canary yellow and rich vanilla, the interior cried out for a spontaneous party, and it seemed that's what awaited Wilhelmina. Thoughts of her own lifeless house with its heavy furniture and drab colors made Will want to hide behind the glittery gold drapes.

A bunch of old clucks filled the seats. Dolly skated through the maze of them, cracking jokes, swinging her arms around as she came forward to greet Will—all noodly limbs and nervous energy. It was as if a dozen puppeteers were pulling her strings. Dolly's hair shone fair to match her manner, light as a champagne bubble. She tamed her curls into a stylish bob. Her blue eyes did not need any makeup to bring out their radiance, but Dolly apparently knew just how to apply the right amount to wow an audience.

Will remembered her sole encounter with Dolly at Brearley the week of final exams. Dolly had made a deal with some seniors with low academic records to provide stolen answers to tests in exchange for cash and ready access to bootleg liquor. And she'd pulled off her scheme. Everyone buzzed about it.

Will had been sitting out track, weak from a lingering cough, when she noticed Dolly sneak under the bleachers with a lanky basketball player. The girl handed over a wad of bills to Dolly, who slipped it down her gym skirt. She didn't see Dolly pass her anything in return, except, she imagined, a promise. Dolly caught Will's eye as she dashed like an Andean Fox out into the open. Dolly winked, and Will didn't even have time to smile; she was so taken aback.

Will wondered if Dolly would remember her. Probably not. There was no reason to. Dolly vibrated with excitement; Will stiffened around people.

Now, inside her lavish manor, she finally twirled her way over to Will. Before Mrs. Raab could make the formal introduction, Dolly leaned over and whispered in Will's ear, "The bleachers, right? Nod if you remember."

Will felt Dolly's breath on her ear. She nodded.

"You'll keep my secret, won'tcha?"

Dolly spoke so softly that Will strained to hear. But she'd transmitted her message with the speed of a white-throated needletail. So, Dolly *had* noticed her. Someone a cut above the rest like Dolly remembered her after one fleeting encounter. She even saw fit to conspire with Will to keep her secret. Well, well, well! That could mean the mirror Will had been gazing into all these years was distorted, twisted to fit the image of those twits.

Dolly took flight once more as the ancient, stoop-shouldered butler wheeled in a tray of tea and set up the Alfred Meakin pot and china with the floral garland borders. The time on the gold Sunburst clock read 4 p.m.

"Wilhelmina, dear, I hear you can speak nine—or is it ten— foreign languages?" the lady with the bluest hair asked.

"Actually, eleven."

"Ohhh! Is it true you speak Persian? I'm told it takes years to master."

"Well, not if you have a system for mastering linguistics. Technically it's *Old* Persian. Mostly spoken in the southwestern part of the region."

"How exotic!"

Soon they were all dusting off their bits of finishing-school French and Italian on her. She indulged them, while she felt someone tapping her foot under the table. Will looked up, and Dolly made a dozing-off face and rolled her eyes. It was thrilling to be part of a secret communication with someone like Dolly. Will usually detested popular types, but Dolly was changing her mind. Perhaps she shouldn't have judged her so harshly.

Mrs. Raab asked Will, "You study birds, dear?"

"Yes. I'm an ornithologist."

Gloved hands found pruned, lipsticked mouths, in awe of such a colossal word from such a young lady.

"Oh, and what birds are native to New York State?"

"Perdix perdix or the gray partridge," Will recited, paying attention only to the feeling of Dolly's now-bare foot rubbing her ankle. "The Phasianus colchicus, also known as the ring-necked pheasant; Bonasna umbellus or ruffed grouse; Tympanuchus cupido or the greater prairie chicken; and Meleagris gallopavo or wild turkey."

"Well, chicken and turkey I know!" One of the biddies laughed.

"Girls, why don't you play a little duet for the ladies?" Mrs. Raab said. "You brought your clarinet, dear?"

Will nodded.

"I'm not in the mood," Dolly said.

Was she joking, Will wondered, as Dolly sprang out of the room, leaving them all to speculate.

Mrs. Raab approached Will. "She's always full of tricks."

Will stood circled by the hens, with nowhere to retreat. On several chairs, she noticed a small bound book with a gray cover and gold embossed letters bearing the title: *Eugenics, Ethics & Immigrants*.

"What brings you ladies together today?" Will said.

Eugenics cut both ways where the Jews were concerned. It seemed prudent to find out where this crowd stood before broaching the subject. Dolly's father was Jewish; her mother, gentile.

"Oh! Well, we're a sort of de facto local chapter of the Immigration Restriction League," Mrs. Raab said. "It turns out that many of us here on Sutton Place and the whole East Side are passionate about Eugenics."

"I see," Will said. "Is that Prescott Hall's book?"

"Indeed!" another hen piped in. "He helped author the whole Immigration Restriction Act six years ago and right now, we need to ensure that the gates stay closely manned, if not closed altogether."

"Yes, for their own good as well as ours," Mrs. Raab said.

"'Their?'" Will asked carefully. "Which 'their'?"

Mrs. Raab looked at her quizzically, and Will immediately regretted pushing the subject. As an outsider, Will felt a kinship with anyone else deemed an "other," but it was foolish to expect the rich matriarch of the Raab family to feel the same way. Clearly, she felt her charity was enough.

Dolly returned with a pewter beer mug raised high above her head. With the deftness of a magician she slid a coaster under it and sat down at the piano.

"A stein for the Steinway." Dolly giggled, rolling out an arpeggio on the keys. "For tips."

The hens laughed. Will kept her expression neutral and opened her black hard-shell clarinet case with a satisfying *clack*. Dolly scanned the sheet music then stage whispered to Will in a perfect German accent: "Der hert auf dem Felsen. D. 965?"

"Schubert?" Will replied. "Ja!"

The ladies laughed. Suddenly Will was the cut-up. This was a first!

She stood at the ready with her instrument and nodded at Dolly. Dolly's fingers moved lightly across the keyboard, the first few notes almost silent, only to be followed by a rush of thrilled excitement like a fox circling a henhouse, and then—nothing. It was time for Will to begin. She exhaled into a few deceptively logy measures and soon they were together. On the white baby grand, Dolly played with feeling; her surprising lack of artifice made Will's body loosen, so their notes could find each other in the ether and dance together.

The two girls played with classical precision, but as the music rose into an aria, Dolly gave Will a playful look. She could hear her change the tempo just the tiniest bit to quicken Schubert's last hurrah with a bit of swing. Will warbled in time and then noticed one of the ladies cock her head. Dolly must've seen it too, and so they retreated back to coloring inside the lines.

They'd never played together before, but this was jazz! Improvisation. Will had no idea that the classics could be toyed with so mischievously, and with such nuance. During another passionate section of their duet, Dolly gave Will that look again. Will waited to see if she would play another trick, but she didn't. Her eyes softened as she looked at Will, and Will's mouth turned powdery, almost too dry to blow; to compensate, she breathed in deep and let a sultry sound vibrate from her horn.

Dolly responded in kind, allowing her fingers to tap the keys with an extra tingle just one octave lower than the score required. The jazzy twist made Will lean backwards—perhaps two inches, no more—and blow a little higher into the sky, as if their notes could meet in heaven, if there were such a place.

At that moment, Mrs. Raab shot Dolly a nasty look and the two girls returned to the predicted fare. When they completed the piece, Mrs. Raab began to applaud, and the ladies followed with slappy seal claps. Enthusiastic as her hands were, Mrs. Raab maintained those icy eyes.

"Darling, why don't you show Wilhelmina your room?" Mrs. Raab said. "No sense letting us old ladies bore you ..."

"Why yes, let's let the young people be young!"

"All right, Mumsie," Dolly said before flitting off to the south staircase and calling for Will to follow.

The paint glowed sunshine. The brass legs on her canopied bed were shined to a glow. White scalloped easy chairs added elegance, while the leopard print rug heightened the energy in the space, adding a sense of unpredictability. Pennants from football games adorned the walls. White wooden shelves held trophies: Tennis. Riding. Skiing. Ice Skating. Golf. Track and Field. Each golden statuette outsized the next. It seemed there was no sport Dolly didn't excel at. On the adjacent wall hung framed photographs of Dolly performing piano recitals. What a thrill to be within these walls.

It was only that morning her older sister ambushed Will with a demand to put on feminine attire.

"You have a social engagement, remember? It's very important you make friends," Estelle said.

"Important to whom?"

"You and Dolly have a lot in common. You're both Jewish."

"She's half-Jewish," Will corrected her.

"Besides that, you girls are geniuses—IQs over 140. When I ran into Mrs. Raab at their department store last week we both agreed. You two should get to know each other before freshman year begins."

"If we were boys, we would have been skipped ahead to college by now," Will said.

"Why would you want to be a boy?" Estelle asked.

It was almost like a challenge. Her sister stood appalled at Will lounging in her silk trousers, legs spread wide, reading Goethe, barefoot and beholden to no one. Estelle appeared dead as a strangled fowl in her sad brown frock noosed by lackluster pearls. Her sister possessed no taste, no refinement. Who was she to judge?

"You both graduated from Brearley with honors," Estelle said. "They're a very influential family."

Everyone knew who they were. Full German Jews on the paternal side, the Raabs were the first and only Jewish family to purchase a home on Sutton Place in New York City. In the spring of 1921, Erich, who inherited Raab's Department Store from his grandfather, and wife Frances, of Irish-Catholic descent, moved with Dolly and her younger brother Sheffy, from the Fox Meadow section of Scarsdale to Number 16 Sutton Place.

Wilhelm Reinhardt moved Momma, Will, and Estelle two miles south, also to Sutton Place around the same time. Wealthy German Jews were beginning to find their way to the East 50s with little resistance.

"Don't be such a prig. You're a year older than Dolly. She's even more academically advanced than you, Will. You're both starting at Barnard in two weeks, and you could use a friend," Estelle said as Waldek opened the car door. "*Especially* one who's a social butterfly."

"Actually, Estelle, that's a misnomer. Butterflies tend towards solitude, with the rare exception of course, such as the South American Heliconius."

"I thought you were an ornithologist. Now you're an archeologist as well?"

"I think you mean, *entomologist*, one who studies insects, not just arachnids, or spiders."

Estelle ignored the comment and sent her on her way.

But now that she was here at Dolly's, Will felt a certain largesse of spirit towards her sister. Dolly pulled out a silver flask from the pocket of a plaid jumper hanging in her closet.

"Drink?" she offered.

The flask fit Will's hand well, and she could still feel the heat of Dolly's grip on it. The gin went down like syrup. She swigged a few more warming little gulps, pretending to be a pro, and noticed those hands. Almost chubby with dimples you'd see on a toddler, they didn't seem to match those long, restless arms. Will stared at them as Dolly lit up a Chesterfield and passed it to her.

"Sit down," Dolly said from the bed with the quilted silver headboard. "Smoke?"

She nodded and took a puff, a couple of gritty bits of Dolly's lipstick sticking to the cigarette. She rubbed her lips together and let out an embarrassing set of choking coughs.

"Easy, cowgirl," Dolly said. "If you can't handle ..."

"I can handle it." Will handed her back the stick. "But I'd just as soon leave it. I prefer liquor to smoke."

"I'll finish this one. Have some more gin."

It felt sharp on Will's tongue after the smoke, but she was getting used to it.

"You're really fine on the keys," Will said.

"Stride baby, stride."

"Hmm?"

"Stride piano—it's a jazz style. Here, I'll show you."

Dolly let the cigarette hang from the corner of her mouth and from under her bed she pulled out a cardboard cut-out of a piano keyboard.

"You buy that?" Will asked.

"No, silly. I made it. Cardboard and black ink."

"Impressive."

Dolly sprang up and whirled over to the Victrola in the corner of her room, flipped through her discs as she puffed, and picked out a James P. Johnson record.

"The old man hates jazz. Gotta practice in secret," she said with an eye roll. "More fun that way. Sometimes I wake up in the middle of the night and can see the music all spread out before me, just waiting for my fingers to bring it to life."

"So you play on this without any sound?"

"I let it simmer in my head, and it comes out even better when I sit down to play for real."

Dolly cranked the volume, pulled up a chair, plunked the paper keyboard on her bed and began "playing" for Will. Dolly's left hand mimed with lightning speed. She'd play a four-beat pulse with a single bass note, octave, seventh or tenth interval on the first and third beats, and a chord on the second and fourth beats. It was the super-rhythmic "oom-pah" sound that Will had heard on Fats Waller records.

"You're pretty good yourself," Dolly said. "We should go check out the jazz in Harlem together, don'tcha think?"

She remembered how she'd squirmed over meeting Dolly. How wrong she'd been.

"Sure," she said. "How'd you learn this technique?"

"I'm a genius, remember?" Dolly laughed. "Besides, ragtime plays it too straight. Improvisation is sweeping the nation."

This Johnson fellow on the record had a lively, jumpy sound. Will could hear why Dolly was so excited.

"Atta girl," Dolly laughed when Will turned the flask over to show there was not a drop left.

"You go to Harlem a lot?"

"I had a gal uptown who showed me the lay of the land." Dolly winked. "You know what a bulldagger is?"

She felt her cheeks flush. Of course she'd heard it. A woman who dressed and acted like a man and liked other women. Will nodded

"Is she ... does she ... live in Harlem?"

"You trying to find out her race, Ace?" Dolly laughed. "Yeah. C.C.'s Black. Or more like what they call 'high yellow.' She really knew about jazz. Great set of pipes, and might delicate moves for a big woman. She told me all about how she learned cabaret routines from her grandmother who toured Europe performing with the pickaninnies."

"The child dancers?"

"Yep. Those dances are supposed to make the southerners all sentimental for the plantation days. Jeez. You know they pretty much bred negroes into slavery. Can you believe that? The master would hop from his white wife's bed to his slave's in the downstairs quarters. He'd have kids who were his—what was the way C.C. put it? Oh yeah—his 'progeny *and* his property.' You know it's amazing that the negroes in this country haven't risen up and staged a revolution. Could you imagine being born a slave? And then being bred like a goddamn animal to breed more slaves so the *massa* has more chattel working for him on the plantation? I mean, think about it, Will. What kind of a savage country is this? Yet it's the negroes who are called savages."

Will nodded, though she honestly hadn't thought much about it before. Dolly surprised her. Behind that symmetrical face, she possessed a radical mind. "You still see her?" she asked.

"Nah, she got rousted by the cops, and nobody seems to know what happened to her. Cops love to raid the joints and it's always gals like C.C. who get the worst treatment. Hey, you know we should go back down there, ask for another round of high tea, and slip a dose of something lethal into one of those old bitch's precious china cups. Wouldn't that be a lark? You could wow them some more with your knowledge of foreign tongues. And me? I can do the slipping in of the poison."

"Poison?"

"Nah, a few crushed sleeping pills. Just enough to make 'em dozy, not kill 'em. But even if it did, what's the loss really?"

"Sure," Will said, attempting nonchalance.

"What, are you scared?" Dolly said.

"No. Scared of what?"

Dolly ignored the question. She slid down to the floor, pulling a well-worn teddy bear from her bed to hug. "Want to play a game?"

"What game?"

"Questions and Commands."

"How do you play?"

"It's a Christmas game I learned from Mumsie. We keep a lid on it around Daddy since Mumsie gave up the cross for him."

"Tell me the rules," Will said, slinking closer to Dolly and impulsively grabbing a fresher-looking stuffed rabbit from the bed.

"The commander bids her subject to answer a question. If the subject refuses or fails to satisfy the commander, she must pay a forfeit ...."

"A forfeit?"

"Follow a command," Dolly answered.

"And if the subject refuses to follow the command?"

"Then she must have her face dirtied beyond recognition by the Commander."

"And I suppose *you* want to be the Commander," Will said.

"It's not a choice. It's my destiny to rule over you."

"How do you figure?" Will said, somehow knowing this to be true.

Dolly lunged at Will, landing her long body on top of her. She made wild attacking sounds as she pounded the stuffed rabbit Will held up as a shield. She sat up then, leaving Will shaking on the floor, hypnotized.

"All right, Teddy," she said, directing her words at the bear. "What do you think of Willsie-poozy? Think she could join our secret little bear-cub club?"

Dolly put the toy's mouth to her ear and opened her eyes wide. Will leaned forward in rapt attention, straining to hear the judgment Teddy would render upon her.

Chapter Two

Will sat at the edge of the Salt Marsh, peering upwards through her field glasses. The way Dolly pounced on her. Why did she do it? Will kept reliving it in her mind. She was probably just playing. Still, the intensity Will felt between them; Dolly must have felt it too. So hard to know; the uncertainty was impossible for Will to shrug off. The distraction of the sticky marsh air helped a bit. She wished she could either see Dolly right this very moment or wipe her from her mind altogether. What was it about this girl?

She caught sight of a Gallinula galeata in her viewfinder. Normally they were hard to spot, given their lack of vocalization. This one had a particularly orange beak, so fiery it made Will blink. She felt a lightness in her chest as she imagined Dolly's symmetrical face—the lively eyes, framed by such harmonious features. She had to take a breath and stop dwelling on Dolly's beauty. It could be the end of her. The galeata flew away, hiding itself in the vegetation.

And it wasn't just her beauty, rather, the alchemy of elements. Dolly possessed superior traits in every category. Except for one. She was far from trustworthy. That much was obvious. Dolly had a sneaky disposition, but even her *bad* side was a perfect match for Will. Ever since she was very young she'd had the same fantasy. Being the abused servant of a beautiful mistress, a Roman Goddess really, from gladiator times. The Goddess would demand she perform some act of madness and Will, barely covered by humble white fabric, would submit. It might involve walking miles barefoot while her mistress, comfortable in a carriage, flicked a riding crop at her, sometimes making contact with flesh, sometimes just frightening Will with the sound, lancing the air with its threat of pain. Will felt every cell in her body moving at hyperactive speed. If she were alone in her bedroom, in the night or early morning, she could relieve the longing. The frustration she felt roiled her and brought a feeling of loneliness with it. She wished she could find a way to soothe herself, but she couldn't. Not today.

Exactly six months since Momma died. Neither Pop nor Estelle remembered, so why should Will—the baby sister—have to remind them? Didn't they care enough to acknowledge the date? She longed to see a Great Blue Heron, Momma's favorite bird. Instead, the sounds of yellow warblers pierced the air, followed by the buzzy-pitched song of the ruby-throated hummingbird. Alone on an August weekday morning, Will imagined herself the last person on Earth, living at peace with her bird companions.

As if in response to her thoughts, she heard a raspy twill. Will pointed her field glasses downward toward the mud and spotted a salt marsh sparrow probing the marsh vegetation, probably foraging for aquatic invertebrates. She could feel the familiar lump develop in her throat. If Momma were still alive, she'd run home to describe her findings. But Momma was gone.

As Momma's symptoms worsened over her last months, it was a relief for Will to see her drift off to sleep. The anguish caused by the rise in blood pressure, the convulsions, and the swelling in her legs from the dropsy—too horrific to watch. Will hated herself for being so weak. Despite her ability to shoot a bird on sight— for taxidermy and research—she shrank from the horrors of the human body. Will herself had been sickly as a child and Momma had coddled her; in return she wanted to be there for Momma. Every day Will faced the irrational fear of blood. Momma's Bright's Disease did not cause bleeding. Still — what if?

Once Momma's breathing shifted to the sounds of slumber, Will would crack open her science journals in search of new treatment modalities and perhaps even an overlooked potential cure. Will's research could not keep up. Momma's kidney nephritis grew more acute until one morning the end finally came.

After the funeral and sitting Shiva, she fully expected Estelle to suddenly take on the mother role, ill-suited for it as she was. In fact, Will had all sorts of contemptuous rebuffs planned should she try and tell her what to do or pretend to nurture her. Instead, Estelle focused her attention on her fiancé. Sanford stood next in line to be partner in his father's formidable legal firm. The two wealthy families approved of the match, and so it was done. Now all that remained was a wedding, planned for the following June, and until then a series of parties to celebrate the upcoming nuptials. It seemed indecent given Momma's recent death, but Estelle and Pop both claimed it would have given Momma such joy. The thought of relatives clucking over Estelle and pitying Will made her wince. She wished she had a friend.

Dolly could be that friend, and oh what an impression she'd make. A real charmer! But Will had to be careful. After so many years without companions, Will had finally begun to overcome some shyness in high school. Her acne cleared up; she'd taken to making dirty jokes in foreign languages and teaching them to the girls, and it was Judie Schneider who honed in on her. She was even so direct as to say, "Don't you get it? I really like you, Will." Will replayed that line over and over in her head every free moment she had. Alone in bed before sleep she would visualize them naked together. Working herself up to the point of high arousal, she would scream Judie's name into her pillow.

That one night Judie slept over they held each other and looked into each other's eyes in the dark. Will had so many times imagined reciting poems from her 1900 edition of Natalie Barney's *Quelques Portraits-Sonnets de Femmes*. But when the opportunity came, she looked at the words on the page and could not move her lips. Finally, it was Judie who put a hand on Will's cheek and Will, feeling as if her fantasy was coming to life, kissed Judie, and to her delight, Judie responded in kind. Will grew so enraptured and must have taken it too far; that was the end of any friendship. Will didn't know what she did wrong exactly, but she knew she had gotten too aggressive somehow. Judie wasn't mean after that, just distant. Will could have sworn the other girls started to look at her with secret knowledge and a new level of contempt.

Having Dolly as her ally would make Barnard so much easier. She wouldn't need to defend herself against the female mob. But she would have to be careful. If she misread Dolly as she had misread Judie, she could destroy the delicate bond they were developing. Thanks to Dolly, she was beginning to feel confident— socially confident—for the first time ever! If, as a close compatriot of Dolly, Will gained popularity and acceptance, then she could finally relax. She wouldn't have to worry about who was whispering what behind her back.

Bird-brain. Loony-bird. These names had followed her for years. As Will's college entry approached she thought perhaps the things that made her different from other girls would serve as an asset. Will always felt as if she were putting on a Halloween mask when she tried to apply makeup. Instead of frittering away hours on such trivialities, she spent her time doing what stimulated her: studying birds, languages, music.

She had already distinguished herself as an ornithologist by discovering a rare warbler in its habitat the previous summer. The varied ways birds learn songs, the undiscovered aspects of their biology, all these things fascinated Will and gave her a sense of peace and self-mastery.

Will moved toward the mucky water, field notebook in hand, ready to jot down the characteristics of the black-bellied plover in her sights. She thought of going back to the car to get her rubber wading boots then remembered she'd subwayed it up to Inwood on the Eighth Avenue line.

She cleaned up in the restroom for the train ride home but couldn't quite slough off the thickest layers of mud from her skin. A bunch of high-school-age kids were playing around across from her, the boys teasing the girls with randy jokes. It was not yet rush hour, and besides, this far uptown in the middle of August, the trains were never crowded. A red-haired boy in a blue-checked suit took the challenge of another boy and began to walk on his hands. Will tapped alternating foot taps to calm herself. *Left, one; Right, two …* The girls tittered and cautioned him to be careful, and Will pulled her legs under her, worried he just might land in her lap.

Sure enough, the jostling of the car threw him off balance and his feet flew downwards, almost socking Will in the jaw.

"Sorry …" He laughed.

She could see he was a little taken aback as he turned himself upright. Was she a male or a female? Colored or white? In her dirty birding clothes of old trousers and Pop's flannel fishing shirt, plus the mud stuck to her pores—she must've appeared quite a sight. When the boy returned to his gang and she heard them say things like, "What is *that* supposed to be? Must be one of those he-she-what-is-it types" she was reminded of every single rotten kid who'd mocked her as a child. Barnard would be different. Will would enter and leave at the top of her class. She would not need the approval of these ruffians. Still, she could feel the tears well in her eyes and she hated herself for being so sensitive. Mercifully, she'd learned long ago to stop her tears before they fell by focusing on an intellectually stimulating subject.

While they laughed Will reached into her canvas satchel and pulled out her copy of Nietzsche's *Beyond Good and Evil*. Chapter One. Page One. She read to herself the late German's words:

"Supposing truth is a woman—what then?"

When she returned home, she announced to her father and Estelle that she wanted Dolly to be her roommate. Could this be arranged?

Chapter Three
Dolly

Dolly took Will's hand and pulled her behind the beat-up old Willys Automobile parked on Second Avenue.

"Are you sure this is all right?" Will asked.

Dolly laughed. What a kidder! "I'm sure it's all wrong which makes it all right."

Will blushed, and Dolly knew she was hooked.

"You've got the nimble way with handling birds," she said. "You use the nail file, okay?"

She could see Will was nervous by the way she used the nail file to pick dirt out from under her nails to kill time.

"Awww, jeepers. I can do it if you're scared."

"I'm not scared. Stand up. The coast isn't clear," Will said.

Dolly saw the frumpy mum pushing a pram and coming their way. "Pretend we're having an intense conversation."

"How did you know she was going to murder him?" Will said.

Go, Willsie. A fellow crime lover.

"Well, I just had a sense. The way she turned on him in the diner. It was as if she'd finally snapped ..."

Once the pram lady had passed they doubled over laughing.

"Come on," Dolly said. "Let's follow her."

They walked a good six yards behind her, stopping to duck behind mailboxes and streetlamps. The playground was pretty active and likely to clear out during lunch for the little brats.

31

Dolly watched as a toddler walked hand in hand with an old biddy to the swings. She couldn't help but notice the fresh, clean teddy bear in the kid's carriage. Her own Teddy was in sad shape at this point.

"Wait for me by the gate," Dolly said, nudging Will along.

"Why?"

"Just scram."

Will shrugged and walked away, then Dolly called after her softy: "Pssst, get a load o' me."

When the kid was up in the air, Dolly grabbed the Teddy and quickly sauntered to the gate.

Once out of the park they cracked up and ran back to Dolly's house on a rush of adrenaline.

They spent the rest of the day playing with Dolly's stuffed animals, from her precious Teddy, to the stuffed bunny she loved best, and a host of other cute furry friends she'd picked up here and there.

Dolly and Will had spent every day that week together, and now the crescendo: dinner with the Raabs! Had the sterling and china always been so shiny? It was as if a wire had been tripped inside her brain and suddenly what was once bright seemed even brighter. Colors she hadn't even noticed before—like the gold leaves of the candelabra on the sideboard—had they always contained flecks of red and orange like the sun? Or just tonight?

Even the old folks somehow seemed more pleasing, especially when they laughed. Daddy appeared more alert than usual. Not griping about his bad heart so much. Mumsie really was a dish—and she knew it, all spiffed up and special tonight in her floral dress with the lace overlay. Uncle David waxed rhapsodic about some legal precedent or another. The timbre of his voice pleased Dolly.

Dolly felt an expansion in her chest. Honest to God she couldn't recall the last time she'd felt this. Well, maybe when she sliced the tires in that pompous-ass teacher's Model T! But she'd been mad then too. As she looked around the table, she felt a peaceful sense of blood ties with her family. Of course her brother was not among them. Good thing the little brat Sheffy was staying at his pal's for dinner! Will didn't seem like the type who was much for kids. No maternal instinct there! And Dolly of course would have been happy to ship off the pest to boarding school anytime! Having Will here was like having the sister, the playmate she always wanted.

She could hear an eight-bar intro forming in her head and plunking out keys that mimicked the ding dong of a doorbell. Dolly pressed her leg ever so slightly up against Will's under the table. Will didn't move it away. No sense denying the truth: Will was a hunter too. A real predator. Sure, Dolly had caught her by surprise that first day up in her room after their little concerto. But she could tell Will was biding her time before making a move. She wanted Dolly to be just as enthralled with her. Go figure that! She was no artist's muse like Dolly, but that face! It was stunning like a movie idol's; you just didn't expect it on a girl. That sharp beak, and those thick lips that knew their way around a reed and plenty more, Dolly would just bet.

She'd once kissed a girl on a dare at a slumber party, but it was more like puckering up to a wet spot on a pillow. No oomph. Dolly had tried to teach a few girls how to kiss up in her room, but they just wouldn't relax—and it made her angry to have to do all the work.

And then there was C.C.

They met at The Nest, a cabaret uptown where Dolly's older cousins took her for her sixteenth birthday. When she and the cousins danced close to the stage Dolly caught a glimpse of C.C. playing the role of a jungle savage—a male—hunting down a female, catching her, and passing her along a row of fellow savages in a heavily percussive dance. When it was time for a break, Dolly brought C.C. a cloth napkin from the table, and C.C. winked a thanks to her.

C.C. made it clear she had no interest in "little white girls." Dolly respected her for it. The Raabs and every white family Dolly knew—rich or not so rich—they all thought they stood above the negroes. Why? This was something she could not understand. They accused Dolly of being selfish and full of herself just 'cause she was so pretty, but really Dolly knew she had a bigger vision of the world than any of her so-called "race."

C.C. would mock her, saying Dolly liked slumming with the colored, but then could go back to having the world on a lily-white platter. She was right. Dolly had a lot more breaks and a lot more choices. But she didn't feel like she was slumming when she was with C.C. She was really living, and learning too. Stuff they couldn't teach at Brearley.

It was C.C. who maneuvered Dolly in to a rehearsal at the Cotton Club.

"See how they make the whole stage look like a primitive jungle scene? That's what they think the whites wanna see. All that gyrating and whooping. That's not what they're doing in the real Harlem. In *Black* Harlem. This is just another in a long line of minstrel shows."

"Well, show me the *real* Harlem then!" Dolly begged.

"What's in it for me?" C.C. laughed.

Dolly hadn't developed her full confidence yet and must have blushed. She liked C.C. She wanted C.C. to like her, but she felt like an awkward schoolgirl in her presence. C.C. had come of age in Philadelphia and left home at age twelve for reasons she only alluded to. But Dolly knew the score. C.C. had had a hard life, but she'd escaped and made it to Harlem.

Now Will. She was different. Buttoned up tight on the outside. She was clearly a nervous Nellie. Yet, mysterious. Dolly couldn't quite pin down what made Willsie tick. It was good to make her wonder about C.C. She could tell Will was intrigued. Of course when she allowed herself to think of what may have happened to C.C. it made her stomach drop. Dolly recalled telling C.C. how much she wished she could be colored sometimes and free to roam with a band like C.C. did. C.C. set her straight on that one, all right.

"You sure are a poor little rich girl. And stupid too, to say something like that."

Dolly smirked, as she was used to girls looking up to her. C.C. was only a year older but somehow seemed more like a woman—

and a man. She had the thinly arched eyebrows and long eyelashes of a woman but the strong jaw and imposing physique of a man. Dolly found that unusual combination so intoxicating, plus she knew about a world Dolly longed to be a part of—the world of jazz.

"You like the music, honey, but you don't know what the life is like," C.C. once said to her. "You'll find yourself some rich white boy and be just like the rest."

Dolly tried to argue, but on what grounds? The attention of boys was great, and sure, she could get plenty of it. But after that one scare with Mr. Debate Team two years before, she'd trained herself to run between the raindrops and not give 'em too much. Just thinking about that frightful spring made Dolly want to toss on a chastity belt and close up shop for good.

She'd liked Mr. Debate Team's way with words on stage, but in his family's garage underneath the staircase he fell silent. It was over so quick she barely knew what happened. He wanted to see her again, but she kept making excuses. She was really mad about the whole thing, and that was before she realized the situation he'd put her in. Dolly thought a guy who was so deft with words, who possessed such wit and confidence on the public stage, would be a real thrill-ride. Guess it had all been for show.

The way Mumsie had looked at her when she told her, "I'm late." You'd think with all their money Mumsie would be glad they could finance getting rid of the little inconvenience. But no, Mumsie said marriage was the only way out. She was still a Catholic despite the conversion—she made *that* clear every chance she got!

Dolly couldn't imagine being strapped with a tot. To live a life of drudgery was worse than death. In fact, she had planned to kill herself if it came to that. Better to die young and pretty and still free than to be shackled to the whims of a husband.

"You can get money from Daddy to pay for this," she'd begged her mother.

But Mumsie stood firm, and Dolly knew why. She was jealous. Dolly had all the charms Mumsie had, and more, and she was young and in bloom. Fine. If Mumsie wouldn't help her, she knew just what she would do. Daddy had a few prize pistols in his office. She would sneak one out and practice firing it out in the woods, then once she had a feel for it she'd eat the barrel.

Dolly wanted to cry with relief in the bathroom when she realized that's all it was—she was just late. Bleeding never felt so good.

"So Wilhelmina, I hear you performed for Frances's women's club this week," Uncle David said.

The linen tablecloth hung over their laps, giving Dolly just enough room to squeeze Will's leg under the table.

"Yes. We played Schubert."

"Next time let's get them on their feet with Wagner!" Dolly said.

"That rabid anti-Semite."

"So what? I don't know about you, Daddy, but his music thrills me."

"Do you know what Wagner thought of the Jews?" Daddy said. "And there was and *is* nothing unusual about that in Germany."

"Erich," Mumsie said. "You're of German descent as well! So are our children."

"And what about me?" Uncle David laughed.

"Yes! Of course and David, and all of your family," Mumsie said. "But we are Americans first. Wouldn't you agree?"

"She has a point, brother," Uncle David said.

"I know what I know," Daddy said. "And things are only going to get worse. It's peacetime and stocks are booming. But the Treaty of Versailles was too harsh, a terrible mistake. It will be the Germans who seek vengeance next time. Real vengeance."

"Come on. They just need to pay the piper and then it's back to business as usual," Dolly said.

"If only it were that simple," Daddy said. "They can't afford to pay the terms of those reparations. And the financial institutions of Europe as a whole were unstable to begin with. Can't you see what a house of cards we've built? I'm a businessman. I know how easily the tide can turn."

Dolly could not believe she had to sit through the same rendition of this song, just in a different key. She moved her leg closer to Will's and could feel Will's body shift towards her.

"Are things really that extreme, darling?" Mumsie said. "Our allies in France and England are making compromises, as are we."

"Your wife is right, Erich," Uncle David said. "The Treaty was signed four years ago and nothing terrible has happened. In fact, compromises are being made."

"Four years ago, eh?" Daddy said. "Let me remind you that mere months ago the French marched in to occupy the Ruhr Valley region because the Germans were not making good on reparations fast enough. And the French are still there, pricking away at the pride of the Germans. None of this bodes well. They hate Jews. And Americans hate Jews too. Just in silence."

"Daddy," Dolly said. "Have you ever considered that the way you feel about negroes is just as bad as the way they think about Jews?"

"Don't be ridiculous," Daddy said. "The Jews are an asset to this country."

"That's not the point," Dolly said. "Negroes were kidnapped and brought here on slave ships, and they still don't have all but a few rights in this country. I mean look at us. The only negroes this family sees fit to keep company with are the servants."

"Dolly," Mumsie said. "Please lower your voice. You'll embarrass the help."

"And it's not as if they're our *slaves*," Daddy said. "We take excellent care of our servants. We treat them like family."

Dolly took a breath. Where to begin? She felt Will take her hand and give it a squeeze. It wasn't a flirty touch. She could feel the difference. Will understood what she was saying.

"How do you like the roast beef, Will?" Mumsie asked.

"I'm curious about your meeting the other day, Mrs. Raab," Will said. "What are you ladies working on?"

"We're having some great success raising money for the Better Breeding Institution in the Bronx."

"Didn't know my mums was in the farming business did you, Will?" Dolly said.

"Oh hush. She's just making fun because we dragged her to the Ulster County Fairgrounds last month to help gather volunteers for the 'fit family' contest."

"I'll say this for you, Frances," Uncle David said. "You don't mind getting your hands dirty."

Dolly placed her hand on Will's knee and gave it a pat. She could feel Will tense up and then relax into it.

"Oh yeah, Will—you shoulda seen her. Mumsie got a little too close to a winning county heifer and had to change clothes mid-speech."

"Wait a moment. I'm confused. *Are* we talking about breeding animals? I know a bit about that as an ornithologist."

"Oh no. Not animals, you see. We're committed to educating the public about breeding better families. Why shouldn't all families have the chance to rise to the level we have? And the case has certainly been made by Dr. Galton, the founder of eugenics, that if man is willing to breed for the best livestock, shouldn't we be just as conscientious about our *own* stock as a species?" Mumsie said. "Has your family been interviewed yet for the Social Register of Families and Better Babies, Will?"

"Not to my knowledge, Mrs. Raab," Will said. "I do some of my birding expeditions in the Bronx. Where in the Bronx is your Institute going to be housed?"

Dolly laughed. "At the Zoo! They're planning on putting negroes in cages again at the Bronx Zoo, didn't ya hear?"

"Dolly!" Mumsie said. "Pay her no mind. We are not putting any humans in a zoo."

"Waaa?" Dolly said. "They did back when *I* was a baby, didn't they?"

"Oh," Will said. "You mean the Congolese boy?"

"Yeah, the one with the monkey and the spear."

"Please! That was most distressing and not fit for dinner conversation, Dorothy," Mrs. Raab said.

"You see, Will? This is what *my* tribe is like. They don't mind ogling colored kids in cages for fun. But God forbid we talk about it at dinner. Now that's the real crime."

"Dolly, you *were* just a baby, and that exhibit lasted only a few days as I recall," Uncle David said. "Although I agree, it was most uncomfortable for the white visitors as well as the negroes. Very sad. But he *was* released to a negro orphanage somewhere down South, I believe."

"Yeah, and shot himself in the heart a few years later," Dolly said.

This was starting to make her agitated. She was glad to have Will here as a witness to see how her family talked out of both sides of their mouths. How could philistines like them think they were superior to negroes or to anybody else?

"Look," Daddy said. "Let's leave the negroes in peace, and let the Jews be as well."

"Unless we start putting the two together," Dolly said.

"What?" Daddy said. "Now you're going to advocate mixing races so it'll be in our family's bloodline too?"

"That would be the worst thing, huh, Daddy?" Dolly said. "Imagine that, Will. Me bringing home a negro to ask Daddy for his blessing to marry me. The ole man would keel over from a heart attack right at the dinner table, wouldn't you Daddy?"

Dolly could see she'd pushed it too far. The vein in her father's head pulsated. She laughed, not knowing why. Maybe it was the thought of what he'd do if she brought C.C. home for a visit. He'd keel over, sure as pudding.

"I do have a heart condition," Daddy said. "Don't test this ticker." But he started to laugh too.

"That's our cue," Dolly said. "Call us when it's time for ice cream!" They ran for the stairs, squealing with laughter.

Dolly flopped down on the bed and pulled Will beside her.

"God, they make me so mad," Dolly said. "Can you believe them?" Will shook her head.

"Well, I for one can't wait till we get to Barnard. Harlem here we come."

Chapter Four
Will

Will had made it through the first days of college without too much fuss, but that was only because she had Dolly as a roommate to help her through orientation. But today was Will's first day walking about solo. She and Dolly didn't share any Monday classes. Acing the academics was no big deal, but dealing with the other girls—that seemed like one of Dante's nine circles of hell. Of course Dolly had assured her that compared to Will these gals were nitwits, but still. *But still what?* She willed herself to focus on something else. The architecture!

Will walked from Hewitt, the dining center, belly full of biscuits, boiled chicken, green beans, and chocolate milk, her eyes locked on the trees as she strode past Students' Hall toward Brooks Dormitory. Known as Millbank, the Hall was comprised of classrooms, study halls, a dining area, and meeting spots for day students between classes. Erected in red brick and trimmed in elegant white stone, the architecture seemed to announce that Barnard was just as much of a "real" campus as Columbia across the street.

The land between Milbank Hall, which housed the students' dining and classes, and the dormitories was separated by a park that had come to be known by all the girls as "The Jungle," because of its lush, naturalistic landscaping. For Will, those four blocks separated the two sides of campus, making New York feel like the ancient city of Mytilene on Lesbos, and Barnard like the academy Sappho created for the education of unmarried young women long ago. In fact, Barnard boasted an annual "Greek Games" event that brought out the whole campus in Athenian garb for sport and pandemonium inside the vast gymnasium. Adding to the timeless effect, Roman columns adorned Students' Hall, along with an imposing arched doorway. Closing her eyes for a moment, Will imagined herself alive and intellectually engaged as a student of the seventh century.

Away from the clutches of Estelle, and enjoying a respite from grief over Momma, Will began to realize that the Sapphic way was not *such* an oddity after all. In fact, Elsie de Wolfe, a neighbor on Sutton Place, the top interior designer in the country—and companion of Bessie Marbury—designed the dormitory rooms. She'd caught glimpses of them from time to time and even heard one of Pop's younger associates at the bank refer to them as "the Bachelorettes" over dinner at the house one night.

Bessie Marbury cut an imposing figure on Sutton Place with her substantial weight and hefty velvet frocks. In contrast, fit and trim Elsie seemed especially demure in lace and pearls. She'd heard from the banker that she practiced the Eastern art of yoga. Apparently, Bessie was the toast of Broadway, a high-powered agent who represented the likes of George Bernard Shaw and Oscar Wilde. This impressed Will who greatly admired Wilde.

Earlier in the century, the Bachelorettes had traveled extensively through France, holding court at the Villa Trianon, which they purchased with their younger friend, Anne Tracy Morgan, and used as a literary and political salon. They barely escaped Europe alive when the Germans invaded. According to the young banker, the Bachelorettes persuaded Anne (who harbored feelings for Bessie) to convince her father, John Pierpont Morgan, to purchase a garbage dump on the East River and build Sutton Place.

To think that Elsie had a hand in creating Will's home on Sutton Place *and* here at Barnard. Will was finding it easier to imagine a place for herself in the world, with her own charismatic and wildly successful companion, of course.

Will slipped through the Fiske parlor where Jane Sterry, one of her hallmates, sat drinking tea and arguing with some of the other girls. Gilt appliqué accented the parlor like the tea rooms of the Colony Club.

"It was only four years ago that U.S. Vice President Marshall cited the fact that girl debaters at Radcliffe upheld the affirmative ruling in favor of labor as a dangerous manifestation of *radicalism* in women's colleges," Sterry argued.

The girls sat beside her on the sofa and at her feet on the carpet beside the unlit fireplace. Not one of them noticed Will.

"If you're arguing about feminism, why not take men out of the equation altogether?" Will said.

"How do you mean?" a redhead in a prim tweed skirt asked.

"Think of *Herland*—Charlotte Perkins Gilman. A country of women. No men seen for two thousand years. And then three American males land there in a biplane and are sure there must be men somewhere. They just can't imagine they're irrelevant."

"But they're not irrelevant," Sterry said.

"In *Herland* they *have* become irrelevant," Will pressed on. "And it was even serialized in *The Forerunner* magazine several years after Gilman's *Women and Economics*, in which she argued that ours is the only species in which females are wholly dependent upon males for survival. And in *exchange* the males extract payment—through sex functions and domestic work—far harder work than what men do. Bees, for example ..."

Sterry jumped on this. "Oh, for some of us it's not work—the sex *functions* as you put it."

They all laughed.

"That's what the author called it."

"And what do you call it, Reinhardt?" Sterry asked. "Or do you even know what it is?"

She was not going to play into the hands of this prom-trotter.

"Well, clearly I've crashed your party. I'll be on my way," Will said.

"Oh, come now," Sterry countered. "No need to get all high hat."

"I'm not," Will said. "Everything's fine."

"I happened to have taken umbrage with the way children were portrayed as the main purpose for women's lives in *Herland*."

Another girl asked Sterry to expound, and Will stayed to listen, hoping she might get a chance to cut her down to size.

"Well," Sterry continued. "Despite the author's feminism even *she* could not see past a woman's role as being first and foremost to bear and nurture children."

"You said 'a' woman's role. Singular. In actuality, she makes it clear that the community as a whole shall be charged with rearing children," Will said. "Unlike our society, from its earliest origins to where we stand today, *Herland* allows for an impersonal raising of children. Do not forget the notion she puts forth that those who are *not* the most maternal of women need not make raising a child their primary focus ..."

"That's not the point," Sterry said.

Will laughed.

"Did you read the book or just read *about* it?"

"Of course I did!" Sterry shouted.

The girls all laughed, and Will saw Sterry's desire to lunge across the carpet and strangle her.

"Wilhelmina, seems like you have contempt for marriage and motherhood," Sterry said.

"I care little for either institution," Will said. "But if these things have import for you, I must say: it doesn't sound like you'd make much of a mother."

"I have no desire to be a mother," Sterry said. "I intend to use my mind to better the world and all mankind—all *woman*kind—rather than just coddle my own little set of brats."

The other girls laughed.

"Well, let's hope you don't indulge in any sex functions that destroy your glorious dream of freedom," Will said. "Good afternoon, ladies."

Will slipped off during the girls' next explosion of giggles and before Sterry could gather herself to toss a verbal grenade. Will could hear her mutter something about Will being a "know-it-all" but who cared? She did know a lot more than that philistine! And she knew this much for sure: she'd won this battle. Let her try that on Will again! She'd put the pompous, hotheaded imbecile in her place once and for all. Will passed through the parlor, hopping up the stairs two at a time, and burst into the dorm room full of vigor, books, and bouquet of flowers in hand.

"Hey Willsie, why the sweat? You run all the way here?"

Will suddenly became aware of the greasy film that covered her skin. Dolly always looked so cool to the touch. She hated the way Dolly teased her. But she told herself to shake it off; the parents had arranged for the girls to room together, and this was the greatest thing that had ever happened in Will's life. Best to focus on that.

"Here. Use this," Dolly said and tossed Will a camisole.

Wiping her brow and upper lip, Will could smell Dolly's scent on the lingerie. Something woodsy mixed with a bright note of orange. She longed to grab Dolly and put her hands all over her.

"I brought some flowers—for our room," Will said, chickening out of her original plan to present them as a gift.

"Looks like you stole 'em from Barn-yard, sticky fingers. Listen," she said. "I think you need a few tips on staying fresh."

A nasty line sizzled on Will's tongue, but she swallowed it as Dolly slid over and patted the bed. Will walked warily towards her, not wanting to get mocked again.

"Plenty of soap and water ... aw who cares ... let's get to something good. Okay," Dolly continued, this time in an exaggerated Patrician accent. "Incidentally, women interested in losing weight would like to know that I lost ten pounds practicing for a fencing scene. I would recommend fencing to any woman who desires a slender, supple figure."

They both laughed, and Dolly blurted out, "Sounds like she just likes being poked."

"Yeah, and doing some poking herself," Will added.

Dolly howled so hard she nearly fell off the bed. Will laughed in unison, not recognizing the wild roars exploding from her insides. Her mouth felt tingly, wondering what would happen next.

"The reason why health experts object to the practice of sleeping on more than one pillow is not to prevent round shoulders," Dolly continued. "But to allow the blood to circulate properly, which is sound sense when you think about it."

On impulse, Will grabbed the pillow from under her head and threw it across the room.

Dolly laughed and grabbed the one from under Will's head and did the same.

"Finally," Dolly said. "Poise and tranquility must come from within."

And with that she smirked and shimmied her skirt up, revealing her step-in chemise. Will looked away.

"You can look, snooks. Unless you find me too *tit*-illating."

Will laughed, then pretended to gawk to keep up the "joke." But Will's heart was beating, and she wondered: was Dolly a prude about anything? She'd heard about schoolgirls kissing, being "smashed" on each other. As long as they had boyfriends too it didn't seem to matter. Well, Dolly clearly thrived on being the exception to every rule, so they really didn't need men to hide behind, did they?

"Hey, I'm sick of these four walls. I know a picture show we should see."

Will felt a rush of disappointment. Why couldn't they just stay in this room alone together forever?

Chapter Five

T he North Side Cinema was located just fifteen blocks south of Barnard. Dolly and Will paid their twenty-seven cents each and sat down for a screening of Oscar Wilde's *Salome*. Will could smell the scent of Adieu Sagesse ("Goodbye Wisdom") on her roommate and moved closer. Dolly, speeding ahead of Will, had bumrushed them into the theater and Will had not had a chance to wash her hands or count steps to their seats. She felt better when she seated herself on an even number of steps rather than an odd. To make up for this oversight she tapped her feet in quarter notes, telling herself that if Dolly spoke next on an "even" tap that would be a sign that Will should hold her hand.

… thirteen … fourteen … fifteen … sixteen … seventeen …

Damn it.

"Hey, check out Pretty Boy and Big Lug, third-row aisle," Dolly snickered.

Will sighed and placed her hands upon her lap. The Big Lug wore a brown suit with a soft collar and no vest, and the spiffy fella sported a Glenn plaid blue and tan suit with a stylish gold-striped tie.

"Let's move up," Dolly said, already rising, bottle of pop in hand.

Why couldn't Dolly be satisfied with just the two of them? What could Will do but get up and follow her? She moved them right in front of the gents even though the audience was noticeably sparse. Will could see by the way he perked up in his seat that he noticed

Dolly. His pupils moved with periscope precision till they captured Dolly's smile in the cross hairs. As the girls moved into their new seats Dolly pretended to trip and fall on the seat right in front of the well-dressed lad. With the grace of an ice skater, she tipped over the seat, giving him a peek of cleavage and "accidentally" dripping pop at his feet.

"Oh gosh. Miss, are you all right?" he said.

"I think so," Dolly said, licking her lips and rising in slow motion—slow enough for him to hop the seat beside her and land in their row, his arm on her elbow.

"Here, let me help you," he said.

"I hope I didn't splash this fine suit of yours," she said, her cutesy choice of words making it clear that this had all been a performance. What an actress!

But he seemed to be cut from the same cloth because he said, "No sirree, Miss," and did a little spin and bow.

Dolly applauded, then looked over the seat with mock amazement as the cherry pop spread like a bubbling river across the cinema floor.

"I'm Joe. This is Buddy."

"Dolly. This is Wilhelmina, but everybody calls her Will."

"Pleased to meet you ladies. Buddy, run up to the concession and grab the ladies more refreshments, will ya?"

Buddy looked a little slow on the uptake, but when Joe tossed him a coin, he caught it and lumbered to his feet. Joe pushed Dolly's seat down as if he was opening the door to a Peugeot Torpedo sports car, and she gave Will a wink and nod indicating she should sit too and isn't this a real lark? The sounds of cracks and pops preceded the first images of newsreel as the house lights dimmed.

Today, the first Detroit-Cleveland passenger air service embarked on an historic journey—of ease and simple luxury, with all the comforts of a railway car ... Back here in the Big Apple the New York Giants beat the Brooklyn Robins 3-0 to clinch the National League pennant and will meet the New York Yankees in the World Series for the third straight year.

The short film started then, a Buster Keaton reel called *The Balloonatic*. Will could hear the giggles and see the "accidental" brush of a leg that passed between Dolly and this slick young beau in response to Keaton's antics.

Buddy shifted his knee closer to Will's. She tried to move away, but he did something she did not expect. He put his hand on her lap and began stroking the tweedy fabric of her dress. She stared straight ahead, her body stiff.

She tried to focus on the screen, but even from her peripheral vision Will could see the brooding Neanderthal shadow of Buddy's profile. What was it with men and movie houses? Will shifted away from him, but he pressed down on her so hard she feared he might leave a bruise on her thigh, or worse slip his hand between her legs. For the rest of the short his hand simply stayed there. As long as she didn't move, he didn't either. She took a deep breath to settle in for the feature.

After the credits, the first title card announced:

"Profound was the moral darkness that enveloped the world ..."

Will's eyes lingered on the words. Joe had whispered something into Dolly's ear that made her coquettishly move her leg and cover her mouth. Buddy sat beside Will crunching popcorn and half-heartedly turning the mouth of the bucket towards her. All Will could do to keep from crying was tap her feet silently and count ... until she saw her.

The first image of Salome, played by Alla Nazimova, was shocking. She wore a strange headdress that conjured up a bright constellation of stars. Her lips were sensual and her eyes as strong and unguarded as any film star. And yet, for someone who starred as a temptress, Will was surprised by who she resembled. *She looks like me.*

Nazimova was older, much older than she, and she wore her masculinity well. The fact that even the character she portrayed served as the object of obsession gave Will a charge she'd never felt before. If she, lacking the "All-American" good looks of Dolly, could lure in the likes of audiences in picture shows across the land, couldn't Will too? She thought about what her powers of seduction were.

Dolly sat unreachable, working her wiles on Joe, that wispy featherweight. Will turned her head towards Buddy and waited for him to return her gaze. He blinked first then shifted uncomfortably in his seat and turned his head back to the screen. She imagined herself as the real Nazimova, full of power and sensuality. Without realizing it, her feet stopped tapping. Buddy took her hand. It felt big and warm. She smiled to herself.

Chapter Six

Joe had suggested sweets after the show. The black-and-white tiled floor of the ice cream shop made Will think of the keys on Dolly's piano. Soon she was replaying in her mind Dolly's impromptu concert after the hen party, up in her bedroom, paper keyboard and all. She looked down into her chocolate soda and tried to imagine being alone with Dolly. In reality, she sat in the back booth at the Etta Louise Sweet Shoppe on Broadway and 110th, where Buddy wedged Will's small body against the wall. She sat there, straw in mouth as Buddy once again slipped a hand onto her lap, and Joe flirted with Dolly across the table. This was all right, for now. At least she wasn't a third wheel.

"You're pretty enough to be in pictures," Joe said.

"Awww, ain't you sweet?" Dolly replied. "And you're right. I've actually been in three, and this summer my parents are paying to send me out to Hollywood to stay at Pick-Fair ..."

Will smirked at Dolly but knew better than to interrupt her little show. Joe actually seemed to buy it. The rube.

"You know I met the star of *Salome* when I was out in Hollywood as a child. She rocked me to sleep on her lap, Mumsie said. I don't remember."

"Salome was no Sheba," Joe said. "Not like you."

"I thought she was fascinating."

Dolly stared unblinking at Will.

50

For that moment the boys disappeared. Will held Dolly's gaze and knew for certain only they existed in each other's hearts. The boys were mere props Dolly had pulled out for amusement; they could end up tossed in a trunk at any time.

"What did you find most compelling about her?" Will asked Dolly.

Will waited for Dolly to say something in code to her, something these boys would be oblivious to. It was then that Dolly turned away from Will and gave Joe an unmistakable look. As if *her* wildness was going to be directed at him. Will's world went silent. It was as if she was dead. Will looked down into the chocolate-speckled ice in her empty soda glass and felt herself float away. Those tiny brown chips transformed into the bits of dirt Pop tossed limply into Momma's grave. There'd be no more sweetness.

Will waited for Dolly to turn back to her, but she didn't. The boys paid the tab and Joe made his move.

"My car's parked a few blocks south. Let's take a spin. You girls are new to Barnard. We're Columbia men, live right by Riverside Park. We can show you all the landmarks."

"Ok, sport," Dolly said. "But we need to be back in half an hour."

This was an outright lie and Will, though deeply relieved, didn't understand why Dolly told it. This could be another secret signal! If Dolly wanted to ditch the boys, could it be she wanted time alone with Will? Of course. Will felt electrified by the spark Dolly lit in her. Dolly played it cool, but she must feel it too. Yes. That must be true. Will was a dark brooder by nature and Dolly a light-hearted rascal. Opposites attract, don't they?

"Ok let's go," Joe said, bouncing out of the booth and holding a ready hand out for Dolly.

What a pesky fly. Couldn't he see Dolly was brushing him off?

Buddy opened the back door of the Ferris Sedan and Will slid in. Will had gone on "dates" before, but only with harmless bookworms, pre-approved by her family. She worried how she could keep this bruiser at bay as Dolly and Joe slid into the front seat. Joe immediately slipped an arm around Dolly's neck and pulled her close, while using the other hand to switch on the radio.

The sound of Buddy's heavy breathing picked up the alluring pull of the clarinet. Will could sense him about to pounce. She decided right then that touching him would be her only chance to stop him from touching her. She'd studied ornithology while other girls pursued home economics. She knew the female northern jacana dominated the male and once she showed aggression, he was helpless to do anything but submit. Without looking at him she put her hand on his lap and allowed him to open his trousers and place her palm around his penis. She was surprised by how curious she felt and by the buzzy groan of pleasure he emitted from his throat.

Buddy placed his hand over hers and moved it rhythmically up and down. She glanced up and watched fascinated as his head bobbed, the eyes on his slack-jawed face rolling back, then popping open to focus on the back of Joe's head up front. She remembered hearing an older boy cousin talk about how men sometimes focused on something like baseball scores to help keep themselves from going flaccid. For all Will knew, Buddy could have been counting the freckles on the back of his friend's neck.

Will felt a curious sense of power as his breathing sped up. She instinctively moved her hand faster, up and down, up and down, up and down, feeling the heat and friction until he exploded into her palm. She wiped off her hand on his shorts then pulled it gingerly out of his pants. The rest of the residue she wiped on the underside of the sedan seat.

Buddy took out a pack of smokes, pounded them against his knee, and lit up.

"Want one?" he asked.

"No thanks," she said.

Up front, Dolly said to Joe, "No, no, Joe. That's a no-no."

Dolly backed away as they stayed lip-locked in a gentle struggle. Joe was no brute like Buddy, but Will could see Dolly did not want him to do anything more than kiss her.

When Buddy stubbed out his cigarette in the backseat ashtray Will leaned forward and said, "Dolly, we should go."

"Hey, I want to see you again," Buddy said to Will.

"Aren't you going to kiss me?" she asked, not knowing where the words came from.

He leaned in and his lips felt surprisingly tender and pillowy against her own. She hadn't noticed how soft and full they were before. Will could taste the cigarette on his breath and tongue. It gave her a slight burning sensation.

"You're a good kid," he said and opened the door to the back seat to let her out in front of Brooks Dormitory.

"How old are you?" she asked.

"Twenty-three."

He was no Columbia man. More like a working stiff if he were that old.

Joe couldn't have been more than twenty. What did Buddy do anyway? How did he become Joe's wingman?

Back at Brooks, Will felt as if she could breathe again. The girls guffawed as they fell into their room.

"Sorry I sic-ed old Buddy on you. He seemed a little slow."

"Yeah, but he was fast in other ways."

"Waaaahhh? Sing, Reinhardt."

"I gave him a French handshake," Will said.

"I don't believe it!"

Will then held up her hand, which still had a few bits of white crust attached, like dried sealing wax.

"Why'd you do that?" Dolly said, her expression dark. "That's disgusting."

Maybe she was jealous of how Will acted like such a woman of the world, while Dolly conducted herself like a tease? Will wondered if she'd made a mistake. She'd been so stupid! She'd just wanted to keep up with Dolly who seemed so much "faster" than she, prove she was no prude, and now their beautiful new friendship might've gotten all balled up—over nothing.

Dolly moved closer to Will and took her hand. She put Will's index finger in her mouth and Will shivered. She then took each of her fingers one at a time and sucked them, never breaking eye contact with Will but maintaining the tiniest curve of a smile.

Finally, she licked the palm of Will's hand and used her teeth to get at the dried fluid.

"It doesn't really taste like anything," Dolly said.

Will smiled. What had she gotten all sore about? She leaned forward, taking Dolly's hands into her own.

"Do you remember the dance scene from today?" Dolly asked.

Of course she did. Salome's dance of the seven veils. They didn't speak another word as Will opened up her closet and pulled out a few silk scarves, one with the monogram of her mother: ER. Dolly pulled out a Bessie Smith 78 and placed it on the Victrola.

As Will wrapped a scarf around her neck and held one out for Dolly, Dolly dropped the needle on the record.

The jazz. The way the rhythmic piano notes punctuated her plaintive wail. Will forgot her own mind and melted into the music. All body now, no thoughts. Will wrapped the jade lamé scarf around the back of Dolly's waist and held each end tightly in her hands, pulling her close as they shimmied and swayed.

"I shall dance for you no more," Dolly said.

"But you must, Salome."

"Not until I extract a promise from you."

"Anything you wish," Will said, the words of the story coming back to her. "I will give thee whatsoever thy soul desireth. What wouldst thou have? Speak."

Will felt Dolly sway in her arms, the music suspending them in a non-linear, nonsensical hypnagogic state. Will had recently read Havelock Ellis's book, *The Dance of Life*, curious to learn the sexologist's theory of "inversion." Yet it was an ornithological aside that stayed with her: the idea that the creation of nests came about as an accidental result of the ecstatic sexual dancing of birds.

"Promise you'll do what I command," Dolly said.

"What is it you want me to do for you? Just name it."

"Is that a yes?"

"Yes," Will said, her breathing joining with Dolly's in perfect synchronicity.

"Good," Dolly said. "Then I'll just keep your promise in my pocket for now."

"Dance for me once more," she said.

"Is that what you want?" Dolly asked. "A private performance?"

Will blushed.

"Do you want me to read your mind?"

Will nodded.

"Your cheeks are red as strawberries. And you know what they say. Tell someone to *not* think of strawberries and that's all they can think of."

"I'm not thinking of strawberries," Will whispered into her ear.

"Then what are you thinking of?"

"Dolly Raab," Will said. "I like the sound of your name."

"Mmmm," Dolly whispered back. "I like the way you *say* my name."

Will took her head and pulled her closer. She put her hand on Dolly's cheek, and Dolly nuzzled her cheekbone into Will's palm. She bit her lip and stared at Will, waiting. Will put her hand on Dolly's neck, but it was Dolly who pulled Will's face toward her own and planted a tender kiss on her lips, and then another. They stopped for a moment to look deeply into one another's eyes. This was the greatest moment of Will's life and she did not want it to end; she knew she must move carefully so this bird did not fly away. Will moved toward Dolly's lovely face and kissed her again, this time opening her mouth. Their tongues played together; they explored each other's lips as their bodies moved closer, and a line from Chekhov's *The Seagull* flashed through Will's mind, "If you ever have need of my life, come and take it."

Chapter Seven
Will

The next night their room seemed lonely without Dolly. Normally an ace at studying, Will just couldn't concentrate, no matter how many times she shuffled papers on her dorm room desk. Dolly had taken off solo, and it was hard for Will to think of anything but her. The way they kissed and kissed. They went no further than that, but the kisses were so tender, so passionate. How could Dolly be out with another girl? But it wasn't like that with other girls, Will told herself. Will might have to contend with this Joe or another boy here and there, but that didn't mean anything; Dolly just had to keep up appearances. Feelings cannot be faked, and the intensity they shared—it was more powerful than anything Will had ever felt in her life. She knew Dolly felt just as strongly, despite how cavalier she acted in other settings. Unless she was misreading Dolly. If only she could read her mind, know what she was *really* thinking. Will paced the room, counting her steps across, back and forth. This would simply not do. She had to take hold of herself.

She put on her reading glasses and focused on a copy of a lecture Austrian-Swiss physicist Wolfgang Pauli had recently given at the University of Hamburg on Quantum Mechanics. Having studied ornithology since early childhood, it was easy for Will to leap ahead to senior classes in the sciences. She wanted to wow her physics professor. She'd heard her talking with one of the lit professors about the Bohemian salons of Paris. Paris must be the place to be. The city of lights, of beauty. Dolly was the most elevated example of a human being she'd ever encountered, worthy of worship. And where else to worship such a Goddess but in the most beautiful city in the world? *Stop daydreaming,* she told herself.

Using her brain would take her mind off her body, and Pauli's theories were of particular interest to her. In his lecture, Pauli proposed a new quantum number with two possible values in order to resolve inconsistencies between observed molecular spectra and the developing theory of quantum mechanics.

He formulated the exclusion principle, which stated that no two electrons could exist in the same quantum state, identified by four quantum numbers including his new two-valued degree of freedom. Will recalled that in the previous year, Niels Bohr updated his model of the atom by assuming that certain numbers of electrons (for exampe: two, eight and eighteen) corresponded to stable "closed shells." Interesting, she thought, how in quantum theory even numbers added an air of stability, which the odd numbers could at times violate.

She chewed on her pencil and closed her eyes, imagining herself as an even number—sensible and serious, while Dolly represented an odd one. One. One. The number one. Will mused over the mystical meanings of Hebrew letters each with its correspondence to a primordial truth. She'd learned the Hebrew alphabet from her father when she was very little, before Momma's illness. Beit, the second letter signified home, while Aleph, the first letter which preceded it signified the one in everything, everything in the one. Dolly is the Aleph! Will remembered her father teaching her about the numerical correspondences of each Hebrew letter. The linguistic and mystical system called "gematria" beautifully mirrored the elegance of quantum physics. Will saw Dolly in all of it. This new direction in scientific theory depending upon uncertainty, improvisation. Dolly, and more Dolly.

Having Dolly in close physical proximity so much of the time made up for all the isolation Will had previously suffered. Yet being in such a high-pitched state of excitement was becoming almost too much to bear. Will felt as if she couldn't exist on the earthly plane without Dolly's body near her, without her beautiful face close by to look upon. It was torment. But she would rather experience it than go back to her life before, the one she lived without Dolly.

By the time Will fell asleep, physics textbook on her chest, it was well past midnight. The sound of the door unlocking woke her. Dolly stumbled in, clearly snookered. She giggled to herself as she tried to kick off her shoes, falling over in the process. Will bolted out of bed and to her side.

"Are you okay?"

"Sure. Don't I look peachy?"

"Did you have a nice time?" Will asked.

"Yeah. *Fine.*"

"You seem a little riled up," Will said. "How's Helena Lances?"

"If you must know I ended up seeing Joe," Dolly snapped. "He whisked me off for a surprise date."

Will didn't want to hear it. She was still left with the same terrible possibility of Dolly falling for another suitor. Which was better—her seeing that boy and probably necking or doing more with him, or seeing Helena Lances, who maybe would take Will's place as Dolly's "other half?" Either way felt deathly to Will. She turned on her desk lamp and immediately wished she hadn't. In the swath of blackness, Dolly could play the part of the sloppy drunk, which could lead to sloppy embraces. The harsh light destroyed the mood.

"Hey," Dolly hollered. "Who turned on the lights?"

Dolly broke into idiotic laughter, and Will's voice turned shrill and accusing. "Were you with Joe this whole time?"

"*Were you with Joe this whole time?*" Dolly mimicked. "None of your biz. And all right, actually I did go see Lances and her tribe for a brief sit."

"How was the meeting?"

"A big joke," Dolly said.

"Yeah?"

"Oh sure, you should've seen this bunch o' half-baked brains with fashion sense straight out of Woolworth's. But I talked them into going out for a little nip after the chat. The whole bunch came out."

"Where did you go?"

"Jelly Roll's on 118th," Dolly said. "That's when Joe took over."

And you couldn't call to invite me.

Dolly laid down on her bed and within a minute pretended to be asleep. Will happily played along, this time making sure to click the light off. She undressed Dolly down to her camisole and lay down beside her. Will could feel Dolly wedge her body up close to hers. She didn't move as Will pet her hair and lightly caressed her back. The feeling of Dolly's ass pressed up against Will's thighs was inebriating. Will considered leaning down to kiss her lengthy torso but felt afraid. What if Dolly laughed or blew up at her? *Judie Schneider.* She'd taken that too far. Dolly was different. Dolly was bold. Was the risk too great? She could always play it off as a joke if Dolly lost her temper. And besides, they'd already crossed this line. Yet Dolly never acknowledged the romance between them in the light of day. Her body craved Dolly's so much.

She leaned in and brushed her lips against Dolly's shoulders. Dolly moaned but did not move. That moan was like a cue and Will felt determined to draw out more sounds, more responses, using her lips like a conductor's baton. She kissed her way to the spot between Dolly's shoulder blades, hearing Dolly's soft growl, but feeling no movement. She wanted to do more, but feared she'd break the spell. Unless Will rolled her over onto her back there was no way to kiss her mouth. Something in Will told her to wait. The waiting and longing only enhanced the adoration Will felt.

She studied Dolly's skin in the dark. There was enough illumination from the streetlights on Broadway to shine a luminous glow across her shoulders. Will could see a constellation of freckles on the back of Dolly's shoulder, a brilliant map to a special place where right now only she was allowed to visit. What would it take to ensure that special status forever?

"Tell me a secret," Dolly said.

Will's heart motored up so fast she thought she might bolt upright. "You're awake?"

"Mmm ... mmm. Go on. Tell me one."

Will tried to think of something, but all her mind could do was jump to wondering what Dolly wanted to hear. She hadn't led a very exciting life. Dolly had been a party girl for years, yet still managed to excel in her studies. Will had cloistered herself away, with her books and her birds. What would thrill Dolly, make her more intrigued by Will?

"I can shoot a bird on sight," Will said.

"That's a skill, not a secret."

"Well, there's more to it than that," Will said.

Dolly rolled over onto her back and looked up at her.

"I'm listening."

"My mother was sick for a very long time, and ... and ..."

Will could feel the ache in the back of her throat, hear the crack in her voice.

"Hey, hey ... it's ok, kiddo," Dolly said. "Come here."

Dolly pulled Will to her chest and stroked her hair with tenderness. Will wanted to weep. This woman was an angel. All superstitions aside, it seemed possible in that moment, in the darkness of their room, that Momma had sent Dolly from the great beyond to love Will.

"Shhh," Dolly cooed. "Now tell me the secret. About the gun."

Will reeled on the inside. Where was Dolly's compassion now? She took a breath. Dolly's presence was enough.

"I had to focus my energy somewhere after Momma died, and becoming a good shot provided me with an aggressive physical outlet. I could then study the birds in the privacy of the science lab. Oftentimes I'd stuff them, teaching myself the craft of taxidermy in the process."

"Where's the gun?"

"It's in the garage. I take it out when I go birding sometimes."

"Can I go with you?" Dolly seemed wide awake now.

"Sure," Will said.

"Hey listen Willsie. That's tough about your mom. Mine's a little too sticky; it's hard to get her off of me sometimes, but I can't imagine losing her. I'm sorry, kiddo. Honest."

"Thanks. I ..."

"I'm tired," Dolly said, and within a minute she appeared to be asleep.

Will wondered how *she* would ever fall asleep, but with her face nestled into Dolly's hair, she did, and slept till sunrise.

Chapter Eight

The next weekend the Schwimmers were all going to Jane Sterry's family's house upstate in Rhinebeck. Helena Lances, who stood at Amazonian height, had started the club, named after her heroine, Rosika Schwimmer, a feminist who'd gained much negative press in her communist homeland. The Schwimmers were just as earnest as Sterry's gang; in fact they overlapped in many activities, including this upstate getaway. They were all boors as far as Will was concerned. Still, Dolly insisted it would be fun. Will and Dolly took Will's Dad's car and stopped along the Bronx River Greenway Trail to practice shooting. Chalk marks on trees directed hikers where to head next, but Will took Dolly deep into the woods. They dodged inky spots of crushed slugs and pulled themselves up through the elevated rocky terrain till they reached a clear secluded landing spot.

"I've been here, I think. The North Trail leads to Scarsdale Avenue," Dolly said.

"Yes, where it meets Crane Road. I once encountered a very rare specimen of spotted thrush in those very woods."

"Huh," Dolly said. "I sure don't miss our old neighborhood. Bor-ing! You have the gun?"

"Yes," Will pulled out the Winchester from under a blanket in the back seat. "Pop calls this his medicine gun," she said, looking through the sight. "Although I don't think he ever shot anything with it."

"Here, let me take a look-see ..."

Will handed the gun to Dolly, who twisted it around like a cheer-leading baton.

"I'll show you how to hold it," Will said.

Will carefully took back the gun from Dolly. The woods were cool at this time of morning. They'd walked deep enough to be protected from the sounds of the road and from random passersby.

"Shhh ... listen," Will had recognized a familiar aural pattern. "It's a cuckoo. I believe it's a black-billed cuckoo, also known as Coccyzus erythropthalmus. It takes years of practice, but over time you can identify any bird through his call."

"Save the lesson for your students. Show me how to work that thing!" Dolly said.

Will shook her head and smiled. "Okay, first we need to determine if you are right or left eye dominant."

"I'm right-handed," Dolly said.

"That's not relevant. Here, take your hands and form a little square, almost like a viewfinder for you to look through ... and then focus on something, keeping both your eyes open."

Will spotted an orange triangle. It looked like a hiking trail marker.

"Close your left eye and see if you can see it clearly."

"It's a little fuzzy," Dolly said, squinting.

"Now your right eye."

"Sharp as a tack!"

"Okay. Mystery solved, Dolly. You're a right-handed shooter."

"I knew it!"

"Now kneel down and I'll show you how to balance the gun for the most precise target practice."

It felt good to be the one in command. She would have liked to have stayed in the woods teaching Dolly shooting tricks all day. But they'd said they'd join the other girls, and Dolly refused to cancel.

"Everybody'll be there. Don't you like to have fun sometimes?" Dolly asked.

We were having fun, Will thought. As they climbed down and across the trail back to the car, Dolly chattered nonstop about guns and boys and whatever other thoughts flitted across her mind. Will said nothing, hoping Dolly would notice the silence, but she didn't.

There were many diversions to choose from on the grounds of the Duchess County Estate. Dolly voted for tennis, and Will went along. Will stood behind the service line of the clay court. The sun shone bright, making it hard to focus. Dolly pivoted from foot to foot, diagonally across the court, her white drop-waist, below-the-knees dress picking up a breeze.

Before tossing the ball, Will imagined it flying right past Dolly, almost skimming her thigh, and bringing up the score to 40/30. She tossed it into the air and smashed it with force, yet it seemed to fly cautiously like a fuzzy duckling. Dolly slid forward in one fluid movement as if she were skating on ice and hit a top-spin shot cross-court.

Will moved center and slammed it hard.

"Nice return," Dolly called over the net with another smooth forehand.

This time Will moved forward and went for a drop shot as if pouncing upon a lumbering animal. It took Dolly by surprise; she tried to scoop it up with a backhand, but no dice.

"Deuce!" Dolly called.

"Deuce," Will called back, bouncing the ball lightly, preparing to serve. They were even now, and Will told herself she could do this. She could do anything she set her mind to. She forced herself to remain steady, not let her hands shake.

"Give it all you've got, including your foots, toots," Dolly hollered.

Will served it hard—almost too long, she feared, but the ball stayed in. This time Dolly hit it back with a forceful backhand. Will had to spring backwards to land in position, but then shot it back. This time, Dolly hit the return with too much force.

"Was that one wide?" she called.

"Yep."

Hard to believe Dolly was playing an honest game. It landed almost on the line, just barely out. In fact, if Dolly had chosen to argue about it, Will would've said it was on the line and let's replay it. Will served hard and exhaled a grunting "huh!" Before she could blink, Dolly appeared just a foot away from the net and lobbed that ball over her shoulder as if she were spooning pudding.

"Ad out," she called.

Dolly tried to fell Will with a passing shot, but Will was able to hit it back and this time it was Dolly who faltered. The ball hit the net.

"Deuce!" Will yelled.

They were even again. Will laughed with relief, then worried for a moment that Dolly might storm off the court. Instead, she kept her usual aplomb.

"Nice, Lucy Deucey."

Just as Will relaxed, Dolly surprised her with a light drop shot. She stood there feeling like a dope, the *thwok* of the ball landing on clay reverberated throughout the court.

"Advantage Raab," Will called, and without thinking, served as if she was warming up, resulting in an embarrassing fault.

She thought for sure Dolly would chirp out a bit of easy mockery. Instead she pivoted from foot to foot, silent enough to be either predator or prey.

"Second serve," Will said, this time placing her feet carefully behind the line, with enough space between them so she could lean into the shot.

The ball hit the sweet spot of her Wrighton Ditson racquet and sailed cross court with perfect speed. Dolly's face alighted with a grin as she lobbed the ball over Will's head, close enough that Will could feel her hair blow back the tiniest bit.

"Game, set, match!" Dolly called.

Will had really thought she had a chance there for a while. It would have meant something to beat Dolly at a sport. Graceful Dolly and awkward Will. Well Will was changing, growing more confident, and she wanted Dolly to see that! But she came up short.

"Come on you two lovebirds," Sterry called out from the gravel lane. "We're going to the lake!"

The moniker gave Will a hidden thrill. She ran to grab a swimsuit with renewed vigor.

After a long swim in bracing water they returned to the bunk before anyone else, giddy from all the exercise. The cabin held four pairs of bunk beds, knotty wooden shelves for a few sundries, and little else. It served as a changing cabana more than a place to sleep, but it gave all the girls the illusion of being away at camp.

Will and Dolly rolled around the bottom bunk, bathing costumes still wet. Will pulled at Dolly's suit, snapping the shoulder strap and laughing.

"Quit it, you dope!" Dolly laughed, gin on her breath.

"It's my bunk. Let me take the top tonight and you can sleep on a wet mattress."

"How about a wet pillow too?" Dolly cried and threw Will's pillow across the room. It landed on Sterry's bed, which cracked them both up.

When Dolly tried to reach across the floor to retrieve it, Will grabbed her and pressed her back down. This time she got Dolly on her back and pushed her chest down with her own while yanking the straps of Dolly's suit down all the way past her rib cage.

"Don't rip it! Joe loves this suit!"

Why did Dolly have to mention that flim-flam man from the movies? It annoyed her that Dolly continued to see him. But he wasn't here now. Will told herself not to sulk. How could she with Dolly's body so available to her, Dolly's mood so playful? They both laughed as Will cupped Dolly's breasts. She'd never done this with anyone before. Dolly's nipples felt hard and her breasts cold from the wet suit, but Will could feel a warmth underneath. Dolly twisted beneath Will, wrapping a leg around her. Dolly kicked Will's ass and pretended to protest as Will yanked the suit down farther. Dolly tried to push Will off, laughing the whole time. Will lightly ran her hand over Dolly's belly then her hands found her way up to her breasts again. Will laughed too, giddy at the way this was turning out. She felt a heat inside her body and a sense of triumph in her mind. She imagined movie cameras capturing them in flattering, gauzy close up. And then Dolly stiffened. Her body simply stopped moving. Will recognized this feeling from having handled so many birds. They only stiffened like this as rigor mortis set in. Will pulled back to look at her. She was no dead bird. But the look in Dolly's eyes scared Will. It was as if she was looking past her, not seeing her at all. Dolly attempted to push Will off of her.

"We were just fooling around," Dolly said, bolting up and fixing her suit.

Jane Sterry stood grimacing.

"Yes, I can see that," Sterry said.

Will sat up, grabbed a towel that had been thrown over a shelf, and started to undress.

"Keep your suit on. I don't want to see any more." Sterry sneered, turning her face away.

"I'm just changing my clothes after a swim," Will said.

"Hey Janey, let's see what you got under yours?" Dolly said, smacking her ass with a towel as if they were boys in a locker room.

"It's not a joke, Raab," Sterry said to her. "You and Reinhardt are perverts, and I know what I saw. And I've heard it's not the first time for you two, either."

As soon as she left, Dolly whipped around and said, "It's *your* fault. I told you there's no privacy here. You can't lock the cabin door. Fucking 'rustic' setting. Jesus! Why didn't you use your head for once? No, you always have to come back for another piece of the pie, don't you?"

"I'm sorry, I didn't hear her coming. I'll bet she was looking to catch us."

"She's going to tell the whole club."

Will waited. Sometimes Dolly just needed to let off steam.

"You know what we should do?" Dolly said, taking off her wet suit completely and signaling Will to turn around and not watch.

"What?" Will imagined herself as the strong Roman servant prepared to do anything to make up for having compromised her beautiful, alluring queen.

"Get her out on the lake for a little rowing expedition. I happen to know she doesn't swim. Boat tips over and …"

66

"No," Will said, slipping into a tennis dress. "They'd know it was us."

"Well, then how about we just go swimming with her? We get her far enough out, push her underwater, hold her head down?"

"You're not serious?"

"As serious as you were before she walked in."

Will felt her heart jump. It wasn't Dolly's dramatic chatter about Jane Sterry—trying to drown her. Some gag! No, it was the way she suddenly turned on Will. Dolly was mad that they'd gotten caught and now wanted to act as if Will were the instigator. But Dolly wanted it too. Will knew she did. They decided to keep their distance—or at least not be seen going off alone together—for the rest of the weekend. She could hardly wait for Sunday night, to be back in their room at Brooks Hall, alone, just the two of them. They could put this ugly incident behind them, and Dolly could fall asleep in her arms once more.

Saturday morning all the girls gathered in the dining room in the main house. Dolly had run off ahead of her with a couple of the others. Will took her time, wondering if she could make it without a meal. The drop in her blood pressure as she bent down to examine the veins of an unusually colored leaf told her that she shouldn't risk it. If she fainted, Dolly would never forgive her for acting like a hysteric.

Will took the long path around and entered through the back kitchen, where a servant in a starched white apron pointed her towards the main room. Dolly sat in the center of a bunch of girls, obviously in the middle of unraveling some wild, twisted yarn. She bit into a piece of toast and jam as if she were a lion attacking prey. She must have cracked a joke, as Will could see the other girls turning red with laughter. Will quickly filled her plate with eggs and toast, grabbed a coffee and juice, and took a place at the edge of the action. Dolly's arms gesticulated madly as she told a scandalous tale of boozers and bootleggers who stalked the waterfront.

Will felt such a longing to touch Dolly that even the protein of the eggs could not give her the strength she needed. She thought she might pass right out there—her head crashing into the Limoges ivory plate.

She forced herself to drink the juice, even though the acid triggered a tightening in her esophagus. Could it be making her physically ill to love Dolly? Maybe. Or perhaps not being able to touch Dolly or look closely at her beautiful face was the cause of her sudden shakiness. If she had to endure this punishment of temporary invisibility, then fine, she could do it. Tomorrow evening they'd be back in the privacy of their room. If Will could just remain low-key and take care of herself and not make a big deal about anything, then Dolly would not be so mad about Jane Sterry walking in on them.

She watched Dolly with hunger now, in sporty top and riding skirt, pushing girlish curls out of her face as she laughed and rolled her eyes, play-acting a couple of characters in the wild yarn she spun. The other girls laughed and leaned in to make sure they didn't miss a moment. Will couldn't hear a word as a pre-fainting buzz began to fill her ears. Dolly was sore and testing Will, but she would prove her mettle, like the loyal worshipful dog she was. She just needed to play it a little more cool, or else she'd blow it with Dolly for good.

When the meal was over, Dolly ran about with the other girls, and Will wandered off to the woods. She felt the pull of a Hawthorn tree. It was short like her, and its rough, gray bark seemed to understand suffering. Will leaned against it, eyes closed.

Dolly's curls. Dolly's curls. Could Will train herself to stop thinking about them? If Dolly did indeed decide to end things with Will, could Will look upon her with fresh, detached eyes? Look back on their love as an experiment? Will had never felt this way about anyone before. She felt guilty for even considering giving Dolly up.

Will opened the door to the dorm that night with a shaky hand. Dolly dropped her duffle and valise on the floor then flopped down on her bed. Will moved the bags to the corner and dropped her own beside them.

"I'm bushed," Dolly said.

Will stood still like a robin at the sound of a hawk, not wanting to make a move. She could hear Dolly's shoes drop to the floor, and the papery swish of the fabric of her dress, as she slipped out of it. Will undressed quickly and thought of apologizing to Dolly for what happened with Sterry.

"Dolly, I just want to say ..." she began.

"Put on some music and come to bed." Dolly patted the mattress.

This time Will knew not to overthink things. She dropped an Ethel Waters record and slipped in beside Dolly, spooning her body with her own. The smell of Dolly, like the earthy scent of the trees in the marsh at dawn. She ran a hand up and down the side of Dolly's arm and listened to the exaggerated yawns. Will had studied the language of birds enough to better understand female sounds than words. The yawn was this bird's way of saying she wanted Will to come to her.

Dolly's hips shifted a little as she hummed along, and Will gently turned her over onto her back and climbed on top of her. Their eyes met. They kissed and kissed, and it was like the whole miserable moment of exposure upstate never happened. Will loved the feeling of her mouth and Dolly's connecting as one. The fleshy softness of Dolly's lips made Will feel as if she were dreaming. She could feel Dolly exploring her mouth and nuzzling her face closer to Will's.

Soon, Dolly was running her hands over the silky night shirt Will wore, then slipping her hands underneath to squeeze her breasts. This was more pleasure than Will had ever felt in her life. She let Dolly unbutton the shirt and put her mouth on her nipples.

"Your breasts are so luscious," Dolly said.

Will moaned and felt Dolly's kisses along her neck and back up to her mouth. There was a tenderness then that Dolly rarely showed. Will caught glimpses of her as they kissed and felt a weakness in her heart from her beauty, her openness to love.

And there could be no question: this had to be love. Every poem—from Sappho to Ovid—finally made perfect sense to Will. It was as if the ancients had written their most beguiling lines in anticipation of the two girls meeting, finding their other halves in each other. As Ethel Waters sang, Will closed her eyes and felt Dolly's hands gently stroke her cheeks. She imagined for a moment that a saber tooth tiger came rushing in so that she could slay the savage beast with her bare hands, perhaps sacrificing her own life, all to prove to Dolly how far she would go to protect her.

Chapter Nine

The next morning, Will pretended to be asleep as she watched Dolly dress quickly through narrow slits of her eyes. She knew she had a meeting with her Latin group. It was such a relief to not have to worry about Dolly being sore at her. She could feel a lightness in her chest. Will had had enough athletics for one weekend, but if she hadn't she might even want to take a swim. She remembered the awful moment Sterry caught them fooling around after the swim. Luckily Will had ridden it out without making too much of it. She'd learned to take Dolly's cues and to say less rather than more.

Dolly kicked the frame of Will's bed, startling her.

"What happened?" Will asked.

"You still owe me an apology."

"What are you talking about?"

"You know what I'm talking about. Rhinebeck. Sterry," Dolly said. "You made a big mistake."

Will felt a prickling of pins and needles run up and down her arms.

"I expect an apology," Dolly said.

Will tried to read Dolly's intentions; she searched her face for clues. Dolly's eyes were challenging. Was she challenging Will as if this were a mischievous dare—just to show Will who was "boss" in a playful way? Or was she angry with Will and on the verge of cutting off from her? Yet how could that possibility be so after what they'd shared last night? Could that have scared Dolly, though? Will had no ambivalence about wanting to be with Dolly—completely, in every way. Dolly, she had to admit, always seemed ambivalent.

What to do?

Will could not think of going to class now. She had to right this wrong or she'd be unable to think, to function. But what wrong had she done? She sat down at the Smith-Corona. If she could finesse the situation, be as hedgy as Dolly, perhaps that would do the trick. This called for guts, though, the courage to risk "blowing" the whole thing.

Will looked at her fingers resting on the typewriter keys.

Dear Dolly,

You have asked me to apologize for the unfortunate incident that took place this past weekend in Rhinebeck. I cannot see how I was the one at fault here who owes you an apology.

The only question, then, is with you. You demand me to perform an act, namely, state that I acted wrongly. This I refuse. Now it is up to you to inflict the penalty for this refusal, at your discretion, to break friendship, inflict physical punishment, or anything else you like, or on the other hand, continue as before. The decision, therefore, must rest with you. This is all of my opinion on the right and wrong of the matter.

Now a word of advice. I do not wish to influence your decision either way, but I do want to warn you that in case you deem it advisable to discontinue our friendship, that in both our interests extreme care must be had. The motif of "A falling out of a pair of muff-divers" would be sure to be popular, which is patently undesirable and forms an irksome, but unavoidable bond between us ...

On Wednesday morning, Professor Hayes stood at the board and underlined the names *Dostoyevsky* and *Nietzsche*. A tall woman with a long neck, she wore a relaxed straight-lined sand-colored suit and tended toward heavy eye contact with her students. Will felt bright-eyed and bushy-tailed and ready to take part in the lesson. Her letter had worked to smooth over the row she'd had with Dolly. It occurred to Will that her every mood had become dependent on how Dolly treated her. Well, if that was the price of admission then damn it she was willing to pay!

The girls sat far apart—Will up front, where she could better see. She kept reading glasses on her desk for when they were instructed to turn to a certain page. Otherwise, she hated to look any more masculine than she already did. Alone with Dolly was one matter but being surrounded by these pretty, well-scrubbed goyim girls made Will feel as if there were a spotlight on her Jewish features— the darkness of her eyes and brow, the thickness of her dark hair, the strong presence of her nose, the olive tone of her skin. Add to that that there was simply something distinctively un-female about her and she knew it.

Will had spent many an hour studying herself in the mirror. Not long after her mother become incapacitated, she started to take long baths and fantasize about what it would be like to be a boy. Afterwards, she would slick her hair back with water and part it sharply like Rudolph Valentino, who all the girls at school giggled about. When the housekeeper was off, she would even go so far as to try on one of her father's starched white shirts and conservative dark ties. She thought she made a rather handsome, sensual, and brooding young man. She'd even kept the starched white shirt, enjoying the way it felt against her skin.

"So, what is the connection between the great Russian author and the great German philosopher?"

"They both thought they were great!" Dolly called out, inspiring laughs. "Super-uber-duber great!"

More laughs, even a smile from Professor Hayes.

"All right, Miss Raab. You woke up your classmates. Now, let's see if we can dig a little deeper. What is the intellectual connection between the two? Miss Reinhardt?"

"Well, Dostoyevsky portrays morality as something that one can choose only if he is so weak to require such a compass to live by,"

Will said, wiping her reading glasses on a cloth for effect. "But the powerful do not need to fall back on such illusions. And Nietzsche, too, saw morality, saw *God* as a fiction created by the weak sheep who wished to follow a so-called 'higher law.'"

"But Dostoyevsky—he *did* believe in God," Dolly said.

"Do we know that *he* did, or are you saying that his novel's protagonist, Raskolnikov, believed in God?" Will replied. "Be precise!"

The class laughed.

"Well, I don't know about Dostoyevsky ..."

"It seems a moment ago you thought you did," Will cut in.

"Yeah, well," Dolly sputtered. "Regardless ... what *Raskolnikov* realizes too late, after he has sinned by committing the worst possible crime ... is that God does indeed exist, and we do indeed live in a just and moral universe."

Dolly paused, then added: "He was a rather serious fellow!"

"Sounds like Miss Raab is giving you the floor, Miss Reinhardt. Do you concur with her conclusion?"

"First, Miss Raab, you are assuming there is a God," Will said. "What proof do we have of that? Second, you are claiming that murder is the worst crime. What about rape? What about torture? But regardless of your careless commentary, Raskolnikov's suffering after his so-called crime is exactly what Nietzsche would expect from such a character ..."

"So-called crime?" Dolly cut in, but Will refused to cede the floor.

"Yes, so-called. For if a superman, an *ubermensch*, a man of greater intellect and self-possession, someone above the common man, the sheep-like follower, were to commit murder it would not be a crime, it would be a mere intellectual exercise, for that man would be above the commoners' law."

"But," Dolly said, meeting Will's eyes. "Who is to choose who is above the law?"

"The superman ..."

"What about the superwoman?" Dolly piped in, lightening the mood.

Will played along, though her prickliness was impossible to disguise.

"Yes, Miss Raab, the superwoman should indeed be included. But regardless of sex, the superhuman is above the law, a master. While all others are mere slaves. According to Nietzsche a slave must know his place and be submissive, not take any self-directed action. Raskolnikov did not realize his station in life. He was not a master but a slave."

"How do you define master and slave, Miss Reinhardt?" Professor Hayes asked.

"That is an excellent question."

"Why thank you, Miss Reinhardt," Professor Hayes said. "Perhaps I shall see about becoming a scholar."

The class laughed, and so did Will. She liked Hayes.

"I think you'd be the cat's meow!" Will said, this time garnering a warm smile from Hayes and Dolly too. "But to answer your question fully, I think master and slave are internal states of mind."

"If internal," Dolly said. "How can they be evidenced? A lot of things can be all in someone's mind, can't they?"

"It can't be proven, but the master mind does not need to offer proof," Will said. "He knows he is a master because of one simple fact: he has no ambivalence about the action he takes. Even an impoverished street urchin could be a master if he is sure of himself and trusts his own mind more than the laws of the common man or the opinion of others. While conversely, the richest of the rich, and the most powerful ruler might be unsure of his decisions, might indeed feel like the emperor who wears no clothes, always fearing exposure."

"And so," said a quiet girl in the back row wearing a smart yellow dress. "Confidence is the key trait of a superman?"

"Perhaps," Will said, taking a moment to think more. "Perhaps it is."

"Then what of false confidence?" the girl in the yellow dress asked, a little more pointedly. "What if a so-called superman took an action that turned out to be the wrong action?"

"He would turn out to be, in actuality, a slave," Will said. "Which is exactly what occurs in *Crime and Punishment*. Raskolnikov should have taken no action for he was a slave on the inside, not a superman capable of choosing and acting upon his own individual laws. That is why he pays such a high price for his mistake—his false belief that he was a superman. For this he is tormented perpetually by guilt."

"But," said Yellow Dress. "What if a real superman, not someone who was a slave on the inside but a true master, chose to commit murder? And what if he got caught? Would that not prove a false confidence?"

"If he were to be caught," Dolly said, "he would not be a superman. For supermen do not make mistakes."

"They are like Gods that way, Miss Raab?" Professor Hayes asked.

"Yes. Or Goddesses!"

More laughter.

"But," Will added. "Perhaps there could be an exception to Miss Raab's rule. For what if this hypothetical superman were to reveal his crime to just one other?"

"But why would he?" Yellow Dress asked. "Why would he confess to anyone unless, as you argue, he were a slave in reality who took an action he should not have and therefore deserved punishment?"

"She's not talking about confessing. Maybe he wants to share in the brilliance of his crime," Dolly said.

Will had to stifle a smile. She knew that Dolly was speaking to her and her alone. They were above these rubes in every way—except for Professor Hayes, of course, but if she'd been in on the joke she would've toasted their brilliance as well. Will felt a sense of superiority knowing she and Dolly were each other's confidantes and so much more. She found so much pleasure in worshiping Dolly.

Years ago, Momma had to pick up Will from camp when Will had developed what the Camp Leah Director called an "unhealthy attachment" to Tamar, a senior counselor. They'd found Will outside the counselor's window in the middle of the night. Remembering that summer in the Catskills, Will could see that she had indeed attached an unhealthy amount of worship to the older girl. She was in no way deserving of it. She was no Dolly.

"So, a superman has no weaknesses?" Professor Hayes said.

"No," Will said. "No weaknesses."

And as she said it, she felt an injection of strength fill her body and steady her nerves. Dolly looked at her, and Will sat up straight, forcing her eyes to project steely-eyed strength. She wondered, as she held her stance, if this is what a man feels like every day of his life.

Chapter Ten

S mall four-tops with white tablecloths circled the crowded dance floor. The band played heavy on the stand-up bass and snare drum. A veritable liquid gold rhythm section. Behind the bandstand a large banner read "In compliance with the Eighteenth Amendment, no intoxicating liquor allowed on the premises." A few corsages were pinned to the edges, making the place feel like a school dance. A bunch of kids had jammed the bar. One boy with a funnel in his mouth hung his head back, while two others poured liquor down his throat. At a half-toppled table closest to the drum kit sat a pint-sized collegian in bow tie and spats surrounded by a minxy set of girls signing the cast on his arm. One of them held a baby bottle for him which he sipped from, leaning his long neck back to gargle with the booze much to the gang's amusement.

Upon entry, a hand waved her over—the girl in the yellow dress, cuddled up all goofy with a young man. She smiled, ready to approach, and then noticed Dolly. The sight of her gave Will a twist of pain in her chest. She never knew quite what to do when they were in public. She had to watch Dolly for cues all the time.

Dolly had befriended the head bartender at Rudy's. In fact, Dolly was practically sitting on the bar telling what looked like a real knee-slapper. Joe from the movies huddled up next to her. He'd been calling on the horn plenty and Dolly had said she wasn't going to give him the time of day, but Will could tell that was a lie. The guy was willing to drop a stack of cash on Dolly, and she wasn't about to turn him down. But Will would have the last laugh. She'd wait him out. Dolly could tease him all she wanted. It was Will who she came home to.

Yellow Dress waved again.

"We're in philosophy class together," she called.

Will approached.

"I'm Maeve. This is my fella Kent."

"Wilhelmina."

Maeve and Kent sat parked at a small wobbly table in the back while rich kids ordered seconds and thirds closer to the front-of-house action.

"Wilhelmina really made some excellent points about Nietzsche in class," Maeve said.

Kent nodded. "Well if Maeve noticed you, you must be pretty on the ball."

"Kent's a reporter," Maeve said. "*New York Spectator*."

"I'm just trying to break in. The boss likes big stories. Right now, the biggest scoop I've made is the dog-catcher snoozing on duty!"

They all laughed and took a drink.

"I know I should be smoother than this, but—boy—does this stuff burn!" Maeve said.

"I'm not a big fan of the taste either," Will said.

"Then why do we drink it at all?" Maeve asked.

"Probably makes a mug like mine seem handsome," Kent said.

"You *are* handsome," Maeve said, predictably.

Will took a closer look at his face. He was a rather ordinary-looking fellow. Small, hooded blue eyes, a nose that was too dainty for a man, thin lips, light brown, almost colorless hair. He seemed benign.

"Are you a philosophy major?" he asked.

"Just a freshman, so I'm undeclared. I guess I'm something of a generalist—I'm a classically trained musician, an ornithologist, linguist ..."

"Wow! Are you what they call a polymath?" Maeve asked.

"I suppose."

Kent looked impressed too.

"I actually covered a nature story last year—and it was about birds."

"What was it?" Will asked.

"Oh, Kent wrote a lovely piece about the seagulls on Ellis Island. It came out at the end of the year ..."

"Thanks, Maeve. Yeah, it was a sentimental Christmas piece. The senior reporters were home with their families and I was out in the freezing cold waxing poetic about birds in New York Harbor like a darn fool."

"I thought all birds migrated in winter," Maeve said. "I learned a lot."

"No," Will said. "Migratory patterns differ widely. Gulls in these parts tend to adapt to cold weather. But I must say, this appears to be a poor decade for humans on Ellis Island."

They looked at her blankly—gentiles through and through.

"Willsie!"

Dolly shimmied over to the table. "I don't think I've had the pleasure."

"Dolly," Will said, "This is Maeve and Kent."

"Swell to meetcha," Dolly said. "Hey Willsie, there's a fight about to break out, stage right. Come with me and help me to pass the peace pipe. Nice to meet you folks!"

Dolly pulled Will away and when Will looked back, she saw Kent slip an arm around Maeve. The band had started up an especially syncopated Charleston, and the dancing caught fire.

Dolly's face gleamed with sweat.

"I've been dancing all night. You see me out there?"

Will just nodded.

"Let's go for a stroll, Willsie," Dolly said, adding, "Don't forget you belong to me."

Will had no idea what Dolly was up to. Could it be she was jealous of Maeve? It was possible. They stepped outside and Will, emboldened by liquor and the attention of first Maeve and now Dolly, turned to her friend and gave her a wink. Dolly moved in close and pushed Will into the dusty bricks on Lennox. Will reached up to put her hands around Dolly's neck. The urge to kiss her was stronger than the fear of who might see.

"I've got a hard-on for you, baby," Dolly whispered into her ear.

The words gave Will a dizzy feeling until she felt something cold and heavy press into her gut.

"What is that?"

Will felt a chill spread through her body as Dolly showed her the pistol.

"Don't piss all over yourself!" Dolly laughed.

Dolly hustled Will out onto 134th Street and whispered "stick close to the bricks," as she led them two blocks south to a walk-up building. Will followed, but not happily. It enraged her that Dolly's beauty, her charisma, made Will such a dope. Then again, it was an honor to be made a fool by such a Goddess. Dolly buzzed in a syncopated rhythm and ten seconds later, the lock unclicked. She led them up three flights of stairs and a winded Will finally asked, "Where are we going?"

"Just follow my lead."

As they approached the fourth floor, Will heard the sound of a Creole-flavored jazz cornet floating out into the hall from number 4R. Dolly knocked with fervor, and a tall mocha-skinned gent in a rust-colored suit opened the door a crack.

"You lost, little girls?" he said, pulling the door open another inch.

"Tubby Arnold will vouch for us," Dolly said.

Will had never heard that name before.

"Tubby? He's here playing the slide. And who you be, girl?"

"Dolly. This is Will."

"Dolly, Dolly, my whole life has been a folly …" the big man sang.

"Come on in. Uh, but first spot me two bits."

"Oh right," Dolly said, then pulled Will aside.

"What's going on?"

"You got two bits? It's a rent party."

Will reached into her clutch for some change.

He gave her a hard look then started to close the door.

"All right, all right. No need to blow your top, Lieutenant. Take it."

He pocketed the coins and opened the door wide, shutting it quickly behind them. How did Dolly know about this place? What it cost? And who was this Tubby Arnold? It was as if Dolly had a whole separate life Will knew nothing about. The apartment opened into the kitchen where greens simmered on the stove along with fatty pork belly.

"Let's get to the booze," Dolly whispered to Will.

The few other white faces in the room were not hard to spot. The railroad-style apartment was packed tight, with a small jazz ensemble playing a set right outside the bathroom. Just cornet, drum, and sax. Will had heard about these rent parties but had never been to one.

"Next up on the keys we gots a man who plays the dozens like his board's got eighty-eight cousins. On loan from down South, here's Speckled Red!"

Wearing a natty tweed suit and a hat too small for his head, the pianist sat down and began to roll out lines in a boogie-woogie style.

Dolly laughed and danced next to Will. "Ain't this grand?" she said.

She stuck her pocketbook under a corner chair as couples twirled in stompy little rounds across the floor and soon, many of the guests coupled off and danced in a languorous sway as the noise dipped into downbeat. Will put her arm around Dolly's waist and turned her around. The music suddenly sped up as if they were playing musical chairs; Will and Dolly giggled and jumped to the beat. Nobody seemed to care that they were two girls. Two older gals, one curvy and dark-skinned wearing a red feathered dress was tearing it up with a slim, dashing lady in emerald silk trousers, shirt, and tie.

An older man with salt and pepper hair and a rough growth of beard looked Will in the eye, smiled, and licked his lips. She instinctively pulled away from Dolly, and Dolly started dancing with a gap-toothed fellow in sunglasses. She'd read about these parties—how they situated the alcohol close enough to the bathroom or to a window out onto an alley so if the law raided, they could swiftly dump the stuff. Prohibition could be a real pickle.

When Will turned back, the gap-toothed man was pawing Dolly, so she grabbed her and pulled her to the liquor station. The alcohol made Will's head whoozy. She closed her eyes and felt the room spin, but when she opened them Dolly was gone. Will put her hand on the back of a stool to steady herself as she scanned the room. In the same corner where Dolly had tossed her pocketbook she saw an older man, noticeably white and noticeably older, laughing with Dolly. As Will got closer though she could see that Dolly was not laughing at all; she was trying to get away from the man.

"Just gimme the goddamn pocketbook," Dolly said.

"Oooh, such language from a young lady."

"Awww come on, buster. This ain't no debutante ball. What are *you* doing here anyway? You look pretty out of place."

"I'm slumming," he said.

"You ok?" Will asked.

"She's fine in my hands," he said.

He placed his arm around Dolly, who tried to squirm free.

"Let her go," Will said.

"Don't worry about this hobo, friend. He says he's slumming but judging by the mud on his spats, he's been walking the streets and eating out of ash cans."

"That's some mouth you've got there," Spats said. "You think I'm so poor, let's see what you can lend me."

And with that he opened Dolly's bag and shot them both a smirk.

"Well, well. You really are loaded," Spats said.

"Look, I can get Tubby over here to take care of you," Dolly said.

"You do that, sis," Spats said, grabbing the pistol and Dolly's small wad of cash.

He tossed her the pocketbook and shoved Will out of the way.

"Grab him," Dolly said.

"What?"

Dolly let out a guttural sound, clearly frustrated by Will's slow response time. Will wanted to be a hero, to save the day, but her head was too dusted up with liquor.

"Come on!" Dolly said.

She followed Spats to a bedroom in the back of the place. The bed was mostly covered in coats. A pretty, ebony-skinned flapper in a shimmery white dress sat on the lap of a man in a tan suit. He rubbed the back of her neck with one hand and held a cigar in the other. With a few nimble steps, Spats stumbled out the fire escape and the girls followed. Dolly had to take off her high heels to do the climb. They each jumped the final step into the dark. Once down in the alley they saw Spats make a dash for the street, but he must've tripped on a bottle because before Will had time to think, he'd dropped the purse and Dolly made a grab for it.

She pulled the gun out of the pocketbook and held Spats in her sights.

What was she going to do, shoot him?

"Ok, kiddo," Dolly whispered to Will and passed her the gun.

Will shrunk back—it was cold and unknowable like black ice.

"What are you doing? Are you off the tracks?"

"You're the one who's going to do something."

Will moved her eyes from Spats, giving him the chance to run— knocking over a trash can as he flew out of the alley.

"God-*damn* it," Dolly shouted. "You let him go. You coward. Gimme that rod."

Dolly grabbed the pistol, and Will felt as if she could breathe again, with the cold, heavy thing out of her hands. Dolly pointed the gun at Will and gave her a look that Will could not interpret. She ran out of the alley, onto the avenue, her head awash in liquor and fear, as she heard Dolly call after her.

Buildings filled her peripheral vision, browner and older than her home on Sutton Place. Like a racehorse she blindly galloped ahead, suddenly free, sensing Dolly was far behind, too far back to catch up. Steam blew out of the manhole covers on the street and in the far distance, Will could see the green light of the subway station. She could leap on the IRT and be home to Momma in no time. But her mind had tricked her, just like it did in her dreams many a night. Momma was gone. Will turned back to see if Dolly was still chasing her. Her ankle twisted on an uneven bit of concrete, and she fell to the ground.

Dolly sauntered toward Will. Her legs looked so pretty parading forth, covered only by her beaded silk dress. She created soft percussive music simply by walking. Will breathed, still sprawled on the ground, relieved at the sound of her.

"It's off," Dolly said, stopping in front of her. "You're a weak sister."

"What?"

"All of it. I'm getting a new roommate. Helena's sick of the bore they stuck her with. We'll swap. It's been fun, Reinhardt. Mostly for you ..."

She walked past Will, leaving her lying there, twisted. Will wanted to ask her for a hand, to help her stand, to get them a taxi, but she didn't. Forcing herself to rise—to stretch her ankle and tell herself she could walk—served as a distraction from the blaring alarm bells screaming in her head: *you've lost her!*

"Please, wait. I'm sorry. I thought you were kidding."

Will was able to hobble up to Dolly, who swung around and spat out the words:

"You would! You don't know how to commit fully to anything, do you? You dabble in birds, in languages, in music, in *me*. But you won't take a risk, will you?"

"I couldn't shoot him, Dolly."

"Well that's okay, I'm sick of you anyway. You had a chance to show your loyalty and you flopped. It's over, Willsie. We're through. I'll bunk up with Helena, say you were all hands in the middle of the night."

How could this be happening? Will feared Dolly and knew she should run. But she couldn't. Then the words and the idea came out all at once, from where, she could not say: "The night of the big Columbia Lions game on Halloween," she said calmly. "We're going to rob those bitches blind."

Dolly smiled. "Go on."

"Chi-Omega. Those blabbermouths let on they're going to be drinking all night during the game and then out cutting a rug with the boys afterwards. By the time they get back they'll be ossified left and right, one more soused than the next. We come in just before dawn. I bet I can swipe a key to the house from Maeve. I'll get us in, Dolly girl, and then we'll rob the place blind and they won't know what hit 'em."

Dolly rewarded Will with a radiant smile.

"Why, Willsie. You do live to surprise, don't cha? Well, that sounds just fine," Dolly said.

Will wanted to cry with relief. If Dolly could warm up to Will again so easily, a shivery feeling inside her warned that she could turn cold again with just as little warning.

"Now," Dolly said. "Let's whistle for a taxi and get you some beauty sleep. Planning starts tomorrow."

Dolly's eyes looked playful again, not dangerous, as she lit up a smoke. Will still wasn't sure if the gun was loaded or not.

Chapter Eleven

Thursday night they met at the library in the stacks of the music section to study Brahms for Friday's theory exam. Will brought a ledger with her, stuck between a textbook on Romantic-Era Composers and a spiral pad of sheet music crib notes.

Dolly lay on the floor reading a pulp magazine, her bare feet up on the shelf, toes tipping into a series of books on Hungarian Folk Dances. Dolly's feet were pudgier than one would expect, almost as if the last bits of baby fat were stubbornly holding on, not wanting to leave her grown-up body. She imagined Dolly's leg wrapped around her neck, and how she would rub her face against the soft fleshy bottom of Dolly's foot, squeeze her heel, kiss her calves.

"Studying hard?" Will asked.

"Mmm-hmm. I've got a real humdinger of an idea for a job we can pull. A little practice in crime before we hit Chi-Omega. Check this out." She passed the magazine to Will.

It was a "True Life Tale," or so the pulp claimed, called "Fire on the Brain." Will gave it a cursory read. An elderly couple sets fire to the horse barn behind the house of their wealthy employers when they unfairly fire them after fifty years of service.

"Great, Dolly girl," Will said.

"No, no, listen, this is something we can do."

Will shushed her, and Dolly lowered her voice.

"There's an abandoned stable on the southern edge of Bronx Park."

"I know it. That's part of the New York Zoological Society's land. How do you know it?"

"I snuck a peek in one of your birding books."

"I'm touched," Will said.

"Look. I found the joint, now you gotta go in with me on the rest."

"And what does that entail?" Will watched as Dolly's feet slid down and back into her patent leathers.

"You steal the gasoline."

"Why steal? I can certainly tell Waldek to pick up a few gallons."

"It's gotta be even Steven," Dolly said. "And we pull the crime together. You bring the gas. I bring the flame."

Dolly leaned in close to Will, so close she could feel the breath from her mouth.

"Write it down," Will said, pulling out the ledger.

"What?" Dolly said.

"I'll pull this job with you, but then you have to give me what I want in return."

Dolly looked at her blankly then tossed her head back as if she was going to laugh, but no sound came out.

Dolly wrote down in their simple code: *RF* for "Fire." No vowels. Consonants backwards.

"And what do you want in return?" Dolly asked, biting her lip and giving Will a secret smirk.

Will wrote down what she wanted:

One hundred percent.

She looked at Dolly, who giggled then looked away. Of course she knew what that code stood for: everything. Why was she suddenly shy?

"Should we crack the books now?" Will asked.

"You crack, while I snack." Dolly pulled out some taffy and started chewing loudly.

Will laughed and said, "Come on, Dolly. Pop quiz. Now!"

"Yes, sir!"

Dolly sat up, suddenly in the mood to play.

"Label the harmony: In Op. 118, No. 2 in A major, what chord does Brahams shift into as the tonic for the middle section?"

"F#," Dolly said, snapping her taffy like gum.

"What type of rhythms does Brahms use in the B sections?"

"Cross-rhythms, natch."

"When does he place a root-position tonic in a strong metrical position?"

"The end of section A."

Will continued to quiz Dolly, in awe of her genius and charisma. Did she ever study? She could argue philosophy and absorb the nuances of classical music theory seemingly without effort. She could befriend a bus driver or a royal prince. Will thought about the promise she held in the ledger and felt herself finally experiencing what others took for granted: good fortune.

At half-past midnight, Will parked the car on West 133rd and sauntered a cool half-block up "jungle alley," as Dolly said it was called by the negro musicians. They landed near Lennox in front of a discrete set of Neo-Greco row houses.

"That's really what it goes by! This block is where all the action is," she said. "Smell a whiff of what's in the air."

Marijuana. The aroma reminded Will of the scent of burning rope, not exactly unpleasant.

"Come on. This is Hansberry's Clam House. You're going to feel right at home here, Willsie."

A big woman in a fur coat looked them over and laughed.

"Should I frisk y'all, or you wanna just cough up extra change to make up for your age?"

Dolly laughed and nudged Will to procure the price of entry.

"Who's that on the keys?" Dolly asked.

Will could hear the syncopated rhythm coming up through the floorboards and rising through her body like a fever. This was hot jazz. They slithered between the patrons making their way to the bar stools. The crowd was a mix of Black and white, and she estimated they were the youngest ones there. Will could see what Dolly meant about feeling right at home. This speakeasy was full of pairs like them. Men and men, women and women.

"Bottoms up."

They slammed the little glass shot glasses, and Dolly quickly slid another dollar from Will's wallet for the next round.

"Let's dance, Willsie."

Will couldn't argue. She followed the beat and it was just like when they first played together. A perfect pair of aces. The gent piano player had a baby face and Will took him to be not much older than them. He wore a spotless white tuxedo, which hugged his burly physique and a white top hat to match. His dark skin gleamed with sweat and he moved his fingers so fast it was as if he had an extra pair of hands.

When the set was over Dolly said, "Come on, I gotta meet him."

The piano player had already started moving in on a curvy older lady with tight kinky curls and pearl drop earrings.

"Hey, do you see what I see?" Dolly said. "That piano player is a girl."

Another woman in high-waisted pants and suspenders casually removed the rich lady's hand from the piano player's arm and dragged her away with ease. Dolly took this as an opportunity to move in.

"Hey, your chops are heavenly, bub!" she said.

"Saw you two kicking it fine. You like the music?"

"Oh hell yeah!" Dolly said. "I'm a piano player myself. Will plays clarinet."

A bow-tied gent carrying a golf club and a heavy glass scooted in between them.

"Thanks," the piano player said and downed the liquor like it was straight from the kitchen tap.

Will wasn't sure if it was the steam bath of the cramped space or the effects of the gin, but when she looked a little closer at the piano player she could see herself in such a costume. Wouldn't it be divine to parade around the party in such handsome duds?

As if reading her mind, Dolly whispered in her ear, "You'd look pretty fine in that tux, Willsie."

Will stood up a little straighter and felt as if she'd already donned a top hat upon her head.

Chapter Twelve
Dolly

The theory exam had gone silky smooth and now Orchestra was breezing along without a snag in sight. The basement room with its soundproofed walls felt like a safe cocoon to Dolly.

"Replace the fourth with a Neapolitan sixth," Professor Wolfenstein directed.

The auditorium was stuffy, and the viola player seemed off-key today. Will kept trying to send her dopey looks from behind her clarinet, but they were in different worlds. She knew what was on Will's mind. It didn't matter. She could give Will what she wanted if that's what it took. Dolly wanted a witness. A partner, yes, because that took away some of the lonesomeness. But having someone witness her talents was divine. Crime and jazz. Jazz and crime. A flaming combination and Dolly knew she couldn't experience the best of both without ole Willsie. This was their moment. Plan and plan and then improvise with the band. She felt her fingers plunking out the physically demanding King Oliver tune even as she leaned into the melancholy Brahms refrain.

This was something she'd discovered after meeting Will—the ability to play classical with her fingers, but play jazz inside her mind. Like an *under*-sound. She couldn't put it into words, but it lit up her insides the way reading the crime pulps behind her school books used to. The teachers never caught on, and her grammar school chums loved her mischief.

Jazz entered her world a short while before the clock struck midnight ringing in a new decade: the '20s! December 31, 1919. Daddy was sick on New Year's Eve and Mumsie outright refused to miss the party of the year, of the decade, the opening party of the decade at that! Twelve-year-old Dolly made a case for going as Mumsie's date, in lieu of Daddy. Mumsie blew that horn with as much passion as Dolly did. What choice did the old man full of aches and pains have but to let the little lassies go on without him? The governess and Sheffy could keep each other company while Daddy rested and the old decade passed into the new.

At first it was all glitter and treats and the thrill of staying up till midnight. But as the hour ticked closer, Dolly grew bored with the grownups and their talk of J. Edgar Hoover deporting Emma Goldman and the rest of the radicals; the Belgians, the French, and the Germans signing the Locarno Treaty. It was all sewn up that there would not be a World War like we just won. It was starting to feel like a particularly dull day at school until Dolly heard someone plunking out a catchy tune on the piano. She slid between the champagne-soaked guests, underneath the wafting cigar smoke, till she came upon a young man in white tux and tails sitting on the bench playing as if the music was writing itself.

"What song is that you're playing?" Dolly asked.

He only lifted his eyes. "Just improvising, little lady."

His voice had an accent Dolly took as Caribbean. She was not used to being at a loss for words—with anyone of any age. She looked at the keys, and he slid towards the bass end, making room for her at the treble side. He ashed his cigarette into an empty champagne flute and began a downbeat rhythm. With a tilt of his head he invited Dolly to join him. Classical piano she knew, and had no problem reading music, but this was something different.

Soon, her fingers found frolicsome little bits to add to the chugga-chugga of his rumbling train. Such an easy rhythm. Dolly didn't have to think, just keep up, slow down, keep up. She watched his hands while letting her own explore. He played at a slower tempo than Dolly expected, so it felt natural to add in plenty of unexpected notes to liven up the steady beat.

They played like that for several tunes, and she asked him what he called what they were doing.

"Jazz," he said. "Wanna learn a song?"

She nodded.

"Okay, just listen."

He played it once, and she could hear the drama in the little underplayed interludes. He told her it was New Orleans-style jazz.

"Now you try it."

She was able to repeat parts of what she heard and add her own little punch. Afterwards he asked her, "You ever hear of the Axeman?"

"I don't know," she said.

"Keep playing," he said. "And listen to a story."

He proceeded to tell the tale of a murderer in New Orleans who came to be known as the Axeman. He'd use a chisel to break the glass on a door, and let himself into a home, only to attack with his axe, night after night, leaving corpses and the maimed behind. And all of this took place this very same year—1919.

He terrorized the city! Families took turns sleeping at night, always needing someone to stand guard against the deadly intruder. And then one day the local paper printed a letter from the Axeman, who'd identified his home address as "Hell." He made a proposition to the townspeople. Proclaiming a fondness for jazz music, he promised that he would be out with his axe after midnight on March nineteenth but would spare any place where a jazz band played. The saloons and dance halls soon filled, and many an improv band set up instruments in living rooms across the city. No victims were reported that night.

"And the song we've been playing," the young man said. "It's called 'Axeman Blues.'"

All through Orchestra Dolly could only imagine fire. The thought of seeing the flames catch and then the whole place sizzle and blow gave her goosebumps.

"Miss Reinhardt, Miss Raab, please stay after dismissal, yah?"

Dolly perked up then and gave Will a wink. After the other girls sauntered out with their instruments, they approached.

"You wanted us Herr Wolfenstein?" Dolly asked with perfect German inflections.

"Oh, yes, Miss Raab. Next time we'll try in E minor. We build even more tension from the composition, yah?"

Dolly nodded.

"So, you have heard of the Leipzig Conservatory in Germany, yah?"

"Yah!" Dolly shouted then laughed.

"Yes, sir," Will replied. "Herr Sigfred Karg-Elert is an alumnus."

"Correct. He studied there and teaches as well. He began with piano and now he is at work on compositions using the harmonium. Very original music! He is actually a close colleague, and he asked me if I could offer up two female students to study there over the summer. Do you think your parents would allow this?"

Will and Dolly both burst out laughing.

"Yes!" Will exclaimed.

"Yah!"

"I mean, we'll talk to them tonight, but they greatly support our studies ..."

"You like for me to call and talk to them?"

This was even better! Will and Dolly thanked the professor and packed up their instruments.

Once outside, Dolly grabbed Will and danced her around the quad.

"We're sailing to Europe in June, Willsie!"

"Well, our parents still have to ..."

"Oh come on. It's in the bag, scalawag!" Dolly said.

She grabbed the sheet music and winked at Will, then set off to meet Joe out on St. Nicholas. He was leaning against that jalopy as if it was a Bentley. Dolly walked over, cigarette in mouth, looked him in the eye with a grin, and waited for him to light it.

"You look swell," he said. "Your hair matches the sunshine."

Where did he get dumb lines like that? Didn't the dope realize she'd been speaking Latin in the morning and playing Grieg and Brahms in the afternoon? All he cared about were her sunshiney curls.

"Nice of you to notice," she said.

"Sure, you don't want to go out for a ride with me instead of working for the family?"

"Nah. It's a family event—the Jewish side of the family. I need to be there. I'll get you your car back in the morning. I'll meet ya for breakfast at Lil's."

"Okay," he said, tugging on his tie and shuffling his feet. "But come in for a little cuddle first, won'tcha?"

Joe opened the door and Dolly slid in, while Joe slipped around to the driver's side.

He leaned in to kiss her, and she drove him crazy by only allowing peck after peck.

Finally, he just lit up a cigarette and put his arm around her.

"You know I'm under a lot of pressure now," he said. "If I don't pull all As this semester the old man's taking back the wheels."

Dolly put her head on his shoulder and held out her hand so he'd pass her the stick.

"You have no idea what it's like," he said. "My whole future is riding on how I do at Columbia."

"It must be so hard," she said, then rubbed her thigh ever so subtly against his to make him *really* hard.

"Dolly ..." he said.

She leaned back so he could kiss her full on. This time she was happy to. Anything to stop his sad-sack speech. Dolly pulled back for a moment to look at his face. Soft baby cheeks, big blue eyes, thick floppy dark hair. She liked looking at him. Just like he liked looking at her. This thing with Will was starting to take over, and she wondered if it would be wise to kill the whole arson plan. Just don't go through with it. Be all *Steady Betty* with Joe. Switch rooms with Will. There were plenty of girls like Will at Barnard. She could find someone to get all smashed on who returned her feelings. She'd get over Dolly.

Yeah, all of this sounded good. But as Dolly heard Joe profess "I love you," when he didn't even know her at all, she realized that she didn't have to do a damn thing she didn't want to do.

"Say it again," she said.

And she made him say it three more times. When he finally looked her in the eye and said, "What about you, Doll?" she pretended not to understand and just asked him for the car keys.

Dolly picked up Will on the corner of Amsterdam and 116th. If Will was all crabby because of Dolly's tardiness it was over between them. But Will stood on the corner, two large thermoses on either side of her, smiling. Dolly honked twice before she pulled up.

"Evening picnic?" Dolly laughed, pushing the door open for her. "You look like an amateur bootlegger."

"Yes, well, what I've got in here will set your insides on fire. That's for sure."

Dolly was glad Will was in a rowdy mood. She didn't need her being a nervous Nellie and ruining all the fun.

"Joe stowed a flask in the glove box. Take a swig and pass it over here," Dolly said.

"So you still seeing him?" Will asked.

"Yeah, what of it?"

"Nothing. Maybe you should have asked him to pull this little job with you."

"Maybe I should have," Dolly said, not falling for her routine. "And then he can cash in on your prize. Would you like that?"

Will fell silent. Dolly took the Harlem River Drive and decided to help old Willsie loosen up with a little hand on the thigh.

"I've been looking forward to this," Will said.

"Where'd you get the gasoline?"

"Trade secret."

Good, the old girl was being playful again. Dolly would have to be careful not to get too edgy with her. Fun Will was better than sulky Will on a job like this.

They pulled onto Webster Avenue just after dusk.

"Let's finish this off," Dolly said, grabbing the flask. "Hold the wheel."

Nice and soused, Dolly drove into a dead end behind a closed Parks Department office and turned off the engine. They each grabbed a thermos, and Dolly led them in silence through the brush to the hilly area just behind the abandoned barn. She loped ahead several feet before she noticed Will was still on the ground, struggling to get some footing with the thermos in her hand. Will could be so klutzy. For someone who went birding in the woods all the time you'd think she'd know her way over some rocks and stray roots. Dolly ambled down, grabbed the other thermos, and hurried her along.

They walked in silence through the long meadow. Dolly's hands felt cold; the temperature had dropped. It was a dry night. She'd checked the almanac and all the papers. This baby was going to burn.

"It's right up around the bend," she said.

She felt Will losing step with her and grabbed her hand in sudden excitement.

"There she is!" Dolly exclaimed.

It was harder to make out in the darkness, but Dolly thought she could see two large boards that formed a misshapen cross over the roof. She hoofed it over the short fence and gave Will a hand to do the same. They tramped through the tumbleweed and pushed open the barn door. Hay bales lined the sides along with broken barrels and crumpled-up newspaper. Maybe a hobo or two made this place home? If they ended up setting a couple of rummies on fire all the better. The hurricane lamp was inside the barrel in the northwest corner, just where Dolly had left it a few days earlier.

She pulled it out and struck a match. Will's eyes twitched back at her with excitement. Maybe she wasn't such a chicken after all. Dolly lifted up her thermos by the handle, and Will did the same. They instinctively clinked them together like shot glasses. Without words they began to douse the place all along the corners. God, this was swell! Dolly could feel the adrenaline rush that only a rousing bit of wrongdoing could arouse. She wished she could watch herself in the act, running about with the gasoline. Sometimes when she was with Will she could see herself from above. Sometimes not. But in the midst of a fine job like this she was too excited to do anything but go, go, go!

The sound of rustling made them both stop and back up slowly, trying to their best to not make a peep. But the figure ran past them, and they saw what it was. A cat! It made a hiss and kept running.

Dolly picked up the lamp and smirked at Will, but the look on Will's face was ghostly. Will pointed with her chin to a nearby stall. Dolly leaned forward and saw a figure rolled under a blanket, asleep. She steeled her nerves and then nodded at Will and tapped the thermos. Leave no witnesses. This was the golden rule of crime.

Dolly approached, but Will gripped her arm so tightly she nearly dropped the canister and doused herself.

Will shook her head "no," and Dolly rolled her eyes. She felt a rush in her belly and she wasn't going to let the old cluck ruin her good time. Whoever was sleeping there couldn't have had a home. He wouldn't be missed. And this could be the experience of a lifetime. Dolly shook Will off as quietly as she could, not wanting to wake the sleeping rube. He was probably dead drunk though, and she didn't have to worry.

They heard another rustle and pointed the lamp down—just a field mouse. This time the barn cat came pouncing out of nowhere and landed on it, holding the helpless creature in its mouth. Then the cat dropped the mouse who lay there, probably playing dead. The cat batted it up in the air, and the poor sucker landed right on the drunken bum! He didn't move though—even when the feral puss sprang back into action and jumped over him to catch its prey.

They looked at each other confused. As the cat took off with the mouse once again in its maw, they investigated the figure.

"It's a scarecrow," Dolly laughed.

Some kid must've rolled him up as a joke. Now that they were safe, Dolly felt an emptiness in her belly, like she hadn't eaten in days. It would have been so good if it had been a real person! Imagine what they could have done. They continued to douse the place.

"What about the cat?" Will asked.

"Cats are smart. All predators are. This one won't stick around once the flames shoot up. Now let's do it."

They stepped outside, thermoses in hand, and Will handed the dirty rag to Dolly.

"You light it," she said.

Will took the matches and struck a flame. Dolly dipped the rag into a little gasoline, stuck it into the fire, and then threw it toward the barn.

"Run!" she yelled.

They stumbled down in front of a tree a few yards away and watched as the flames spread, eventually enveloping the whole place in a gorgeous cloud of color.

"It's beautiful," Dolly said.

"Like the poplars in Van Gogh's 'Les Alyscamps,'" Will said. "The yellows burning at the edges and fiery orange, just like the fire."

"Kiss me," Dolly said.

Will grabbed her and pressed her lips into Dolly's. Dolly opened her eyes to witness the destruction as Will's tongue entered her mouth.

Chapter Thirteen
Will

Everyone in town would read about them!

BARN BLAZE IN BRONX

"They have no idea who did it," Dolly boasted as they hustled into a practice room waving the newspaper.

"Read it to me," Will said, indulging Dolly, as she warmed up on her clarinet.

"Abandoned horse barn in Bronx Park set ablaze early Thursday evening. Traces of gasoline found indicate the work of an arsonist was at play. No witnesses. The police are looking into the possibility of this being the work of Klansmen, as there was a recent cross burning at a local synagogue just north of this secluded spot in the Park ..."

They looked at each other.

"That's odd," Will said. "They think Jew-haters did this?"

"They're grasping at straws. Look! The column's just an inch, but the picture says it all."

Nothing left but charred remains where once stood a simple shelter for animals.

Will wanted to ask Dolly why she loved to destroy things. What was the thrill for her? But then Dolly sat down at the piano and plunked out a gorgeous Chopin sonata. Dolly stared into Will's eyes the whole time, and suddenly the question seemed crass and insignificant.

"Wanna do something?" Dolly said.

"What?"

Dolly pulled out a Swiss army knife. "Swiped this from Joe's room," she said.

What had she been doing in Joe's room? Had they snuck into his Columbia dorm? When? Will had had it with Dolly and wished for a moment she had the guts to grab the knife, slice Dolly's throat, and then her own. It seemed as if only through death could they be together forever.

"Give me your finger, Willsie."

Unable to deny her and longing like a hop-head for her touch, Will complied.

Dolly held her hand and told Will to open her fist. "Don't you think it's time we took a blood oath together?" she said.

Will just nodded as they stared into each other's eyes. She was terrified of blood. But she trusted Dolly. This was a way to make the two of them into one and connect them forever. And it had been *Dolly's* idea. That's what made this so beautiful.

"I can't look," Will whispered.

"I'll do me first," Dolly said, pricking the pad of her index finger.

A tiny drop of blood rose from the wound.

"Now you."

Will looked away and in a second felt the prick of pain. And then relief.

"Press your finger into mine and look into my eyes," Dolly said. "And you're the wordsmith. Make with the poetry."

Dolly smirked to cover the sentimentality of her request.

"Let this blood oath unite us forever, through time, space, and eternity. May nothing separate us from this moment forward."

They sat on the floor like that, leaning against the soundproof wall of the practice room, in silence.

"Let's go back to our room," Dolly said.

They lay on Dolly's bed and with low bass rhythms and scratchy-voiced Bessie Smith singing to them on the Victrola, Will allowed her hands to explore every curve and muscle of Dolly's lithe body. Her hands felt just as natural making love to Dolly as they did fingering the keys of her clarinet. Will spooned Dolly from behind, nuzzling the back of her neck and running her hands over her body. Kissing Dolly's back felt like something she was born to do, and she knew she'd gladly commit any act of childish vandalism to do this again.

The sounds of Dolly's growly little moans were better than jazz itself. When Will felt Dolly reach back and begin to lightly touch her inner thighs, a deep thrill rushed from her toes all the way up to the crown of her head, the surprise trill of an arpeggio.

Their bodies grew more and more heated. When the record scratched to a stop, Dolly turned to Will and smiled, cueing her to get up and choose the next platter. Will's mouth slid down to Dolly's hip as Ida Smith sang "Crazy Blues."

Dolly smiled and mumbled something about—"our bargain." Will could not make out exact phrases; her ears were tuned into the music and the throaty, longing tone of Dolly's voice.

She kissed her way around to Dolly's thighs, her inner thighs. Will moved so slowly cupping Dolly's cheek, finding a delicate spot on the underside of her ass, just where her thigh met her bottom. It was there that she explored with the lightest touch of her lips. Her tongue tasted Dolly for the first time. Soon Will felt the dreamy smoothness of Dolly's legs resting on her shoulders. And with help from a little oil, a little more gin, Will gently but persistently slid her entire hand inside of Dolly. It was then that she looked into Dolly's eyes. They telegraphed a kind of painful pleasure they never had before. Will held complete control over beautiful Dolly's body, and she felt a combination of aggressiveness and protectiveness that intoxicated her. As she held Dolly before sleep, Will asked, "What are you thinking?"

"You've fucked the words out of me," Dolly laughed.

Will kissed her shoulder, laughing as well.

"But there is something on my mind," she said.

And then there was a pause. Like the caesura in an elegiac couplet. Would Dolly profess her love, Will wondered, her heart suddenly exposed. Or would she bring up another goddamn crime?

"It's a fragment from Sappho," Dolly said.

"Mmmm," Will moaned.

"'But I love extravagance,

and wanting it has handed down

The glitter and glamour of the sun

As my inheritance.'"

Will luxuriated in the poem and the suggestion that it was she, and only she who provided Dolly with the extravagance she lives for. In between waking and sleeping, a couplet came to Will:

Gliding your slopes has left my mouth swollen,
filled with your secrets as sleep pulls us down

She'd write it down in the morning. No poem was worth taking her hands off Dolly for.

Chapter Fourteen

Halloween night. The campus seemed unusually empty as most of the parties were happening across the street at Columbia. A stray bunny in floppy pink ears or Cleopatra with jewels of the Nile clattered by. Once the coast was clear, Dolly and Will moved nonchalantly through the quad.

Chi-Omega occupied the third floor of the southeast corner of the quad.

"This way," Will said.

She'd cased the joint for a week, determined that everything about the robbery go right. It was easy to swipe Maeve's key from the locker room while the girls changed after track. And now, hearing the click of the lock turning in the tumbler with Dolly's hot breath behind her ear, Will felt like she was exactly where she was supposed to be.

The suite of rooms spread out before them like the numbers on a roulette wheel. Will made a conscious effort to think the way Dolly did. To appreciate the thrill of doing something wrong, committing a crime, taking what wasn't hers. So far it was the sound of Dolly skulking beside her, following the beckoning arrow of her penlight that made Will feel alive. She didn't care about the jewels and frilly dresses of the Chi-Omega girls.

"Look," Dolly said, spying a jewelry box on a nightstand next to a picture of one of the lesser-known Chi-Omegas and some football player.

"Holy moley! This ring looks like it's worth a mint," Dolly said, slipping it on her finger and pointing the light so Will could get a glimpse. "I know a fence who lives up in Pelham who could unload this rock for us."

Dolly and her criminal lingo! Will just nodded and slid around the corners, aware that someone could walk in at any time. She had a satchel in her hand and she opened drawers looking for any obvious valuables. Her hands indiscriminately grabbed at change and dollar bills, charm bracelets, and beaded purses.

On the floor next to one of the beds was a grooming kit—scissors, tweezers, makeup. Is this what women used to make themselves more womanly? Will spied a jar of Brilliantine stuck behind some pink stationery. It must belong to the beau of one of these girls. Will nabbed it. She wasn't sure why.

Shining a flashlight into the corner, she saw on the desk—a typewriter. Will recognized the machine, the coffee-stained gray plastic cover carelessly tossed behind it from when Babs and a couple of the other sisters had joined Dolly and Will for Latin cram sessions. Letters addressed to Miss Barbara Lufrane sat beside the sparkly Underwood.

They both heard the sound at the same time. A bottle smashing on the street below followed by a swell of high-pitched laughter. Some of them must be coming back. Will grabbed the typewriter and shoved it in the sack.

"What the hell are you doing?"

"Come on. This is perfect. It's heavy. It's personal," Will said. "More than just grabbing some green glorious. It really messes with them. Who would do this and why? Let them wonder!"

"All right fine. Now shake a leg; we need to be yesterday's news!"

They dropped the stash in their dorm and costumed quickly, over swigs of gin. As Dolly painted on cat makeup in the bathroom, Will sat before the desk mirror with a pair of scissors, cutting just a curl here, and just a curl there, as she slicked back her looks with the Brilliantine. She wasn't sure if she'd gotten her look just right, so she slipped on her glasses to examine her work more closely. Very suave.

She remembered being seven years old and finding a pair of scissors on her mother's vanity table. Taking them in her hands, she wondered what it would feel like to cut her unruly curls. The first click of the scissors sounded so satisfying as she watched the ringlets tumble to the floor. She cut again, but soon she saw how lopsided her head looked. Will went downstairs to look for her mother in the parlor. When Momma saw her she shrieked, "What have you done?!" She took Will upstairs to even out the cut.

"There," she said, brushing hair off the back of Will's neck. "There's the little boy I always wanted."

Tonight, I will be Valentino.

They hurried out into the brightly lit streets of Harlem, finding a welcome place to celebrate on Halloween night. They could access Moonglow on West 129th with a special knock and a nickel. Dolly, dressed as a cat, wore a beret with pointy velvet ears sewn on, black whisker makeup, green eye shadow, and a tight little black dress with a tail attached.

Will wore a pair of black trousers with her father's starched white shirt, a black bow tie from their old butler, and her hair, shiny and slick and exotic. With Dolly on her arm she felt alive, fully alive, for the first time in her life.

For a quick coin they were able to score some room temperature gin.

"I don't know why you had to grab that typewriter..."

"Just drink, Dolly, drink. We scored. You got your wish."

"You're right, kid," Dolly said. "We really stuck it to them, didn't we?"

"We were way too smart for those bubbleheads."

They ching-chinged, then went quickly for another as the music played. Will looked at Dolly and Dolly looked at Will, as couples— men and women, men and men, women and women found each other to sway in the night. Dolly smiled, and Will felt Dolly's fingers tickle her palm and pull her close, so they could dance to the sultry sound of "Jazz Vampire."

And where there is a little jazz, you'll always find me near.
Cause I'm a jaaaazzz vampire...

A drunken roustabout in sailor garb began shouting and shimmying to his own psychotic beat and the girls slipped into the bedroom where they found a wall to lean against. Other lovebirds filled the bed.

Firecracker specks ignited the blues of Dolly's eyes as she smiled at Will. The sweat, the worry, the sadness, all the inward and outward signs of self-loathing disappeared, and Will entered a new body, one that wanted another woman—this woman. She only had to take three steps.

Will's eyes locked on Dolly's and she could see her own joy reflected in them. No longer was she a mass of awkward parts; she had received the spark of life, been re-animated. The thrill of the robbery, the cat ears, the gin. They blended in with all the costumed guests. Who knew such freedom could exist in plain view?

The only way to mark such a moment was to kiss her, the woman who destroyed the old sad-sack Wilhelmina and connected the electric charge to create the new and masterful Will.

As she brushed her lips against Dolly's, she closed her eyes, and soon their tongues touched. The ardor of their mouths pressed together, the force of Will's hands pushing Dolly's above her head as Dolly thrust her hips against Will's, it was all the instruments of the orchestra coming together, the song they were meant to play the first time they'd met.

Will paid a pretty penny to get Dolly's flask filled and hailed a cab to ride them back to Brooks Hall. Inside the taxi, their hands found each other. When Dolly got into bed next to her, she seemed shy like a child. Will wrapped herself around Dolly's body and pulled her close, holding her as tight as she could, laughing at the tiger growls they both emitted. They grinded against each other, kissed, and ran their hands through each other's hair, but Will could feel Dolly's reticence and it made her panic. To assuage her fear, she kept the action moving. And yet, she could sense there was something different. A chance not just for sex, but for love.

They kissed and kissed and kissed some more, getting up to light candles, to put on records, and dance. Playing "Jazz Vampire" again and again. Growing tired and falling into bed. And once in bed, she could feel Dolly's passion for her. The feeling of Dolly's tongue, her lips working up Will until she couldn't take anymore and then finally exploding in Dolly's mouth—it finally allowed Will to relax, to trust. This wasn't the transactional game they'd played before. This wasn't part of a deal or contract. It was real.

Dolly fell asleep while Will kept vigil over them, over this night. Will could hardly rest. Having Dolly near, being able to touch her naked body, it was too exciting. To share a bed. This was what she wanted all the days of her life, even if she hadn't always known. It was like the beautiful love between men during the times of the Greeks, and the even more beautiful love between girls hinted at in the picture shows and in the timeless stories of Sappho, the contemporary French poetry of Natalie Clifford Barney. She fell asleep just before sunrise, imagining the two of them living in France, the free life they were meant to lead.

When Will woke up, Dolly had already left for class. She wondered for a moment if she had dreamed it all. Then she rolled over onto her belly, saw the cat ears on the floor, and smiled. What a beautiful dream! And it was true! Will wanted to hear their song on the phonograph again, "Jazz Vampire." She bounced out of bed and dropped the needle on the record. Her eyes still filled with sleep and heavy with gin, she thought she saw a white mouse on the floor. It was just an envelope! Everything seemed like a passage lifted from the pages of Lewis Carroll.

She bent down to pick up the envelope, excited. Dolly's first love note to her! From the bottom drawer of her desk, she pulled out her horn-rimmed reading glasses. She wanted to savor every word and every indentation of Dolly's pen. For a moment she felt jealous of the pen and ink themselves for being close to Dolly.

She sat at her desk and used the letter opener to break the seal. It was Barnard stationery, which seemed so quaint. This would always be the place that brought them together. The letter inside was typewritten, and it only took a moment to see it was an official missive from the Dean of Students.

It has been brought to our attention ... upon the request of both families ... change of dormitory rooms ... effective immediately.

They were separating her and Dolly. No. They could not. She would not allow it. She thought of getting dressed and going out on campus to find Dolly, but Will suddenly felt weak. She crawled back into her bed. Thoughts of needing to rise and go to the toilet to vomit competed with feelings of longing for Dolly.

Her thoughts then turned to who—*who*—exactly could be behind this scheme to separate the two? Of course, Jane Sterry came to mind. They really should have killed her when they had the chance. Dolly was probably just joking around, but maybe she wasn't? Either way, if they'd drowned her like a rat they'd be reveling in their love, not fighting for it. Timing! Timing! Why was Will so gifted in the art of patience and timing while watching birds, and so lacking in it in the world of humans?

She kept willing herself to get up and out of bed, but even her rage at Jane Sterry couldn't energize her. She must have drifted back to sleep. She had no idea what time it was when the knock at the door came.

"Come in," Will called.

It was her sister, Estelle.

"Oh...I see you're not dressed. I'll come back in thirty minutes," she said.

"All business, Sis?" Will said.

Will sat inside her room, Estelle standing opposite her. Estelle brushed invisible lint from her tweed jacket as Will glared at her. She pretended not to notice and leafed through a book on ornithology on Will's desk.

"The white-breasted nuthatch," Estelle said. "What species is it?"

Will knew the answer of course: Sitta carolinensis, a North American songbird, Chordata of the Aves class, native to North America and unlikely to migrate far from its home. Estelle used to quiz Will on the particulars of birds when she was younger and in need of company. Well, she didn't need Estelle anymore.

"Let's wait until Dolly gets back before we talk," Will said. "This is utterly preposterous."

"Dolly is with her family, and they're explaining it to her as well."

"Explaining what exactly?"

"Sister dear, I don't need to use tawdry language, but we know that Dolly has been a bad influence on you."

Will shot up and looked at Estelle with what had been brewing her whole life: unadulterated hate.

"Don't you insult someone you can't understand, someone whose IQ exceeds yours by upwards of twenty points ..."

"I don't care how high her IQ is. Her tendencies are abnormal, and the family can't have her pulling you down into depravity. There I've said it plain as day."

"Are you basing these assumptions on the rumors of some jealous teenage twits?"

"No, Wilhelmina. Sanford did some digging so we could place ourselves on the offensive just in case more came out."

"And?"

"Has Dolly ever mentioned a negro named Celia?"

"No, who is she?"

But as soon as the words left her lips Will remembered. The infamous "C.C." who Dolly sounded all smashed on.

"She's a vagrant who hung about in Harlem and was taken in by the police after a raid. They arrested her for several acts of vice; she was often mistaken for a male predator. They were not setting bail and apparently it was the night of a big snowstorm. All criminal proceedings were being delayed. Your friend Dolly came to the precinct barely dressed for a spring stroll and tried to bribe a police officer into letting this negro go. She was sent home to her parents, who said they would deal with it."

"Estelle, I won't hear any more of your crass assessment of Dolly. This sounds like more loose talk from a very stupid class of female. And I know just the one. She's another freshman here and ..."

"I'm afraid the evidence is rock solid and comes from a reliable source—Dolly's family. Dolly's father was going through heart problems before and they didn't follow up on this negro's foul influence on your friend. This Celia woman was released a few weeks after the whole debacle. But they've made sure to be thorough this time. Dolly's uncle is a lawyer and agreed to personally make sure that this negro was put away for a very long time. Did you know she has a baby too?"

"What baby? What's going to happen to it?"

"Well, clearly this woman is an unfit mother, and the State will take charge of the negro child."

"You don't have to keep saying negro. They're human beings, Estelle. Just like us. Does Dolly know what her family is up to?"

"She will. You'll come to thank me later on, Sister, for giving you a chance to start fresh. She'll be in a different dorm and, with the exception of classes, you must now keep away from her, completely."

"You can't dictate what I do. I don't live with you anymore! And you're not my mother!"

"If Mother were alive ... well ... here's the letter we received, Will. I know you're upset, but ... just read this."

There is no question that these two girls have crossed the line into depraved acts and if not immediately separated they will spread their perversions to the rest of the school body.

Will's eyes passed over the words again till tears made it impossible to read. Jane Sterry and probably her malicious followers were behind this. Accusing the two of them of perverted acts. Will threw it down on the floor

"Bunk!"

"Well, if it is, then just keep your nose to the grindstone and let the rumors die down."

Estelle looked over at the pile of loot in front of the closet, including that sweet little typewriter. They hadn't had time to even hide the goods. Will wondered if news had already spread on campus about the robbery. She didn't care. Estelle was not about to beat her gums about it and bring more "shame" upon the family.

"Don't supply them with more material, all right?"

"Or what?"

Estelle paused.

"Will, Dolly's family is on board. If anything happens between the two of you—we'll separate you for good. Transfer you both to colleges out of state, and you'll never see each other again."

Will did not take a breath as the words sank in. *We'll separate you for good.* Let them try. Will would sooner kill Momma if she were alive—that's right –Momma!—than be torn from Dolly. What had Momma done for her? All the love in the world, and then complete and total abandonment. Her father was absent as usual, leaving the dirty work to this dullard, this savage. How dare she come in here and play judge, jury, and executioner? The love Will felt unconditionally for Dolly could only be matched in this moment by the unmitigated and pure hatred Will felt for this person who stood before her, staking claim to her because they shared the same blood. Well, she and Dolly had shared much more, and their life together was just beginning. Someone would pay for this, and soon.

Will wondered what it would feel like to squeeze Estelle's throat till she lost consciousness, so that the last image the prig would hold in her mind for all eternity would be that of her own sister, wielding merciless power over her, like a peregrine falcon swooping down on a bank vole.

Part II
The Crime

Chapter Fifteen
Dolly

The sounds of Marjorie Hammond doing her facial exercises in the next bed scratched inside Dolly's eardrums.

"Could you can the sound effects, Hambone?"

"It's important for keeping my skin tight. And stop calling me that."

"Oh Jeez. Your skin's tight enough for my money. But why don't you get some beauty sleep? That's your best bet. Besides, the sound of your jaw opening and closing for an hour is giving me the heebie jeebies. You're starting to sound like a skeleton clattering around in the next bed."

"I'll just be a few more minutes," Marjorie said.

It was enough to make you want to take a hammer and knock her head open. Dolly thought. *Keep her skin tight! She wears so much powder who can tell? What a pest and a bore.* Dolly wondered if she could sneak over to Will's hall to check on her. From what she'd heard, Will broke down like a basket case. Hadn't left her room in days. No sign of her in classes. It had been two weeks since the big scandal. So what? Some loud mouth yapping about the two of them being queer. Dolly had enough fellas in her little black book to fight that rap and everybody knew it. It would blow over, junk like this always did.

Meantime, there hadn't been enough attention paid to the robbery. That was a thing of beauty. But only a bunch of huffing and puffing sorority wives crying the blues about their missing stashes. Hardly anything to write home about, after all that excitement. And Dolly wasn't even given a chance to go back to the room to collect her share of the goods after the folks got a load of the story.

She'd clipped a one-inch report in the paper about a college break-in, but it had been deemed a basically harmless prank. If only they knew what Dolly was capable of! She did not like the direction things were going in. Cops oblivious to the brilliance of their crimes, parents treating them like babies—sent to separate rooms.

Who did their families think they were anyway? Dolly couldn't say for sure about ole Willsie, but speaking strictly for herself, she knew that no cage could contain her, no set of rules, no parents, no Deans. Sure, she'd play along—pretending to be through with Willsie—but it was all an act. Dolly would see her when she wanted to and make Willsie *do* whatever she wanted her to, and that was that. Fat chance they'd even find out once Dolly started meeting Willsie in secret, something she had every intention of doing! She realized she better make her move soon before weepie Will bid the world goodbye by hopping it in front of an A train.

Dolly threw on slippers and headed to the hall to dial up Will. If she didn't, she'd die of boredom.

A female voice answered.

"Wilhelmina please," Dolly said, adding a lilt to her voice.

"Who may I say his calling?"

"Her cousin Bess."

"Just a moment please. Wilhelmina!" the girl called down the hall.

Dolly heard rumbles of chat and held the line for at least a minute.

Finally a sad "Hullo."

"Hiya cuz. How you feeling?" and then in a whisper, "Don't say my name."

"Uh-huh."

"I wanted to remind you that cousin Nick's birthday is on the eighteenth."

They'd set up a code weeks before just for kicks. Nick meant St. Nicholas Avenue. And eighteenth meant eighteen hundred hours, or six o'clock.

"So set your watch, ok? Get the picture?"

That meant we're going to meet at a movie house.

She repeated the message once more to make sure down-in-the-dumps Willsie understood and then hung up.

Alone in her room, Dolly pulled open her underwear drawer. She slipped on a cream-colored crepe-de-chine combination made of silk and decorated with embroidery and lace. Opening a bottle of Adieu Sagesse, she anointed the sweet spot between her breasts that she often caught Will ogling.

She was glad she'd left enough time so she wouldn't have to rush. If only this dorm had a place for a bubble bath, she could really luxuriate in her preparation. Watching the way Will looked at her was such a kick.

She couldn't believe the numbskull they'd stuck her with. Marjorie Hammond! Who were these prison screws at Barnard to keep her and Will apart? It was probably Sterry who was behind it, or maybe that moron sister of Will's. Boy, wouldn't it feel good to slice that cluck's neck, see if she ran around Sutton Place like a chicken with its head cut off.

Dolly looked at herself in the mirror. Yeah, she was a knock-out. She could see for herself! Sure, she had a little bit of a goofy, crooked smile, but that only added to her charm. Who could blame Willsie for falling for her? Her own face was so pleasing she wished she could kiss it herself! But it wasn't just that. She hadn't ever felt so connected to another human being. There was something about allowing Will to see all of her—her crimes, her body, her jazz. She could be completely free with Will and that's what they wanted to put an end to. Try and force Dolly to be like the other sheep here and just find a husband and pop out some little brats.

What about Sterry, though? Yeah, she probably did turn them in after all. Dolly remembered the look of disgust on her face when she caught her and Will playing around. She'd bet that in ten years Sterry herself would be running a college. All any of them wanted was to tell Dolly what to think, what to do. Well, good luck to all of 'em.

And was she going bats or was all this eugenic breeding stuff an American version of Nietzsche without the nuance? For hell's sake they both were about the same thing: deciding who was at the top of the food chain and who wasn't! But there was one significant difference. Nietzsche knew that it was the *ubermensches* of the world who singled themselves out for top dog status. Then as individuals decided who was worth living and who was worth breeding out!

Wasn't jazz all about having free will to make your own choices in every single moment, every single measure? Hell yes. It stood to reason then that jazz was the art of the individual player who, if he wanted, could riff off of another individual if that individual was in the goddamn mood and had the goddamn chops! Jazz musicians couldn't be told to "play this" and "play it this way." That's not how it worked. Not real jazz at least. Pure jazz.

She could hear Helena's voice from around the corner and made a quick slip into the stairwell. Dolly watched through the glass as Helena and her minions passed by. She took off her shoes and silently padded down the steps to the lobby.

"Stepping out for a smokedety doke," she muttered as the revolving door slid her onto the street.

There were about fifteen people in the theater. Dolly walked through the dark aisle and heard a "pssst" from behind her. Will waved her over from the back row. Even with Will's eyes facing the screen, Dolly could tell she was thinking sentimental thoughts. She decided to cut the horse manure and get down to business. She had not forgotten the way they tried to ruin her good thing with Willsie. Who did the families think they were, and these mopes in the administration at Barnard? It roiled Dolly to have to be shamed and punished by these imbeciles.

She whispered as softly as possible into Will's ear, "Just listen while I tell you the plan."

Dolly knew that the brush of her lips against the invisible downy hairs of her friend's ear would put Will into high alert.

"So you're going to stop going to classes for a week."

Will shuffled a bit in her seat.

"Then you act like you're grievin' in the gutter so bad you can't get out of bed. Your sissie-pie Estelle will hear tell of this and come a-running. Then you give her some silent treatment and finally break down, 'I miss Momma!'"

Dolly could feel Will shrink back, horrified.

"Hear me out. Here's the kicker. You say Dolly Dolly Dolly only Dolly understands. You get her to call me on the phone right then and there, and I tell Sis I'll talk to her alone—in person. I'm sure she'll give me a lot of slaps on the wrists and warnings, but I'll turn on the ole Dolly charm and let her know I have your best interests at heart. If she gives me any guff I'll hardball her with 'Sure, you can call off your wedding and be your sister's keeper, or let me tend to her. Easy does it.' You got that, Willsie?"

"Come with me to the powder room," Will said.

Aw come on.

But Dolly followed. Will probably needed to get her paws on Dolly. She had no self-control when it came to that stuff, or at least when it came to Dolly's body. Poor kid. They waited for an old bag to re-paint her lips and then, just as predicted, Will grabbed Dolly.

"Okay, okay," Dolly said, laughing but sharing a passionate kiss.

"I just want to say," Will said. "I'll do anything you want. I can't believe what your parents did to your friend?"

"What friend?"

"C.C."

Dolly pushed Will away. What was this, a joke? But from the look on Will's face, she knew it wasn't. She made Will tell her everything. And at the end of it, Dolly walked into a stall and vomited. She kept retching even when there was no more bile left.

Chapter Sixteen
Will

The girls shared a good laugh when, one week later, Dolly moved back into their own room. Watching Estelle and that fool fiancé, Sanford, carry in Will's books while Dolly lounged about in a camisole, already queen of the castle—it was such a goof! Money talks and so does a suicidal threat from a bereft daughter. Dolly's plan had been brilliant, but Will had to give herself a hand for sealing the deal.

Once the girls were alone in their old room again, Will's near-operatic grief easily abated thanks to the good cheer of Dolly. Will knew Dolly thought she could be such a pill with her moods. But she was fun too, wasn't she? Dolly loved a prank, and Will had shown herself up for the job more than once. The fact was Dolly needed a witness, a pair of hands to applaud her, and Will was happy to oblige, as long as she got what she needed from Dolly in return.

They'd spent Thanksgiving break lolling around Will's mostly to show Estelle how trustworthy they were. Playing cards with Pop was about as wild as they got. But by Saturday night the girls had grown stir crazy. The garage adjacent to the building was quiet as they approached sleeping Waldek at the gate, a Polish newspaper spread across his stout belly.

"Hey," Dolly whispered. "Let's break in and take one for a joyride."

"Just wait," Will said. "I've got a surprise for you. Excuse me, Waldek."

"Ah. Miss Reinhardt. How do you do this evening?"

"Very well. Can you bring the Stutz around?"

"Yes, Miss Reinhardt."

He scooted off, the darkness beyond the entrance camouflaging him. Once he'd been swallowed away out of sight, Dolly pitched the idea of stealing a car again.

"I've *got* me a car now. That's the surprise," Will said.

"What? Spill it."

"Pop got some new wheels—a Ford Model T. And gave me his old one."

"Hmm," Dolly said when the wheels rolled up. "His Stutz Bearcat! This heap's got potential. Keys, please."

"Forget it, Sis," Will said. "Thanks, Waldek."

The car shone raven black and had too much va-va-voom for Pop to comfortably drive. This was no banker's car!

Dolly seemed impressed as she walked around the vehicle to inspect it. The roadster boasted a "dog house" hood, open bucket seats, a tiny "monocle" windscreen in front of the driver, and a cylindrical fuel tank on a short rear deck. They squeezed in, and Will drove them up Third Avenue, then across 57th Street, where Dolly catcalled and whistled at the sight of Carnegie Hall.

"Forget that jazz," Dolly said. "Let's hit Mama Pearl's."

Located just south of the Cotton Club on West 140th, Mama Pearl's was not Whites Only and didn't charge so much for hooch. The house band was in the middle of a fast rendition of "Chimes Blues," and the girls hovered near the stand-up bass player, cups of gin in hand.

"You ready for that Constitution quiz?" Will asked.

"Oh jeez. Don't talk to me about school when I'm getting tight. That's why I dropped Sterry," Dolly said, chugging her drink, then finishing Will's with a wink.

"What are you talking about?"

"What? Nothing. Hey, let's dance, come on." Will didn't budge. It wasn't like her to turn down Dolly, but she was miffed. Just the sound of that girl's name from Dolly's lips sparked rage, and she knew Dolly could see it in her eyes.

"Come on, Willsie. You know Sterry had a little frosh crush on me. So what? It's not like she'd ever do anything about it. She's a square. I mean I see her just to keep her from blabbing, but it's ho-hum."

Will was still silent.

"Let me get us some more drinks, come on."

Will glared.

"What? You're giving me the cold treatment? Come on, Willsie. Let's go if you're done with this place."

But Will grabbed Dolly by the wrist, hard.

"Hey! Easy, jealous lover," Dolly laughed. "What are you getting so sore about?"

"Tell me about you and Jane Sterry."

"There's nothing to tell," Dolly said, suddenly playing it cool, watching the band.

A few minutes passed and when the band shifted into the soft version of "The Sheik of Araby." Will whispered, "Maybe we should have drowned her like you wanted to."

"Huh?"

"That day in Rhinebeck," Will said. "We could've gotten her out of our hair for once and for all."

"Ha! Good one, Willsie."

Will gave Dolly a look that showed she meant business. She pulled Dolly close and they swayed to the music:

I'm the Sheik of Araby, your love belongs to me.
At night when you sleep, into your tent I'll creep.

Dolly snuggled close to Will as they swayed on the floor. She ran her hands up and down Will's arms, and Will felt the shivers her touch elicited. She pressed her hips against Dolly's and looked into her eyes. She tried to telepathically transmit her thoughts: *you belong to me.*

They took Will's car back up to Chum-Chum's. Dolly asked the band to play "Jazz Vampire." The girls swayed rhythmically to the song as the Harlemites looked on.

"Let's take a ride ..." Will whispered. Once inside the Stutz she turned to Dolly. "I thought we could drive out to the cemetery."

"What, and rob a grave?" Dolly laughed. "Where's the fun in that?"

Will wanted to say something but feared she'd sound too emotional. Why could Dolly never maintain a serious mood?

"Look, bully for us for the burglary job, but I've been thinking. We gotta do something big. Something that'll have them beating their gums about us for years."

"Like what?"

"You know like what," Dolly stared into Will's eyes. "I'm thinking of a word. If you know me, Will, if you really know me, you'll be able to read my mind."

Will knew instantly as she gazed into the dark, dilated pupils of Dolly's pretty blue eyes. She didn't want to say it, even though she knew Dolly was just joking. But Dolly poked her in the ribs.

"Come on, Willsie."

Will just laughed as she hit the gas then turned onto West 130th Street. She was just cruising now. Dolly placed a hand on her thigh, and Will stiffened. She pulled the car over near some dumpsters where no one was walking about. Will leaned closer and pulled Dolly in for a kiss.

"No," Dolly said.

Will was not about to hear that word. Not tonight. She'd had enough of being controlled by other people—Sterry, Estelle, and now Dolly herself.

"Yes," she said and pushed her body into Dolly's.

Dolly tried to wiggle away.

"What are you going to do, scream for help?" Will said.

She didn't recognize her own voice. It was hard and mean and didn't care about anything anymore.

"Say the word."

"What word?" Will said, having forgotten Dolly's childish game.

"It's something big only you and I can do together. It's going to be perfect. Just tell me what word I'm thinking of. Prove you can read my mind. Prove you understand me more than anyone else."

Dolly's voice penetrated Will's resistance. It was just a silly word. Why not?

"Murder," Will said.

Dolly laughed and lit a cigarette. "Yes. Yes! Dammit, yes! You crazy kid!" Still guffawing, she puffed and passed the smoke to Will. "A perfect murder. The kind only a brilliant pair of *ubermensches* could pull off. It's something that's never been done, and *we* are the only ones brilliant enough to do it."

"You must be kidding."

"Come on. Put your money where your mouth is. Has all that talk about Nietzsche been just a lot of hot air?"

"Dolly, as *ubermensches* we don't need to *prove* anything, do we?"

"If you are showing fear now, Willsie, then you're out of the game. I thought you were above human emotion. I thought that after what happened—the way they tried to keep us apart, make us obey them like sheep—that you'd be ready to step out of their world and step into our own."

"What do you mean?"

"I mean this is something that we do together. Just us. There's no God to witness this. We're the only witnesses."

"Why?"

"That's easy. Because we want to. They tried to split us apart. They destroyed C.C.'s life. What are they going to try next, once they find out they can't stop us from thinking the way we think, living the way we want?"

"Look, we turned that one around. We're living together again," Will said.

"Do you think that's going to last forever? You know they're on to us."

And Will did have that feeling. The more in love with Dolly she felt, the more she feared losing her. "My Pop is okay," she said. "He's good, actually. A good man."

"Yeah, but he's weak. Sorry to say it, Willsie, but since your Momma died it sounds like the old man is just shuffling through life waiting till his time is up. And it's that shrew of a sister of yours who's pulling the strings. And once she gets married. Oh boy! You know what's going to happen?"

"What?"

"That fiancé of hers will be the boss. And he won't like having some freakish half-girl-half- boy, smart mouth in his family. And I'll bet he's got a family that will like it even less."

"I can handle Estelle."

"Sure you can, but she'll be his underling. And then I'm telling you what's going to happen next. She's going to say, 'Oh don't worry, Wilhelmina's a normal girl underneath it all. She just needs a decent husband.' Yeah, well so next thing you know they'll arrange for you to marry some guy they pick out for you. I mean, come on, Will. Picture yourself in a wedding dress for a second. Go on. I'm serious. Close your eyes and try to imagine that scene."

Will closed her eyes. She felt as if she needed to belch. Something stuck in her chest, causing a heavy ache. Seeing herself standing so awkwardly in a white dress, with some dead-in-the-eyes man. It was unnatural! She knew that's how they looked at her. She took a breath and saw something different. It was a wedding, all right. But she wore a white tuxedo and tails, and it was Dolly who stood beside her, in a white gown. Tall and fanciful with sparkle piping on the sides running over her hips and down her legs, just as Will's hands wanted to.

She opened her eyes. Why couldn't she just be with Dolly and go away with her and live together as one? They did have the Europe trip to look forward to, but that was just a brief schoolgirl trip.

"But how's this ... this idea ... going to change anything?"

"It's called revenge, Willsie. All their talk of morality. When they're the ones who are full of hate. They think their lily-white, square lives are worth more than any queer's, more than any negro's ... you know my motto—live and let live. Well, they couldn't do that could they? They couldn't just let us be, could they? What's so wrong with what we're doing anyway? Who are they to pass judgment on us, think of us as inferior to them because of who we are—what we are—when we're above them in every way imaginable. Let's do something that bonds us together forever."

Those words pulled Will closer to Dolly.

"And listen. We can approach this like an experiment."

The thought of science calmed her. Dolly was right. Why did murder have to be so emotional? What had emotions done for Will but caused her torment? She imagined approaching this entire hypothetical scenario like a scientist.

"Yes," Will said, her pulse slowing. "Killing a human being could be just as easily justified as an entomologist killing a beetle on a pin. A mere experiment."

"We should make it look like a kidnapping," Dolly said. "That way we can make some big dough too!"

"Do we really need it?" Will asked.

"It's part of the game," Dolly said. "Besides, money is money."

"That's not good enough Dolly. It just doesn't feel right. We have all the money we could ever need for a lifetime through our parents."

"Look, Willsie. How long you gonna be a dupe? If you don't think you can do it, then I'll do it alone."

Will paused. She thought about what it would be like to go to Europe with Dolly with enough money to stay there, leave the families behind, start a new life.

"We'd need a weapon to kidnap someone," Will said. "Something could go wrong."

"Let's keep it simple. Kidnap somebody we're physically bigger than. A kid, for instance."

"I dunno," Will said.

"Look, we grab a kid, send a ransom note ... have the parents running all over town to meet our demands."

"And maybe we knock the kid out and leave him somewhere with a big bump on his head," Will said.

"No. We'd have to really kill him. Can't leave anyone alive who could identify us."

Will was silent.

"So, it's a promise? You're in?"

Will nodded, then realized this was all Dolly's idea. She had to toughen up and quick.

"Rather," Will said. "It's a deal. You understand? Part of our bargain."

Dolly smiled and then moved closer to Will. She leaned on Will's shoulder, and it felt so loving and sweet. So natural. Will wondered if she would lean in to kiss her. If she didn't then Will would grab her. The equilibrium she'd felt a moment before when she had her scientific mind at work had disappeared. The heat from Dolly's body, just inches away electrified Will.

"But just one thing, Willsie."

"Yes?"

"I'm in charge. When it comes right down to it. You know that don't you?"

"I ... I think so."

"Let's play a game."

"What game?"

"Ruler and servant."

Will could feel the flush rise in her cheeks. "What do we need to play it?"

"Just our imaginations and a typewriter."

All thoughts of Dolly's wild bluff disappeared, and the promise of Dolly's body, her love, filled Will with anticipation. It seemed as if Dolly found Will just as irresistible as Will found Dolly. The game they played of who was in charge merely added to the excitement. Will wanted to use the typewriter she'd pinched from those sorority girls. What sweet justice. All this talk of murder was fun to talk about, thrilling really, but Dolly and her body, that was what was real. Flesh and blood.

Chapter Seventeen

The typewriter seemed to emanate a glow from the dorm room desk, as if it were a Giza pyramid from Ancient Egypt. Will had already broken in the stolen Underwood taking notes for Latin cram sessions with a small study group. But how glorious to use the hot machine for something as intimate as this. Will couldn't believe her luck. A rare opportunity to use the power of the written word to impress Dolly! The physical world of athletics, the social world of parties—these were areas of potential humiliation for Will. But on the page, she could slide into Dolly's brain and stay there, like an organism capable of growing inside her.

February 1, 1924

Dear Dolly,

I write this of my own free will and at no one's behest but my own. This letter is a proclamation of my willingness to enter into a ruler/servant compact with you. As part of this compact I hereby swear to follow your commands (as long as they remain serious—trivial ones shall not be included in this agreement) and fulfill your desires of body and of mind.

As your servant, I am bound to fulfill your desires and obey your (serious) wishes.

Should I refuse or hesitate in acting upon your commands I must submit to the punishment of your choice.

To prove to you that I am worthy of the title of number one servant, I will lay out for you the different ways in which I have come to know you, and then you can tell me whether you believe I have earned this honor.

Will paused and looked over at Dolly lying in bed reading her pulp magazine.

She knew she had the power to do things to Dolly no one else could. She still wasn't sure whether Dolly was going all the way with Joe or exaggerating. Either way, it seemed all for show. What she shared with Dolly was the real thing. Joe served merely as a mask Dolly could wear to appease her family. Will understood that. Perhaps Dolly had some real interest in boys, but it was clear that her passion remained with Will.

The question was—should she put into words the things that brought Dolly to life in bed? Will's intuition told her that Dolly might be embarrassed to read such details. Better to just show Dolly how in tune with her body she was. Music and movement, action, impulses, these were the keys where Dolly was concerned. Will looked at her lying there, her toes tapping out a rhythm on the foot of the bed. The shape of Dolly's calf exerted a pull, like the undertow dragging her out to sea. Will's eyes lingered on Dolly's calves, and then she sat down on the bed, the noise of the springs suddenly a crow's screech. She had to be careful.

"Whatcha reading?"

"Buzz off and finish my letter," Dolly said.

But she was smiling.

Sometimes when Dolly was rude like this—with a grin on her face—it meant she was inviting a little roughhousing. Will grabbed the cheap paperback out of Dolly's hands and tossed it across the room.

"Hey! Go pick that up. I command you."

"Uh-uh," Will said. "I only comply with serious commands."

"Oh, yeah. Let's see what you've got banged out for me so far."

Dolly sprang up so fast Will didn't have time to catch her. She wasn't sure if she wanted Dolly to read her draft. It was a work in progress. Her desire had been to give it to her when it was fully refined and able to be used as the ultimate tool of seduction.

"I don't like all the parentheses," Dolly said.

Why must she always be so damn rude? Will *knew* the parentheticals were distracting and took away from the power of her missive, but the letter was not finished yet.

"That's it!" Will said and pulled the white paper from Dolly's hand. "Now it's your turn to write a letter to me."

"Whaddaya mean?"

"Don't play dumb blonde. Use your imagination."

Dolly moved a step closer to Will and stood up straight, showing the inches she had on her.

"Don't forget who's the ruler here."

"Out in the world, yes," Will stated. "But in this room, I'm the ruler."

Where these words were coming from she did not know. But her hands spoke a special language that Dolly could understand, a language Dolly would obey. She grabbed her by the arm and pulled her towards her with a sudden strength that startled them both. She smacked Dolly hard on the ass and ordered her to put a clean sheet of paper in the typewriter and begin her letter. Dolly submitted. She bent her over the chair so that Dolly's breasts slid over the top, and her outreached hands could touch the keys to type.

"What should I write?" Dolly asked with a grin, and Will knew what she wanted.

She lifted up the shimmery green dress and smacked her over her pink silk knickers repeatedly. Dolly let out some exclamations, but she didn't try and push Will off. Will continued, only allowing her an occasional pause to type.

Dear Will:

I submit to your corporeal commands and do not question them. This is what I want, and you are the only one I deem superior enough to fulfill my desirres

"Good girl," Will said, then slapped her ass once more. "But correct that mistake."

Dolly xxx-ed out the error and fixed it.

"Hey Dolly!"

The voice of Sterry came from the hall accompanied by a couple of loud knocks.

Will could feel her chest fill with the heat of panic. Was the door locked?

"Yeah? Coming!" Dolly yelled, writhing out from Will's hold.

What if Sterry heard something? That girl had it in for them. But then Will looked down at the page as Dolly straightened her clothes and fixed her makeup. Will could see that she'd spanked Dolly so hard she'd cried. Why hadn't Dolly let Will hear her? It made Will feel a deep tenderness towards Dolly, the way she let Will take charge of her body like that. Hell, what if Sterry *did* hear? So what? Let her know damn well that Dolly belonged to her and her alone, and to bugger off!

Dolly shot Will an angry look, and Will slunk down onto the desk chair, quietly removing the letter.

"What's the buzz, Sterry?" Dolly asked, opening the door.

"Your guy's calling for you," Sterry said.

"He's on the horn now?"

Sterry nodded, and Dolly bolted to the hall.

"Hi Reinhardt," she said, barging in without an invitation.

Will nodded and slipped the letters from the desk into her science book.

"We're in physics together," Sterry said. "And I can't seem to find my book. Can I borrow yours?"

Will just stared at her with hatred. Sterry was trying to intimidate her, and this time she wasn't going to give in. She wanted to stand right up to her and say "What's your angle, Sterry? If you have a point to make, make it. Or else be on your tedious little way."

But in Sterry's face she saw a willingness to fight, to try and separate her and Dolly again, and suddenly Will had to sit down. The letter from the school, the letter to the families—the threat of never seeing Dolly again. She felt a little queasy and held her book to her chest.

"Jane, I'm sorry. I feel a little ill. Please excuse me."

Will took the book and ran out into the hall, past Dolly who had slid to the floor and was cradling the phone like a puppy. She made it into the bathroom and, with the stall locked, she suddenly felt like she could breathe.

"I need that book, Reinhardt," Sterry said, coming in and knocking on the stall door.

"Give me some privacy, Sterry!" Will yelled, then immediately regretted her tough tone.

"Give me the book, Reinhardt."

Will remembered the time Waldek was late picking her up and she had to run back to school and hide in the bathroom when two rough girls chased her in. It turned out Waldek had had a family emergency, and it was Estelle who came and found her. Will sat hyperventilating on the floor of the stall and strangely, when Estelle knocked and identified herself, Will crawled out under the door on the floor like a soldier slinking through enemy lines.

"My God, Will. This floor is unhygienic. Why all the theatrics?"

Will stood up, walked right past Estelle, right past the bullies (knowing they'd avoid her with her older sister behind her), and decided she'd never lose control like that in front of Estelle again.

Will slipped the two letters out from the book and slid them into her bloomers. She feared that Sterry would hear the rustle of paper as she walked by, so she simply dropped the book at her feet and scurried off. Sterry exclaimed something, but Will didn't bother to listen. She stormed back into her room, slammed the door, locked it, and threw herself on the bed.

"That bad, huh?" Dolly said with a laugh.

Will hadn't seen Dolly poking around inside the closet.

"That Jane Sterry. I'd like to strangle her."

"We had a good chance to teach her the dead man's float, but you went all yellow."

"Big mistake," Will said, sitting up. "So, what did Joe want?"

"Me, you idiot," Dolly laughed, ignoring Will's distress. "Actually, he had his bowtie in a knot 'cause I gave him what-for the other day. Seems he's got marriage on his mind, old girl."

"Is that why he called ... did he pop the question?"

"No, but he's sniffing around and getting serious about burying his bone in my yard till death do us part! Hey, got any gin?"

Will felt dizzy and didn't think gin was such a good idea, but she pulled a stash hidden in her bookcase, took a swig, and passed it to Dolly.

"So," Dolly said. "He wants to meet the family. I have a feeling he's going to ask Daddy for his blessing. Can you beat them apples?"

Will reached for the flask and took another swig. She held onto it and tapped her fingers in a rhythmic pattern. *If Dolly speaks next on an even number, she'll marry him ...*

"So listen, I want you to be there for this little date, okay Willsie?"

An odd number! Will *knew* she would not marry Joe. She just knew.

"What do you want me to do?"

"Just keep the conversation lively. Get into some friendly debates with the old man. Anything to avoid giving Joe the floor."

"What's the end game here, Dolly? I don't understand."

"That's up to you," Dolly said. "My father is not so keen on the idea of giving me away."

"Oh yeah?"

"I think he'd rather I marry a Jew. Even though *he* didn't!" Dolly said. "Dance up some diversion and before you know it, the night will be over and Joe will have to come up with plan B."

Will knew Joe had every confidence he could win Dolly. And what father wouldn't give his blessing to a rich, clean-cut Columbia man despite some initial resistance? And especially after this perversion scandal. The world was unfair. She and Dolly made a far better team, a more holy and superior union than Dolly and Joe. Will hated to even couple their names together. For a moment she saw a flash in her mind of an engraved wedding invitation bearing the names "Joseph and Dorothy." It was time to let Dolly know she was serious.

Dolly's father sat at the head of the table with his wife to his left. Joe, the guest of honor, sat to Mr. Raab's right. Dolly sat beside Joe and across from Mrs. Raab, and Will sat opposite her. The kid Sheffy squirmed in a chair next to Will.

"More wine, Mrs. Raab?" Joe asked.

Mrs. Raab accepted Joe's offer and clinked glasses with him. It was Shabbat, and they were the only two gentiles at the table. Will pushed her glass toward Joe and caught his eye. As he refilled her chalice, she cleared her throat.

"What are your views on Prohibition?"

"Well ..." He laughed, turning to Dolly. "I like to look reasonably at both sides."

"What does that mean?" Will pressed.

"It's the law, but I'm a guest in the Raab house and my mother raised me with Southern manners."

"I can see that, Joseph," Mrs. Raab said.

Why don't these two just get married? Will thought they seemed better suited.

"Dolly said you're interested in the law?"

"Why yes," Joe said. "I am. Sorry, I was expecting Dolly's father to grill me tonight."

He laughed, and Will caught Dolly poking him. Having her touch him in any way made Will want to smash the chalice and slice his throat.

"I suppose I'm just curious," Will said. "If you were a lawyer, an officer of the court, would you willingly indulge in illegal activity such as imbibing liquor?"

"Well, the question is hypothetical. I am a student, not yet an attorney. I will, however, say no, I would not imbibe."

"Spoken like a boy, not a man," Will said under her breath.

"What?" Mr. Raab asked.

"Nothing, sir."

All eyes turned to Erich Raab. His skin had a slight yellow pallor of ill health and his jowly cheeks gave him a slumbering look, like a bear just awakening from hibernation. His eyes stared dark and alert, making him just as dangerous as a resting sloth bear. He chewed on his brisket with a loud gnashing sound, a king who cares not for dainty gestures. Why did he seem more manly in this young man's presence? Will wondered what he had been like when he was younger, before his heart condition. She suspected by the way he grabbed for a dinner roll to sop up bloody gravy on his plate, that his ravenous appetite made him quick and forceful when his appetites prevailed.

"Joe," Mr. Raab said. "Wilhelmina has a point. Shouldn't a lawyer abide by the rule of law?"

"Well, yes sir, of course," Joe said. "I intend, when the time comes ..."

"And if you *were* to choose the rule of law, you'd be going against the Jewish law we abide by in my home, in Dolly's home. We drink wine on Shabbat."

"Sir, I didn't mean to offend you in any way. I'm humbled by your hospitality and ..."

He couldn't argue his way out of a family row much less a court-room. This mock trial at the Raabs revealed his embarrassing lack of backbone.

Then Mr. Raab started to laugh. A slight rumble in his belly rose up into a full-throttled guffaw. Will didn't know what to expect, but she heard Sheffy start to giggle and then saw Dolly muffle a laugh as well.

Sheffy leaned over to whisper something into Will's ear, but the whisper was spoken at full volume.

"Daddy's going to say something funny."

"I'm a salesman, Joseph," Mr. Raab said. "No different than being a lawyer. We can sell silk stockings one day and kitchenware the next. Just like a good attorney can fight for a victim on Tuesday and defend a murderer on Wednesday. The one link in the chain that must be strong as steel and absolutely unbreakable though is salesmanship ..."

Joe nodded and smiled as if he'd just received a call from the Governor giving him clemency. She couldn't believe that all he needed to do to make good after so many blunders was to simply grin and listen at the foot of the castle's king.

"And don't be taken in by my husband's sudden religiosity. We haven't had Shabbat in a year, perhaps more?" Mrs. Raab said.

"Why did we stop doing Shabbat, Daddy?" Sheffy asked.

"Well, the laws are changing. The secular laws. It might be time to act American, completely American."

"Then why are we doing Shabbat tonight?" Dolly asked.

Mr. Raab smiled. "I guess I keep a leg on either side of the fence," he said.

Will felt something under the table. The brush of Dolly's foot against her leg. The feeling electrified her. Mr. Raab's voice lowered into the bass strings on a classical guitar. Deep, pleasant, and muddy, like a painting of water lilies by Manet. All Will could see were Dolly's mischievous eyes staring back at her—an invitation. Will knew then that Joe was a lightweight, just as she had thought from the beginning. He was no threat to her. She had the masculine qualities he lacked: bravery, integrity, rationality. It was ironic that she had been born a woman. And yet, had she been born a man would this thing between she and Dolly have been so strong? Wasn't it truly the delicious details of what they did with each other, what they shared as two women—wasn't that what added the charge that galvanized their relationship? Everything seemed clear now. Will had nothing to worry about.

And then Joe took Dolly's hand in his own.

Dolly's foot slipped from Will's leg, leaving Will with a ghost-like feeling, as if a limb had been amputated and lost to her forever.

Chapter Eighteen

Lying in bed in their dorm, it was hard to stop thinking about Europe. Getting out of the country with Dolly, grabbing some cash on the way out through a smart little kidnapping and blackmail. Dolly was worked up about committing the perfect murder and Will had to be honest, the talk of it excited them both. But when it came right down to it, it would be enough to grab a kid from behind to ensure he didn't see them, knock him out, get the money, and be all set to sail. It was thrilling to think about, but she needed to calm down. This level of intensity was hard to take.

Will closed her eyes, imagining all the different realities that could exist for the two of them. Ultimately, each possibility led to the same image—her arms around Dolly, kissing her. The warmth between their bodies forming a tender bubble of protection around them. The slam of the door jarred Will from these pleasurable musings.

"Wake up!"

"I wasn't asleep," Will said.

"It's time to pick a date. Enough stalling."

Will knew what date Dolly was referring to, but she preferred to imagine this experiment in murder as a mere possibility. To start to make movements that would lead them closer to *enacting* it suddenly seemed, well, beside the point. Utterly unnecessary.

"I've been studying this new quantum theory of physics, Dolly ..."

Dolly pulled open the closet as Will ignored her question, pretending to study.

"Which one of these frocks should I wear to see Joe tomorrow?"

"You're still seeing him?"

"Well, I got lonesome chum, when we were separated. I'm not sure if I should string him along or let him down easy."

"You mean you don't like him?"

"I like *certain* things about him, one big, throbbing thing in particular," Dolly said with a wink. "So, what about that date, Reinhardt? I'm itching to go through with our plan."

The thought of Dolly with that numbskull boy was enough to make Will want to explode. But Dolly had her, and she had her good. The only way to *really* ensure she'd choose Will over Joe was to do something with Dolly that Joe wouldn't have the guts to do in a million years.

"All right then. January."

"Too soon. We need time to plan," Dolly said. "Plot all the small details. That's where our genius comes in."

"All right. How about May twenty-first?" Will said. "It's the day classes end, but grammar schools are still in session. And besides that ..."

"We're heading to Europe June first!" Dolly said. "That's cutting it too close."

"Well, let's get all our ducks lined up first and then pick a date. Why decide now?"

"You're just stalling. You're not serious about this."

"Sure I am," Will said. "I was thinking we could grab a kid from behind and blindfold him before he sees us. Then send a letter to his parents and keep them running around before we return him."

"Return him? No way. We gotta see this thing through. Nobody's as smart as we are, and it's all in the planning. Don't think halfway."

Will could see the excitement the fantasy brought to Dolly's eyes. Dolly's nerves were like strings vibrating building to a crescendo.

"So how much should we ask for?"

Dolly smiled. "How much spinach? Hmmm. I think some of these millionaires could plunk up $25,000 easily enough."

"That's too much," Will insisted. "For that large an amount they'd likely bring in the cops."

"Ok, twenty ... and the key here is picking the right kid. It's got to be one with a father who's not a tightwad. You know he's gotta be willing to cough up the cash for the little brat!"

"He's also got to have it at the ready. I say ten. Any higher, they may need more time and we want this to happen quickly."

"Fine," Dolly said. "Now the question is where? How to find the right brat?"

"My birding class is full of kids," Will said.

"Yeah, but you're their teacher. We can't have any connection to the vic'."

"We can drive to Brearley and see if we can pick up a stray."

"Nah. Not Brearley."

"Still too much of a connection to us?" Will asked.

"There's that, plus I want a boy. It should be a boy," Dolly said.

"Why? What's the difference?"

"It's just what I want, okay? Let's get on with the plan. The Collegiate School is our best bet."

"You have a boy in mind?"

"Well that little brat Sheffy would be a great choice, don't you think? Love to see him on the slab ..."

"Your brother, huh? Very funny. We have to be calm and rational. No emotions involved."

"Like men," Dolly said. "Okay, you got a point. No crime of passion!"

Dolly lay down on her bed and reached out a hand to lure Will close. Will checked to make sure the door was locked, then gently but firmly rolled Dolly over from her side to her back and then laid down on top of her. Will looked deep into Dolly's eyes. She deftly took Dolly's arms and pinned them over her head, then leaned in for a kiss. Dolly allowed it and smiled her coquettish smile. She then squirmed out from underneath Will and said she had to take a whiz. Will wanted to follow her but resisted the urge.

"What family?"

"*That* we'll only know the very day of. The letter is gonna be a strictly 'Dear Sir.' Now comes the fun part, Willsie. Rehearsal."

The two sat on the floor of their room, drawing out their plans. They'd nixed several ideas as too complicated and finally decided to place the ransom note in the father's mailbox after the killing. Killing the child was necessary, Dolly insisted. No witnesses. She was on a tear, and Will let her wear herself out. Dolly's idea came from a detective story, as did her certainty that they should instruct the victim's father to go to the bank and ask for denominations of twenties and fifties and include only old unmarked bills.

"Hey, you know what would be tops—if they go into your Pop's bank to get the green?"

"No," Will said. "We can't have anything traced to us."

"If it happened, it would just be a coincidence anyway. Relax. Now I say we give a lot of specific instructions about how to box up the cash. Keep 'em busy and focused on the details."

"We need a car," Will said, "to pick up the kid, but it can't be mine."

"Sure it can be. We smear the license plate with mud the way bootleggers do when they're smuggling hooch across the border."

"Dolly, come on. My car is too easy to make. Be reasonable. How about renting a car?"

"Women can't rent cars, so that won't work," Dolly said. "We could steal one! Betty Pearson keeps a car near campus."

"What do you know about stealing a vehicle?"

"I've got nimble fingers, Willsie."

"Even so, we have to avoid involving anyone we know. There has to be no connection."

Dolly paced around and then suggested getting a hop-head to steal a car for them—pay him off with dope and then knock him off.

"Think of *Crime and Punishment*," Will said. "We can't pile up a bunch of bodies. We have to stick to our plan."

They rattled off a list of possibilities such as taxis and public transportation, but those were obviously not viable. The idea of renting a car kept coming back as a necessity, but how?

"You're chickening out," Dolly said.

"Don't bo sullen. If we want to commit the perfect crime we must make sure the automobile cannot be identified."

They both seethed in silence.

Finally, it was Will who approached the mirror above Dolly's bureau. "We could disguise me as a man."

Dolly smiled. "I'm listening ..."

"We create a fake identify for me as a man," Will said.

"Phony references and all," Dolly said, smirking.

"So even if they trace the car somehow, they can't trace who rented it because *he* doesn't exist."

Dolly started laughing, rolling over with glee.

"This is great, Willsie! Your best yet!"

"But we should take the car out first, so it doesn't look suspicious."

"Aw, come on! You're like some twat who won't put out. Stop stalling!"

Will insisted she was not, that the planning was what would make this perfect.

"Okay. Okay," Dolly relented. "I'll serve as your reference. Mr. So and So. You know I can disguise my voice pretty well. I can teach you a few tricks from my old prof so you can too. Your voice is much huskier than mine to begin with, so it'll be smooth sailing."

Chapter Nineteen

Raab's Department Store in the Garment District was crowded that night. She noticed how many blonde *shiksas* worked as shop girls here. As Will looked around the menswear section she noticed that Raab's only sold shorter coats for men. How different their two families were. Her father would never shop here. He felt a kinship with the "old country" and his Jewish faith more than the fellows at the bank would believe.

Will had spent her whole childhood immersed in science, in languages, in music. But the infusion of Dolly into her world added a delicious element of theatrics. Everything between them felt like a performance, a form of heightened reality. Props. Costumes. Magic. The bustling holidays were the perfect time to shop for makeup, clothes, wigs—the whole look Will needed to pull off if she was going to pass as a man. The stores would be so crowded, no one would remember seeing the girls. Dolly looked around for the perfect tie.

"Why not swipe one from your Dad? He'll never miss it," Will asked.

But within minutes Dolly made her motivation clear. She picked up a simple blue and white stripe—as bland as a banker's. So bland Mr. Reinhardt could have actually worn it.

"Oh," she said, holding it against Will's chest, "Don't you think Joe will love this? I hope he thanks me in smooches and a nice poke."

Sure it was all talk, just to tease Will, but Dolly knew the words would burn. Will frowned. Dolly pressed the tie against Will's sternum and stared into her eyes, unsmiling—a dare. Will couldn't help but stare back and imagine the feeling of being dressed in men's duds, out on the town with her. Then Dolly dropped the tie and slipped it into her purse.

Outside Will said, "It's your father's store! Why rip off a tie? You don't need to."

"Of course not, bubs," Dolly said. "But I *wanted* to. You should try it yourself. Steel your nerves a bit. You've got to enjoy crime for crime's sake, Willsie!"

Will could never understand this part of Dolly. It seemed so childish. But thanks to Dolly's slippery fingers, Will had a few sets of male clothing at her disposal, and she was excited to move on to the next part of the costume. And it was probably safer not to connect them to Raab's Department Store, should any trouble arise.

A month later, in the dorm room Will sat alone before the mirror. After making sure the door was locked, Will placed the small, round mirror on her desk and tipped the glass upwards till she had the right view. She gazed at the picture of Douglas Fairbanks and used it as a model for her mustache. Once glued on straight, she took a pair of small scissors from the barber's kit and trimmed it.

The color looked a little too chestnutty. The mascara brush helped to darken it up a bit to match Will's hair. She spread a bit of charcoal on her forehead and rubbed it in, penciling a few creases to add age. She did the same under her eyes. She used a fine helping of Brilliantine to comb her hair into a slick patent-leather style. She combed down the head and angled to the back of the crown, creating a distinctive part that made her look rather handsome. Dolly had been gradually trimming Will's hair, so the shorter length did not appear shocking. Her eyebrows needed bushiness, so she rubbed them a bit to make them appear a little lived in. Yet something was missing.

Will looked at a picture of Dolly's family hung above her bedside table. Mr. Raab's complexion was too fair. She found no inspiration there. Her own father was too old and deeply Semitic-looking to use as a model for the kind of man she wanted to be. She picked up a bunch of Dolly's screen magazines and flipped through them. Most of the movie stars were too dapper. Will wished to fade into the crowd, so as to avoid capture. But she wanted something distinctive that strangers could focus on without realizing it. An article about John Barrymore which included photographs of his portrayal of *Dr. Jekyll and Mr. Hyde* caught her attention.

It used the opening quote of the picture.

"In each of us two natures are at war—the good and the evil. All our lives, the fight goes on between them, and one of them must conquer, but in our hands lies the power to choose, what we want most to be, we are."

In top hat and tailored waistcoat as Jekyll, Barrymore looked elegant, dashing. But his hair grows and he takes on a savage appearance as he transforms into Hyde. His smile becomes that of a lecherous drunkard. It was compelling to stare at, but Will did not want to make such a disturbing impression. Hyde's face contained a deep crease between the eyebrows, and Will thought that she might be able to capture a subtle variation of this look with a bit of eyebrow pencil.

She slipped into the men's trousers, button-down shirt, suit jacket, and tie from Raab's. Lacing up the black wingtips, she felt a surge of energy. Will walked around the room, swinging her pocket watch carelessly knowing time was as much a man-made construct as gender. She took a gander of herself in the mirror. Her portrayal of a man was quite convincing. She did not resemble a girl dressed as a boy. She had the bearing and the features of a young man.

Will's limbs felt so much looser, not having to keep her legs so close together. She felt her breasts through the linen of her shirt. She could take a scarf and bind them, couldn't she? But the fit of the suit was loose enough, and she did not want to *be* a man. She wanted to simply dress like one.

Something was missing. What? Music!

"Bo-Weavil Blues," the newest recording by Ma Rainey, all wrapped and ready to be dropped on the phonograph. It inflated Will's body with the power of strut and sureness.

When Dolly's key clicked in the lock, she stood upright.

"Well, well, well, Mr. Ballantine," Dolly said, using the alias they'd come up with. "What brings you to my room?"

Will smiled and took a seat on Dolly's bed. She patted the mattress, never breaking eye contact.

"Oh, I don't know, sir. I'm a little nervous," Dolly said. "I'm not supposed to have any gentlemen in my room."

"That's not a problem," Will said, lowering her voice but an octave. "I'm no gentleman."

Will rose up and grabbed a flask from the old banged-up clarinet case she never used anymore. She poured a couple of swigs down her throat then coaxed Dolly to do the same.

"Care to dance?" Will asked once the liquor made its way down Dolly's throat.

She put out her hand like a real gent, and they danced, bodies in rhythm.

There was no reason *not* to kiss Dolly. She was biting her lip and batting her eyes, really pulling out all the feminine wiles. Will pulled her close, and with strength and boldness she didn't realize she had, she slipped Dolly into a surprise dip and then lifted her up like a tender hubby in the picture shows, carrying his bride across the threshold. They laughed and flopped onto the bed. Dolly, normally a nervous chatterbox, didn't say anything. Will kissed her neck, so long and elegant, and felt the luxurious touch of Dolly's hands, loosening her tie.

The next day they met at the music room where Dolly sat at the piano, noodling on the keys, cigarette hanging from her lips.

"All right," Dolly said. "Stand up straight, chest out. But not so stiff. Shake it out, will ya? Ok, now chest out proud. Let's begin in middle range. You're an alto anyway, so this should be easy breezy. Start with scales and we'll take it from there."

Dolly was a good teacher. Will could hear herself keeping tune and lowering an octave without being directed. Dolly's pretty face and graceful hands inspired her instead of distracting her. They were a perfect team.

"Ok, let's try 'My Buddy,'" Dolly said. "You know this one, right?"

Dolly sang, her voice smooth and sleepy, her lips turned downward, suddenly too sad to look up.

Miss your voice, the touch of your hand
Just long to know that you understand
My buddy, my buddy
Your buddy misses you.

Will opened her mouth, about to smack Dolly with a rude comment. Who was Dolly to mock her and Buddy? But she took a breath and decided to sing instead. Maybe Dolly had chosen this song out of a sincere desire to make this one of *their* songs. She never could tell with Dolly.

Will began to sing the song.

"You're getting there, but don't lower your chin. You're crushing your larynx. Let's try the next verse, chin up ..."

With Dolly's guidance, Will's voice lowered of its own accord, as if that deep, male part of her always existed within. It only took someone like Dolly to bring him out.

Chapter Twenty

The spring migration walk through Inwood Hill Park had turned out to be a popular class. Much older ornithologists took students through Central Park, but this marshy area uptown felt like home to Will, and she knew there'd be much to see on a beautiful May morning.

"There, down on the ground to the right," Will said. "It's a palm warbler."

"The one bobbing its tail?" a high school boy asked.

"Yes, remarkable rhythm don't you think?" Will said. "One of its habits is its bouncy tail-bobbing. This species is known for planting its nests on the ground. Unlike most warblers it spends most of its time below foot level. This is just the time when these birds pair off. That's the male guarding the nest."

The students took notes, and Will peered through her field glasses, then continued, climbing up a steep incline.

"Look," Will said. "There in the red bush. A ruby-crowned kinglet."

"Wow! You can't miss him," said a married female student. "A real redhead."

"Yes, beautiful specimen. These birds will forage quite adventurously—at all levels. You may see them examining foliage and tree limbs for food, and sometimes they'll fly right out to catch insects in mid-air. Still, if you look at another kinglet, like the golden-crown, you'll find that this little redhead does more hovering and flycatching. You won't find him hanging on trees so much."

The next morning, Will drove downtown to the Ziegfried Hotel and while Dolly waited in the car, Will sauntered inside. She could feel a rattling inside her fingertips, as if she'd been playing clarinet for hours with no break. The excitement of the brush of trousers against her legs made her stand up straight. What would she do if she was recognized as a girl? Nonsense, she told herself. If it weren't for the girls' clothing she normally wore, she'd have been mistaken for a man a good deal of the time. Somehow repeating the word "*Ubermensch*" in her head helped her walk in with confidence.

The man at the front desk sat stamping cards; he looked up with a smile as she approached.

"Good afternoon, sir," he said. "May I help you?"

She breathed in and smiled. He bought it. She wished Dolly could be beside her to witness the success!

"I'll need a room please," Will said, practicing the octave method Dolly had taught her.

"How long will you be staying with us, sir?"

"I'm in town on business. About a month." Will made sure not to lower her chin.

"Fill this out, please." The concierge passed her a card and a pen.

Will registered as Kenneth A. Ballantine of 302 Oak Street, Elmira, New York. She was dressed in a man's brown suit and hat and carried a small suitcase containing books to give it weight. The bellhop escorted her to Room 1031. Will waited a reasonable length of time, then rejoined Dolly outside.

Later that day Will entered Barclays Bank downtown and opened an account under the name Kenneth A. Ballantine, giving the Ziegfried Hotel as her local address. The bank clerk asked Will if she knew anyone in the area, and "Ballantine" replied in the negative but supplied the names and addresses of several people in Elmira.

"Just wait here, Mr. Ballantine," he said. "And we'll have you finished off in a jiffy."

She nodded, worried that a smile would reveal her sex. While she waited, Will took *The New York Times* that lay on his desk and picked it up to occupy her jittery mind. The headline spread across the full page, as did two drawings of two world maps, side by side. One map was almost entirely shaded in throughout Europe. The map beside it only highlighted Germany, Great Britain, and a few other small lands.

AMERICA OF THE MELTING POT COMES TO END

Effects of New Immigration Legislation Described by Senate Sponsor of Bill—Chief Aim, He States, is to Preserve Racial Type as it Exists Here Today

HOW NEW LEGISLATION WILL CHANGE THE FLOW OF IMMIGRATION FROM EUROPE TO THE UNITED STATES

By Senator David A. Reed, Pennsylvania (R)

The immigration policy upon which the two houses of Congress have now substantially agreed marks a new departure in the American attitude on this subject. Until now we have proceeded upon the theory that America was "the refuge of the oppressed of all nations," and we have indulged the belief that upon their arrival here all immigrants were fused by the "melting pot" into a distinctive American type.

Until the years 1853-85 the sources from which the greater number of our immigrants came were the same sources from which our country was originally colonized, and as result of this fact, the immigrants were easily assimilated in our population upon their arrival here. Beginning about 1885 new types of people began to come.

"Good news at last, isn't it, Mr. Ballantine?" the clerk said, indicating the *Times*. I have your paperwork ready."

Two days later, Will and Dolly drove to the Rent-a-Car Company on John Street in the Financial District. Dolly sat in the car parked four blocks south, and Will went in and spoke with Franklin Richardson who had recently sold his young car business to Jack Avis.

Will introduced herself again as Ballantine, explaining she was a salesman with the Abbey Manufacturing Company who happened to be staying at the Ziegfried Hotel. She had an account at Barclays

Bank and wanted to rent a car and would be happy to make a deposit. Will as Ballantine offered four references, three in Elmira and one in New York City—Lewis Carlton of 121 East 29th Street whose number was Murray Hill 4568. Dolly!

As she wrote the information in more masculine, blockish script, a matron entered with a young lady who appeared to be in her charge. The matron explained they were visiting the area on holiday and looking for a gift shop, a place that sold handkerchiefs.

"Oh yes," Richardson said. "Over on Pine Street, there's just such a place."

He pointed them in the right direction, held the door for them like a gentleman, and then licked his lips once alone with Will . "I'd like to take a bite outta that one. Whaddaya think she's about fourteen, fifteen?"

"Hard to tell," Will said. "I didn't want to look too closely with Grandma right there."

"Good man," Richardson laughed, slapping Will on the back.

Will kept the car for several hours then returned it at 4:37 p.m., having driven only nine miles, paid the bill, and obtained her deposit. Before leaving, she asked Richardson if an ID card might be sent to her hotel so that the next time she rented a car she would not have to provide references. Two days later Will felt more assured; they visited the rental car place and this time Will, disguised as Ballantine, chose a Stutz similar to her own but in dark blue. She paid a $35 deposit before obtaining possession of the automobile.

Will and Dolly next went to the Ziegfried Hotel to retrieve Ballantine's suitcase, pay his bill, and tell the clerk to hold any mail addressed to him. They wanted to keep an address for this fictitious man, should the cops trace the car. But there was no longer any need for them to physically go near the place again. All they required was Ballantine's suitcase and that would be that.

Will turned the key to Room 1031, entered, and locked the door behind her. She imagined for a moment what it would be like to actually be Ballantine. Could she pass as a man and live somewhere with Dolly as husband and wife? But why? Sitting here on this spring, utilitarian bed Will knew she did not want to change herself.

She recalled leaving the suitcase on the wicker bench at the foot of the bed, but it was no longer there. The maid must've cleaned the room and moved it. Will didn't like the thought of anyone touching the case, even though it was merely a prop. A busybody maid would be able to see that no one had slept in this room. They should have made a mess of the sheets.

Will looked about, but the case was not in obvious view. She opened the closet. It held a few hangers and shelves. No suitcase. She looked in the bathroom, even though there was no logic to that. She told herself to pretend that she was indeed Ballantine. There was no reason to panic. Look under the bed. She disturbed the beige dust ruffle and peered beneath the box spring. Nothing. After examining the small room several times, Will exited and walked calmly back to Dolly in the Stutz and told her what had happened.

"What do you mean it's not there?" Dolly said.

"Don't get excited. I have an idea," Will said. "Why don't you call the hotel and pretend ..."

"What? No smart ideas. No calls!" Dolly exclaimed. "Maybe the maid got suspicious 'cause the bed hadn't been rumpled. Maybe she told the manager, and they confiscated the suitcase."

"Dolly, you're overreacting. All we have to do is ..."

"All we have to do is hit the gas. Now come on, we're gone like yesterday."

"No, no," Will insisted. "If we had nothing to hide, we'd ask for the suitcase and pay the bill."

"There's not going to be any *we*, Jack, unless we get a hustle on. Now, come on, let's find another hotel."

Will went along with Dolly, but unlike past times when Dolly had gotten upset, Will let it roll right off her. As a man she felt less vulnerable and was able to look at Dolly as overly emotional. How had she not seen that before? Perhaps, she realized, because she had been equally emotional. Well, something had changed since she'd taken on this male disguise. It was now Will who possessed her rational powers in full. Or perhaps it was just that people had started treating her with more respect.

They decided upon The Savoy. Will registered and asked the clerk to hold any mail that might come for Ballantine and to have the ID card sent to the Savoy instead of The Ziegfried.

Will trusted that on Tuesday Dolly would visit the hardware store they chose in Canarsie, Brooklyn. They'd decided Dolly should dress in unfashionable rags, a wool hat atop her head, and non-prescription glasses from the drugstore, all to purchase a chisel, some tape, and three green plastic seed planters.

The day arrived without much fanfare. On the morning of Wednesday, May 21, the girls attended their 8 a.m. American history class, and at 9 a.m. Will attended a French poetry class. At ten, Will and Dolly attended their Russian Literature class and at noon, classes over for the day, they took the train downtown to pick up the rental car they'd left parked on East 74th Street. Dolly picked up sandwiches at the Spotlight Diner while Will changed out of her male garb in the car with the shades pulled down.

They drove across town to West End Avenue and 77th Street. In a few minutes, it would be time for dismissal at the Collegiate School. The girls watched limousines and town cars pull over to pick up the boys.

"The baseball field is around the corner," Dolly said. "Park across the street."

The ball game went on for about fifty minutes, during which time they assessed the worth of each boy.

"Clifford Bergen's father is a tightwad. He'd just as soon let the kid drown like a kitten then part with a sawbuck."

"My Dad says Donny Martell's dad is worthless," Dolly said. "Not liquid in the least and lousy with debt."

Dolly pointed out that the rich boys of Collegiate came from well-connected families, just as the rich girls of Brearley did. The game started to break up.

"That one. Roger Meyerson. Follow him," Will said.

He was by himself, distractedly tossing a baseball in the air as he turned the corner.

"You know him?" Dolly asked.

"Estelle used to babysit for him."

But just as they closed in a high school kid, probably his brother, ran up from behind and grabbed the ball. They laughed and jostled as they paraded home together. The last one out of the park was Eddie Diller.

"He's the one," Dolly said.

"Yes, his father has dough and is not afraid to spend it, but he's blue-chip stock all the way, my father says."

"And he played with that little twerp Sheffy on Saturday. He knows me! He'll trust me. Just watch."

They drove up behind him, and Dolly rolled down the window all the way.

"What are you doing?" Will asked.

"Just drive ... slowly," Dolly said.

Chapter Twenty-One

I n a matter of days they'd be sailing for Europe. Their wild plot, all of it would be put behind them and they'd create a life as artists together in Europe. Dolly couldn't see it now. Will was the more mature of the two. But she'd follow Will's lead once they were out of this oppressive country once and for all.

"Hey Eddie."

The boy turned around and looked at Dolly quizzically.

"I'm Dolly Raab. You played tennis with my brother Sheffy last weekend."

"Oh, oh, yeah. Right."

Eddie approached, confused.

"This is my friend Wilhelmina. We were running errands for a dance at our college. You need a ride home?"

"Oh ... that's ok."

"It's no trouble," Dolly said. "I wanted to talk to you about a tennis racket, actually. Something I'd like to get for my brother. It's a Wilson. Get in ..."

"Well ..."

"Ah, come on," Dolly pressed. "Keep me awake. As you can see my pal is the silent type!"

"All right then," Eddie said, sliding in.

Will could smell the scent of dirt and sweat on the boy, the scent of spring heat. The temperature in the car seemed to rise when he entered it.

"You're on 63rd?" Dolly asked.

"67th," Eddie said. "But you can take the long way. I'd like to put off homework as long as I can."

"Funny kid," Dolly said. "School boring you?"

"Nah. In fact I'm an ace at debating. I won the finals last week. It was on capital punishment?"

"Oh yeah?" Dolly said. "Which side were you on?"

"Against. I don't believe in an eye for an eye."

"Very big of you," Dolly laughed. "Hey, how old are you anyway?"

"Fifteen."

"You look younger. I mean no offense."

"Well," Eddie said. "I'll be fifteen in September. Just a few months."

"Big man," Dolly laughed. "Don't you think he's practically a man, Will? Not a child, that's for sure. You got a girlfriend?"

Will glanced over; Eddie blushed.

"He does! What's her name?"

"I can't tell you." He laughed.

"What, is she younger? Her Pop would kill you for getting her in trouble, right?"

"Gee, you sure don't talk like a girl," Eddie said.

"Yeah, well. Times are changing. So spill it. What is she twelve—eleven?"

He laughed. Why was Dolly making idle conversation? With each little joke between the two, Will felt like she would lose control. She wanted something to happen or to get him the hell out of the car. She thought for a moment about saying something, anything, to get him out of the car, but no words came to mind. It felt like they'd stepped onto a carnival ride, and before they could think twice a bar dropped down and locked them into their seats. All she could do was stay on till the music stopped and the ride came to a halt.

"Wait. Oh no! I got it. She's *older* than you?"

He laughed.

"Why you nasty little brat! Come on. How old? Sixteen?"

"Yup," he said.

"Or almost sixteen?"

"Well," Eddie said. "Almost."

"You love her?"

"Yup," he said.

"You want to marry her?"

"Yup."

"Well, forget it, kiddo. Ain't there laws?"

"Oh yes," Eddie shot back. "And they said you can get married at age fourteen in New York State."

"Don't the folks have to sign off on it?"

"A mere incidental," Eddie said. "My parents never say no to me."

"Hey Will, I like this kid. Don't you like him?"

Will said nothing.

"Did you hear me, Will? Don't you like him *a lot*?"

Will muttered a yes. She knew what Dolly meant. The father was eating out of the kid's hand. That made it all the more likely they'd made the right choice. The father would pay up immediately. All well and good, but Will wanted out of this car. This didn't feel like a game anymore. Her heart beat faster and she could feel sweat on her hands as she gripped the steering wheel.

"I'm not a kid. I'm old enough to join the army if I want to."

"What are you screwy? You definitely have to be older than you are."

"Well, technically you have to be sixteen and have your parents' consent. But you know I have a cousin who fought in the War. He lied about his birthdate and fought on the ground in Europe. He was only my age!"

"Must've been taller." Dolly laughed.

"Actually, he was. So what's this about a tennis racket? And either of you got any chewing gum?"

Will drove through the park as planned and everything started to speed up. The sound of the kid's gasp was more than Will had planned on. She stole a look at Dolly, afraid to catch Eddie's eyes. Dolly's expression made it clear: it was too late to stop now.

The sound of the blows against his skull came so quick, a staccato measure. Will could barely keep her eyes open to drive. Her head felt light. Did Dolly have to do this? How could he keep struggling? He must be strong. When the drops of blood splattered against Will's face, she felt certain she'd pass out at the wheel. But the white line on the road remained steady and so did she. She thought she heard herself scream out something and Dolly shout back in anger.

Will's hands on the wheel felt as if they might float upward, as if gravity were an illusion. She wasn't sure if her hands were real for a moment. They looked ghostly. There was nothing to do now, Will told herself, taking a deep breath and forcing herself to show courage, nothing to do but see this thing through. Dispose of the body. Follow the plan.

Will headed west to the parkway to take them to Inwood Hill Park, West 218th Street. The area around the Salt Marsh near Spuyten Duyvil Creek was deserted, and Will pulled the car onto a small patch of woods, where trees would give the Willys cover.

"Get the blanket and rope from the trunk," Dolly said.

"Hold on, we agreed to wait till dark," Will said.

Her voice sounded normal. Good.

"Fine."

They stopped alongside a quiet trail to turn around and Dolly climbed into the passenger seat again, leaving Eddie dead, quiet, and still alone in the backseat.

Will drove a quarter mile, then turned down several deserted roads where they parked. Will removed Eddie's pants, shoes, and stockings. They buried his belt and school pin in one spot, then dug another hole about six yards away to bury the rest. Will noted the particulars of the nearest trees, as landmarks in her mind. Just as she did when birding. They then drove aimlessly for a while, waiting for darkness to shroud the burial. There were still a few hours to go.

Will performed these acts in a trance-like state. The woods were so familiar, she was able to move from action to action by using the same motor skills she might use while taking a class on a birding expedition.

"I'm starving, sis," Dolly said, breaking the silence and lighting a smoke while Will drove east.

They stopped by The Dewdrop Inn, where Will got out and bought them each a frankfurter and root beer, which they enjoyed in the car. Will watched her own fingers as she bit into the frank, noticing the dirt under her nails.

"Dolly we can't just ..."

"Willsie. The time to eat is now. We need our strength to finish this thing. The time to talk is later."

Dolly clicked on the radio, and they sat chomping while listening to Ma Rainey.

"Fine sound on this record," Dolly said.

"I think she's got two guitars playing with her."

"Yep. Pruit twins. They make it sound like she's all alone on a desert island," Dolly said.

"Nothing like the sound of it."

Dolly turned off the radio and washed down her frank with some root beer. She leaned on Will's shoulder and sang another Ma Rainey tune, "Prove it to Me" a capella. Her voice twanged with a whistley pitch and a slow, sad rhythm.

How different this would have felt a day earlier, Will thought, the food going down with a bitter swallow. There was no idyllic "Herland" where they could live together. And besides, Dolly would find that world too goody-goody. She'd heard of jazz musicians who led "the life" in Europe. It could be true, couldn't it? There was Sappho, Natalie Clifford Barney. There had to be others who'd found a way.

They could put this behind them, sail to Europe to put the finishing touches on their musical education, and start a life together. Will's father was easy and would be a soft touch for Will. He felt sorry for her, she was sure. She'd lost her Momma. And now that Estelle was betrothed, well, Will knew her sister was only being dutiful by keeping an eye on her. In reality, she'd be relieved to have Will take an ocean liner far, far away, only to communicate once in a while by postcard.

Will rested her head on Dolly's and told herself to just get through this next series of steps. Complete the plan and get to Europe. And once there they would create beautiful music, dedicate their great minds to science, philosophy, the humanities, and in doing so elevate the world to a greater state of beauty and understanding.

As sunset approached they called home to let their parents know they'd be late. They drove around until it was dark enough and made their way to a culvert they had scouted out weeks before, located near a set of railroad tracks.

They dragged Eddie out of the car and used the robe he was wrapped in as a stretcher to carry him closer to the water. His body felt heavy. His brown eyes, still open, stared blankly.

They rolled Eddie out of the robe. She took the bottle of hydrochloric and poured it over his face and genitals to obliterate his identity. Will pulled on rubber hip boots, took off her jacket, and carried Eddie's body into the water while Dolly walked upstream to wash the blood off her hands. Will pushed Eddie's body as far as she could into the narrow pipe, then climbed out of the water and took off her boots. Dolly, picking up Will's discarded jacket, joined her as she put her shoes back on, and they walked back to the car together.

"So we slip the letter in their box as we drive by and that's that," Dolly said.

Will nodded.

The letter, both agreed, was perfect. It struck just the right courteous, professional tone, but with a strong underpinning of threat.

Dear Sir:

As you no doubt know by this time, your son has been kidnapped. Allow us to assure you that he is at present well and safe. You need fear no physical harm for him, provided you carefully follow these instructions. Should you, however, disobey any of our instructions even slightly, his death will be the penalty.

1. For obvious reasons make absolutely no attempt to communicate with either police authorities or any private agency. Should you already have communicated with the police, allow them to continue their investigations, but do not mention this letter.

2. *Secure before noon today $10,000. This money must be composed entirely of folded bills of the following denominations: $2000 in $20 bills, $8000 in $50 bills. The money must be old. Any attempt to include new or marked bills will render the entire venture futile.*

3. *The money should be placed in a large cigar box, or if this is impossible, in a heavy cardboard box, securely closed and wrapped in white paper. The wrapping paper should be sealed in all openings with sealing wax.*

4. *Have the money with you, prepared as directed above, and remain at home. See that the telephone is not in use.*

You will receive a further communication instructing you as to your final course.

As a final word of warning, we are prepared to put our threat into execution should we have reasonable grounds to believe that you have committed an infraction of the above instructions.

However, should you carefully follow our instructions to the letter, we can assure you that your son will be safely returned to you within six hours of our receipt of the money.

Yours truly,

George Johnson

Will drove past the brownstone on West 67th Street.

"Okay I'll hop out here," Dolly said.

Will watched from the rearview mirror as Dolly ambled towards the Diller's home, stopped to light a cigarette, and then casually looked around. Will kept watch to make sure no one suddenly came around the corner. Dolly walked up the few steps casually, slipped the letter in the box, and skipped down the steps and back to the car. Will had to tell herself to drive nice and easy. Every cell in her body wanted to race away as fast as she could. But they needed the power of invisibility.

Chapter Twenty-Two

W ill could only stay calm by sticking to the plan. They'd decided to visit with Will's Pop as part of their alibi. Before going in, Will suggested they check out the rental car. The red spots were hard to miss.

"Relax," Dolly said. "Get some rags from the garage. We can clean 'em up well enough."

They used some cleaning solution they found and scrubbed as hard as they could.

As they were going at it, Waldek approached.

"Miss Wilhelmina," he said. "I oiled the brakes on the Stutz just like you asked. Quiet as a mouse now. You won't hear a thing."

She thanked him and then bid him goodnight, but she could see he was curious about what they were doing. Before Will could panic Dolly jumped in.

"We had a little too much fun last night," she said with a wink. "Spilled some red wine in the back seat."

"You want for me to clean it?" he asked.

"Nah!" Dolly said. "We got it."

Inside, Pop was home early and the three sat down at the card table to play some gin rummy. Will felt squirmy in the Queen Anne chair and wished she could jump from her seat, grab Dolly, and run. She hated her home. The federal-style dark walnut and blue tones were so depressing! They made her feel trapped like a stuffed bird, displaying what it once looked like alive. She'd come to life when she met Dolly and now they'd taken a life, and Will wanted to just give up. It took too much energy to keep playing this game.

Thank God Dolly had enough vivacity for the two of them. Besides, being a good cover for where they were that night, they could let the old man see for himself how well his daughter was doing and how charming her friend still was. They had agreed, at Will's insistence, that Dolly—the consummate performer— should play the role of sweet, young girl. None of her mischievous behavior. Pop didn't go in for that sort of thing.

Pop pulled out the gold pocket watch from his vest, a gift from Momma, and noted it was getting late.

"You're welcome to stay over, Dolly," Pop said, after winning another hand of gin rummy.

"Oh, thank you, sir. But we were going to meet some of the other kids to celebrate. End of the term. Go team!" she laughed.

He gave a soft smile. Will squinted her eyes and tried to imagine Pop loving Dolly like a daughter. His eldest was leaving home. What if Will and Dolly came to visit the old man more? True, Will was Momma's favorite and Estelle, Pop's, but Momma was gone now, and Estelle was getting hitched.

"So it's a promise, Mr. Reinhardt. We'll be back soon. Just not tonight. It could be a wild one. Just joshing. Come on, Will. Let's hit the road."

Will followed along, barely kissing her father goodbye.

"Let me drive," Dolly said, once they'd stepped onto the pavement. "You look a fright. Let's go to Chum-Chum's and wind down."

The place was packed elbow to elbow, but Maeve caught a glimpse and waved them over.

"Where's your guy?" Dolly asked, pulling out a chair; Will followed suit.

"He's actually working on a sizzling story."

"Oh yeah?" Dolly asked, moving in close. "What's the scoop?"

"I don't know much. My roommate took the call. All I know is he's working late on a hot case," Maeve said. "Hey aren't those fellas your beaux?"

Joe and Buddy walked towards them, Joe with an extra spring in his step. Oh, this was not good. Will started to feel that sick feeling again. Too much happening too fast. Buddy put a paw on her shoulder and when she looked up, he was smiling. This was the first time she'd seen him lift the corners of his mouth. She smiled back and for a moment felt what she supposed was a "normal" sense of attraction to him. Why, she wondered? But she knew. Everything felt vivid, like a slow-motion dance in a picture show, complete with cryptic titles and orchestral soundtrack. Tonight, instead of watching a moving picture, they were part of it.

Then she looked at Maeve and wished Maeve would just hold her in her arms and tell her everything would be all right. And Dolly, Dolly ... what had they done?

Estelle's voice screeched in her mind. What a bad influence Dolly was. Estelle was a fool and no friend to Will, that's for sure. And yet, everything could have been different if Will hadn't fallen for Dolly. Buddy felt like such a safe choice, strangely soothing and compelling in his quiet manner. Maeve—well—she was just a regular girl, probably not very interested in other girls. But who was to say? She seemed to like Will. Everything could have been different. Everything.

She tried to take control of her mind. She knew she was being ridiculous. There was no way to trace the crime to them. Two young women would never be suspected. This little test proved their theory. They were above ordinary human beings. And despite Will's momentary revulsion at the splatter of blood, it had all gone perfectly. She told herself to focus on now, this moment.

Dolly made jokes, and Joe laughed as more kids came in to join the fun. Introductions were made and once again, Joe sent Buddy for refreshments, this time promising to pick up the tab.

"You seem pretty tight already," Buddy whispered in her ear. "Wanna dance?"

She was surprised that Buddy was as light on his feet on the dance floor as he was lumbering in everyday gait.

They danced to "Hard Hearted Hannah (The Vamp of Savannah)."

"Listen to this line, 'Brother, she's the polar bear's pajamas.'"

"Clever. Are you a musician?"

"Yeah, I play cornet—jazz."

"I play the clarinet."

"You sing?"

"A little," Will said.

"My band's looking for a gal out front."

"I'm a little shy, Buddy."

"Yeah, but you have something deep inside."

He leaned in closer to her and looked her straight in the eye.

She felt something in her heart. What was it? It was a physical sensation, something adrenal quickening the pace of her pulse. But she also felt a curiosity. She wanted to kiss Buddy, to be distracted by his lips, to try another way.

"Kent! Kent! Your seat's all warmed up and waiting for you!"

It was Dolly, hollering across the room and practically carrying poor Kent to his seat. Will moved to re-join the gang at the table, but Buddy held her arm.

"Stay with me. Your friend's a real—chatterbox."

Maybe she didn't like boys, and they didn't like her, but she could like this man. He seemed to appreciate the real her, and there was some connection between them. Maybe it could grow into something?

Then she remembered: the boy, the culvert, and Dolly.

"I'm sorry, Buddy, let's just sit down with them for a bit."

She even took his hand and pulled him over.

"All right, big newspaperman, do tell! Your girl let the beans spill that you're in the middle of a big case. What's the story?"

"Whoa, easy, Dolly."

"Sure, sure. Have a little nightcap, take a load off," she said, moving quick to pour Joe's drink down poor Kent's throat. "Now come on!"

"Okay, okay," he laughed, clearly enlivened by the booze. "Well, you know the park up in Inwood?"

Will felt suddenly disembodied. It was as if she were hearing the words and watching the scene from above.

"Inwood Hill Park?" Dolly said. "Will, you go birding there, don't you?"

"I have, yes," Will said, pulse starting to race. The calm had only lasted a moment.

"Well, some railway workers who were cutting through the woods happened upon a dead body."

"Holy smokes!" Dolly cried. "It was a bootlegger. I know it! I can feel it in my bones."

"Unless they start bootleggers as kids, I don't think so."

Will held her breath and felt her eyes start to blink. She willed them to stop. It had to be a different child.

"A kid?!" Dolly exclaimed.

Couldn't she keep her mouth shut?

"Yeah, that's all I can say for now. You'll read about it in the morning papers."

"Aww, come on," Dolly said. "Pleeeease, Kent-o. You gotta give us more. You broke a big case. We can't wait till sunrise."

"I didn't break it," Kent said, "I was typing up some copy when this call came in about the body, and the city editor sent me up there. Just the right place at the right time."

"And I guess that kid was in the wrong place at the wrong time," Joe said.

"Did you see the body?" Dolly asked.

"I did. Pretty sad to see a dead kid. He was just about twelve."

"Twelve, huh? What a mystery. Who could he have wronged?"

"My girl loves mysteries!" Joe said.

"How you can call me your girl is a mystery to me, bub," Dolly said, then kissed him on the cheek to show she was teasing.

Will wanted to cry. After all she'd sacrificed for Dolly, how could she play best girl to Joe?

"Come on, Willsie. We gotta go splitsville."

Will breathed. Dolly had changed her tune.

"What for?" Joe asked. "And if you really gotta go, I can drive you."

"Will has wheels. We don't need your old jalopy," Dolly said, grabbing Will and making for the exit.

They left Chum-Chums and drove several miles north, Will behind the wheel.

"They don't know anything yet," Dolly said.

But Will felt a certain calm, as if it would all soon be over. They'd never considered the possibility of being caught. Now, it seemed probable.

"The story's breaking," Dolly said. "We've got to clean up the car, get rid of all the evidence that ties us to the crime."

Will felt Dolly's panic, the jangle of her nerves, and something inside her shifted. A feeling of calm flowed through her.

"Fine," Will said. "But, we can still take a bite at the apple and see if we can get the ransom."

"What are you talking about? The case is going to be all over tomorrow's papers."

"Yeah, but the papers aren't going to get delivered till six a.m.," Will said. "So we change up the plan. We get Mr. Diller on foot at a hot pace and keep him moving. Dollars to doughnuts he's not going to see the paper. Might as well take our shot."

The two spent the next hour parked out of view, cleaning out the blood spots from the back seat of the rental car. Somehow at this late hour it felt to Will as if only they two existed. But the world felt like a dark lonely place too. Will couldn't believe they'd actually gone through with it. She had assumed that Dolly just enjoyed the crazy scheming. That's what Will enjoyed. Not for the planning itself, but because it allowed her intimate time with Dolly. Even up until the very last minute she thought Dolly would say to the boy, "okay kid time to get lost, dinner's getting cold." But it all happened so fast. And now it was done. And it was Will's time to collect. She would not go soft now. They could end up in prison or hanged if caught; the only reason to live now was for Dolly.

Chapter Twenty-Three

After all these years studying birds, Will felt comfortable in the early-morning hours. At 5:45 a.m., they sat in the rented Willys, down the block from the Diller home, and watched as the old man opened the door. It must be Mr. Diller. He looked as if he'd slept in his clothes from the night before—rumpled trousers and shirt, loosened tie, and haggard face. He opened the mailbox and took out the white envelope. Dolly must have gotten through on the payphone down the street without a hitch. The paper would not arrive for another hour at the earliest. They had studied the route.

Will watched as Mr. Diller looked up and down the block. She was too far down the street for him to notice, and she could see from the jerky way he moved, like a man in spasm, that he couldn't really focus on anything except what was in that letter. He disappeared inside, and Will counted to sixty before she drove down the block to pick up Dolly.

"The ball is still in play," Will said.

They drove next to the drug store on Lexington and waited.

Will wanted to say something about how slim the odds were that another young boy's body had been found in that very same park, but she chose to focus on the road. Once inside Moe's Pharmacy, Dolly traded a nickel for a slug and called Diller's number.

"The line's busy."

"What? Try it again."

166

"We told them to keep the line clear. He's going to pay for this," Dolly said.

"Oh, yeah? We already killed his son."

Will immediately regretted this slip of temper, but Dolly just laughed.

"Oh, yeah. That's right!"

The pace was heady; adrenaline carried them, as if they were staying up all night for finals. The main thing for Will was to keep emotions at bay. If an image of young Eddie popped into her mind, she'd replace it with a bird. She tested herself on the scientific classifications of the Rainbow lorikeet, native to Queensland, Australia. Part of the Animalia kingdom, a member of the family of Psittaculidae ...

"It's ringing," Dolly whispered, covering the mouthpiece.

Dolly changed her posture as she inhaled to deep her voice.

"Is this Mr. Diller?"

"Yes, yes, this is Bernard Diller speaking. My boy is safe?"

"Did you prepare the money as instructed?"

"Yes. I have the money. How is Eddie?"

"Your boy is fine. As soon as this call ends, proceed to the drugstore at 33 East 61st Street. Wait for a call in the phone booth to the left outside the front door. Do you understand?"

"Yes. Yes. May I please speak with Eddie? I just want to hear his voice ..."

"Remember, the address is 33 East 61st Street. Further instructions will follow."

They gave him thirty minutes for the walk. He was an old gent. The phone rang several times, and Dolly looked at Will a little jittery. The store was just opening up.

"Hello, is there a Mr. Diller outside the store waiting for a call?" Dolly asked, lowering her voice and allowing Will to share the earpiece with her.

"No," an old man's voice said. "Nobody there."

"Can you check please?"

"Hold on."

They waited, and the man returned to the phone a few seconds later.

"Nobody out there, sir."

"All right. Thank you."

They stepped outside, and Dolly lit a cigarette.

"Why don't we drive past his house again?"

"Nah," Dolly said. "Too risky."

She started to walk, and Will followed.

As they passed a newsstand they both saw the headline.

BOY FOUND DEAD IN INWOOD PARK

"The jig's up," Dolly said. "Come on. Let's get lost."

Will could see Dolly's eyes dart back and forth, as if the cops were surrounding her, like in one of her detective stories. It was as if when Dolly ran hot, suddenly Will could remain cool. She bought the paper, slid onto a bench in front of a candy store, and read the story.

"We knew this already," Will said. "From Kent. They found the body. But they still have no idea *who* the kid is."

"Come on! It's been hours since the paper got the scoop. They must know about the kidnapping by now. And even the most piss-poor gumshoe could put two and two together and get four."

Dolly was regressing. It was up to Will to remain adult, *rational*.

"You're getting too excited. We have to see this thing through to the end. It's an experiment and it's not yet over."

"Are you bats? It's done, you dumb Dora. Let's ditch the car and then lay low."

"I'm going to call again," Will said, turning away from Dolly.

But Dolly grabbed her roughly by the arm.

"*You* were the one who insisted on that spot. You knew it from your goddamned birding. Well now they're going to be on us like vultures thanks to your bright idea."

"We wiped out his identity. The acid."

"You think parents can't identify their own kid's body? Jesus you're a numbskull."

"Stop attacking me," Will said. "You'll only upset yourself more."

Where did those pedantic words come from, Will wondered. She could tell they only sparked more fury in Dolly. Then she remembered: Estelle. That's exactly the kind of thing Estelle would say.

"And we can't ditch the car. I'll dress up one last time and return it. Then that'll be the end of it. It's true, we lost our chance at making ransom, but we are still in the clear. There's no way we can be connected to the crime."

Will felt a sense of relief at Dolly's panic. They were even now. Neither was immune to a case of nerves. She'd rather Dolly be the one to get shaky. From a logical point of view there was simply no room for both of them to give in to fear. Let Dolly worry; Will would take care of everything. Dolly's fear made Will feel protective, stronger. She was in charge now.

Mrs. Raab hugged Sheffy to her breast as Will and Dolly watched.

"Oh it's just awful. Simply awful. This could have happened to Sheffy!"

Will sat at the kitchen table, telling herself to remain calm, pretend they were in a picture show. The news had broken early that morning, and the phone kept ringing.

"Miss Jacobs, ma'am."

"Nettie, thank you," Mrs. Raab said as the maid handed her the phone.

"Rona, it's awful isn't it? Who could do this?"

"Nettie, take Sheffy outside to play in the sprinkler, will you?"

Once the girls were alone with her, Mrs. Raab went silent.

It was Dolly who shifted the mood, bursting into tears.

"It *could* have been Sheffy, Mumsie! And what would we have done then? We'd be sitting in this kitchen making preparations for a … Oh god … Oh god …"

"It's perverse!" Mrs. Raab shouted. "That's what it is! Whoever did this should be tarred and feathered."

Will leaned back as if watching a play, wondering where those tears of Dolly's came from. Could she be feeling true remorse? What a relief it would be if Dolly were softening. She would need Will to lean on; they would be more alike. She would drop the joking mask at last, and Will could be with the real Dolly.

Mrs. Raab opened her arms to Dolly and pulled her to her breast. Mother comforting child. The image made Will want to cry for herself. For should they get caught, who would cry for her?

"I think I need to take a walk, Mums," Dolly said. "I just can't ... I just can't ..."

Dolly wiped her eyes and headed for the door.

"I'll go with you," Will called after her.

Once outside Will recognized Dolly's familiar smirk.

"I thought for a moment you were feeling regret."

"You don't know me very well, do you?" Dolly said, but her tone was playful as she threw an arm around Will.

"I know you better than anyone knows you, Dolly."

"That's not saying much."

"Now we share something that unites us forever," Will said, pulling Dolly into an alley and pushing her up against the bricks.

"Easy, tiger."

Will looked deep into Dolly's eyes and said, "You know that we're one now, don't you?"

She didn't even know where these words were coming from. Had the murder given her a strange freedom? If she was not a super-woman before, had she transformed into one now?

Dolly said nothing as she moved towards Will, putting her head on her shoulder. Will opened her arms and held Dolly close.

"Don't ever let me go," Dolly whispered.

Will breathed in deep as if with the snuffing out of one young life, her own young life was about to truly begin.

"Never, never," Will said, thrilled to be reassuring Dolly at last.

To hold her like this, with her guard down, was everything to Will. Will noticed for the first time a tiny speck of amber in Dolly's eye she'd never seen before. How many other intimate glimpses of her body and her soul would she behold, now that this one act had bonded them for life and till death do them part?

In a moment Dolly's eyes flickered, like a film strip cutting to the next shot.

"Come on, kid! Let's go check out what's going on at the Diller's."

They walked across the park and stopped at a newsstand on Columbus. The story had made all the front pages. Will plunked down a coin, and they grabbed the paper.

BODY OF DROWNED BOY
FOUND IN SALT MARSH

"Look at this spread! It's just like in the detective stories!" Dolly gloated. "They think he drowned! The rubes!"

Very little text filled the front page of May 24, 1924 edition of *The New York Daily Spectator*, but the pictorial accompaniment on pages nine to ten were spread out like pieces of a photographic puzzle.

Search for Slayers of Edward Diller: One of the Most Baffling Crimes of Record

Seek to Pierce Mystery of Diller's Death: *This photo was taken at the inquest held yesterday into the murder of the fourteen-year-old school-boy whose nude body was found in the Spuyten Duyvil Salt Marsh. Acid was used to obliterate the sex of the child.*

School Which Edward Diller Attended: *Classes were not held yesterday at The Collegiate School on West End Avenue and West 78th Street. Several instructors were being questioned as the principal assisted in the search for the slayers.*

Found Body: *Stanley Staszalek, laborer who discovered the body of Edward Diller in the culvert.*

Quizzed: *Peter Rogers, Athletics instructor at the Collegiate School, snapped at the inquest.*

Scene of Kidnapping: It is here on West End Avenue and 74th Street that Edward Diller is suspected to have been kidnapped and whisked away in an automobile.

Rendezvous Appointed by Kidnappers: It was in this East Side drugstore that the kidnappers of Edward Diller expected to meet the father with the $10,000 ransom. (See Story page one)

Expert Studies Typewriting of Ransom Note: Left to Right: Lt. Michael Shoemacher, Barton Elwich, typewriting expert, Sgts. Marcus Ellery and Gavin Schoels studying the note which kidnappers sent to Bernard Diller.

"Incredible!" Dolly said. "Come on, let's go investigate."

"Don't be so rash. We should lay low, don't you think?"

"You lay low if you wanna. I'm being au-nat-ur-al and checking out the scene. Hey, there's Kent!"

Dolly skedaddled across the street, and Will followed cautiously.

"Kent! What's the latest, kid?"

Will approached and nodded at Kent.

"So? Any suspects? Mums and I were just talking, and we think it's just beastly. I saw in the papers they're questioning some of the teachers. Any of them break yet?"

"Whoa! Whoa! Dolly, I've got work to do ..."

"Did you talk to the handyman yet?" a middle-aged reporter asked Kent.

"No, I ..."

"Handyman? Do you think a working stiff did it? Jealous of the rich kid? Desperate for dough?" Dolly said.

The older reporter smiled at her.

"Friend of yours, Kent?"

Will didn't like how this man looked Dolly up and down. She could practically hear the wolf whistle.

"Yes. This is Miss Dolly Raab. She goes to Barnard with my gal Maeve. Dolly, this is Steve Reilly, senior reporter at my paper."

"Pleased to meet you, Miss Raab."

"Dolly, please!" She squealed with razzle-dazzle. "You know I was just saying to my mother it could have been our sweet little

Sheffy who was taken and brutally … It's so awful, isn't it? I mean Sheffy *played* with Eddie."

"Did you know Eddie Diller?" Reilly asked as Will moved closer to Dolly, hoping to get her out of there before she flapped her gums too much.

"Well just a little bit. I mean he was just a neighborhood kid, a friend of my kid brother's. He played tennis at our club a handful of times. He had a mean backhand."

"Do you have any idea who could have done this?"

"If I were you I would definitely go a little rougher on the teachers. I mean they're all hands, if you know what I mean. There's a couple who've never been married and like to spend extra time 'mentoring' the kids, and I just don't buy it. These guys …"

"Which one?" Reilly asked. "Any names?"

"Grebstein teaches science and let's just say it wouldn't surprise me to hear he'd experimented on …"

"Dolly," Will said.

"Oh sorry—this is my friend—Miss Reinhardt. We go to school up at Barnard College."

"Very impressive," Reilly said. "… And pricey."

"Yeah, I know we were born into hideous wealth! Heck if we were younger it could have been us. In fact, Mums is so frightened she wants me to move back home and never leave her side. But I have a feeling whoever did this wasn't interested in girls, if you know what I mean."

"So is there anything in particular about this Grebstein fellow? Is he the type you're thinking of?"

"He was pretty grabby according to a couple of old beaux of mine who studied … under him."

Will couldn't believe how risqué Dolly was being. This wasn't like their joking around together, nor was this even akin to Dolly's naughty flirtatious gags with Joe. This fellow was a real reporter. Kent had wheedled his way into a position of importance on the case due to his good timing and eager-beaver attitude. But Kent was still one of them—a kid really.

Reilly. He looked at Dolly with predatory eyes. Will didn't know if he wanted to neck and nuzzle Dolly or catch her in a lie. But maybe she was just being paranoid. They didn't know anything. And they *wouldn't* know anything if Dolly kept her mouth shut.

"But he's not the only one. I'd also look into the music teacher, Meyer Rodgers—boy that one can sing soprano, if you know what I mean. I've seen him looking too long at the boys. Pretty light in the loafers, let's just say."

Will started to move forward when she felt a tap on her shoulder. She turned around.

"Maeve!"

"It's awful, isn't it?" she said.

"Yes. Yes. Awful."

As Will said the words, she felt a strange desire to put her arms around Maeve, to comfort her as her boyfriend might, if he weren't so busy. She put her hand gently on Maeve's arm, and Maeve took Will's hand and held it.

"I just want to cry," Maeve said. "But we all need to be strong, don't we? This is our community. This young boy could have been a member of any of our families."

"I see Dolly has a lot of ideas," Maeve said.

"Yeah, her mind always runs a mile a minute. Almost as fast as her yap."

Maeve looked at her, and Will smiled. Was it Will's imagination or did Maeve rub her hand against hers, the way, well, the way Dolly did sometimes when she was feeling a little moony.

"So what about Eddie Diller?" Reilly asked. "How would you describe him?"

"Well, he was a decent ball player, the kids all said. Mums and I came to watch Sheffy recently, and Eddie caught a coupla fly balls like there was nothing to it."

Reilly penciled a few words in his notebook.

"But he was also a real know-it-all," Dolly added. "In fact, if you were looking to murder a kid, a cocky-little-son-of-a-bitch like Eddie Diller would be the one!"

She laughed, unaware of the impact. Will heard the awkward silence and passed Dolly a secret look she hoped would not be caught.

Then for a quick save Dolly said, "Hey come on! Gallows humor. I just keep thinking this could have happened to my baby brother."

But it was too late. Her callous dismissal of the boy struck a terrible chord. Everyone heard it and looked at Dolly like something was truly wrong with her. Will could see it too. But she still found her face impossible to look away from.

Chapter Twenty-Four
Dolly

Ditching Will had been a chore. She had to promise to meet her at Etta's for a soda later that afternoon. Ever since they did the deed, Will acted like she owned her! It was getting hard to breathe.

KIDNAPPED BOY DIED FIGHTING

Dolly grabbed the broadsheet, the May 25th edition of the *New York City Tribune*. She crossed the street to read it start to finish. It was strange. She didn't remember him "fighting." That part was a bit hazy. But going into the woods in the dark of night. What a thrill to remember! She looked around, considering the option of ducking into an alley. But the lede made it clear: these cops were chasing their own tails! They naturally assumed a couple of men did it. If only they knew. Dumb doughnut-eaters underestimated the strength a girl is capable of.

If the belief that the boy's death came while in the hands of men whose one and only object was extortion is correct, the police have nothing on which to work except the tracing of the typewriter and a few other odds and ends clues, it was admitted.

One objection to the "kidnapping for ransom" theory was in the question of why would they take a fourteen-year-old boy? Many

wealthy families live in the neighborhood. Would kidnappers not
have taken a much younger child if their game was ransom money?

They didn't know anything! The plan had worked. Dolly phoned up Will and made a plan to meet.

♫

At Chum-Chum's that night, the crowd was in full force. When Dolly saw Kent roll in she called him over.

"Here's our man of the hour! What's the latest, Kentsy? What's this I hear about them doing something heinous to his anus?"

Will shot Dolly an angry look, but Dolly just ignored it.

"Well," Kent said. "That does suggest a homosexual may have committed the crime. I mean a normal guy wouldn't ..."

"Kent, please don't," Maeve said. "Who are you or anyone to judge what's normal?"

"Oh, come on, Maeve. A line has to be drawn between humans and savages, don't you think?"

"So you think homosexuals are savages?" Maeve asked.

"Read what they did to the boy! Oh forget it. I just came for a quick drink with my girl."

"Well, you've got all of us here hanging on your every word," Dolly said. "Come on, what's the latest clue in the case?"

Dolly made sure to set him up with a shot of gin. The guy really didn't seem to like the spotlight, so it was hard to work the usual schmaltz on him. You just couldn't pour it on thick. But he was a lightweight, and after they raised the glasses and the booze slid down the hatch, she found him easier to wheedle. Plus, Dolly could see how bushed he was. The bags under his eyes puffed up like balloons every time he blinked.

"What time is it now? It'll be in the early edition ..."

"Whoa? Spill, brudder, spill! That's just a few hours from now. Have they caught the guys?" Dolly said, her eyes sparkling at Will.

It was great to be able to share this with ole Will. She maintained a blank stare. Almost *too* blank. But no one was watching Will. She made everyone too edgy with her awkwardness. You'd think liquor would loosen her up, but she seemed to have a glass leg. Dolly was dying to hear the news but also wanted to freeze this moment in time. This was it! It was happening! They'd done something more dangerous than anyone could ever dream of. Sure the ransom angle had gotten bungled, but still, they'd done it!

"They haven't found the culprits, but a big lead just came in."

Everyone leaned forward. Dolly tried to think of a line, but her nerves shorted her circuits for a rare second.

"They recovered glasses by the site of the body."

"Glasses? What kind of glasses?" Dolly asked.

"Eyeglasses. They were too big for a kid, and besides, the family confirmed that Eddie Diller didn't wear glasses. He had 20/20 vision."

"So the vic' had 20/20 vision," Dolly said, buying time by dropping police lingo she'd read about in detective stories. "Do they think the specs belong to one of the killers?"

"Well, likely so. I had a hunch when the railway worker who discovered the body turned them over ..."

"*You* had a hunch? You mean this is your scoop?"

"Well, it was just dumb luck."

"It sounds very smart, and isn't it Sigmund Freud who said there are no accidents? Tell us more, Kentsy."

"Well, it was just instinct. I asked to look at the glasses, and I just tried to slip 'em on my face to take a peek. They were tight on me but definitely grown-up spectacles. The detectives tried 'em on the body, and no dice. They were way too big."

Dolly looked over at Will, who was reflexively checking her purse. She gave her a look to tell her to cut it. Will was a walking confession. Some *ubermensch*! What a dupe! Of course Will would screw things up like this. The little klutz. Dolly would have never done something so idiotic. And Will liked to brag about her high IQ. Higher than Dolly's. But Will was a nervous Nellie. She didn't have the daring to be a master criminal.

"Was there anything special about the glasses?" Maeve asked.

Little smartie. But Dolly wanted to hear the answer.

"No, they look like a common pair of reading glasses. But it's the first major break in the case."

Will wasted no time returning to the dorm to search for the glasses.

"She's not going to find them, is she, Teddy?" Dolly said, addressing her stuffed animal. Since the crime, Dolly had taken to carrying her little childhood bear around with her. She'd joke to the gang that she was scared since the kidnapping, but really it was nice to have someone to talk to.

"I admit it was an unforgivable error," Will said.

"Well, that's so big of her, isn't it, Teddy?"

"Dolly please, talk to *me* not the bear. Besides, if I may say this in my own defense—when we were leaving I asked you to grab my blazer. I had laid it neatly on the ground. And if memory serves—you carelessly grabbed it by the tail, and it was almost certainly at that moment, in the darkness that the glasses fell out ..."

"*Grabbed it by the tail,*" Dolly mocked, then threw Teddy to the floor and slammed the heels of her hands into Will's chest, knocking the smaller girl onto the bed. "Don't try to put the finger on me, Reinhardt. You didn't want to do this in the first place. Sure you could plan a crime, but when it came right down to it, at every turn *YOU* were the one who lost your nerve. Being a master criminal does not just take brains, it takes guts."

"Dolly, calm down. This does not change anything ..."

Will hesitated for a few seconds, and Dolly wanted to strangle her. She would do this from time to time. This cuckoo bird spacing out. Like she was suddenly asleep.

"What?!"

"I'm sorry. I was just thinking. What if I drop by the police station and I say that I go birding in that area all the time and it's possible I may have dropped my glasses ..."

"No. No. You'd crack up. You'd get us in a worse jam."

"Why? I think it's quite reasonable ..."

"No!" Dolly said. "Now come on. You know how you are about neatness. You have a place for everything—*one* place for everything! Let's look again."

"Ok," Will said, this time resigned. "But you're not going to find them."

"How in hell could you be such a stupe? Look, can they trace them, do you think?"

"They're a very common prescription," Will argued. "Half a degree of astigmatism or something, the doc said. There must be a jillion pairs like them in the city. So I don't think there's much chance of their being traced. On the other hand, I've got all the alibi in the world for them being found there. You know I go birding out there all the time. Hell, I've been there—right at that same spot—half a dozen times in the last couple of weeks. I had my birding class in those woods just this past Saturday. I have a number of respectable witnesses to corroborate. Whaddaya say I go in and claim them. Kinda spike their guns in advance."

"Naw, I think that'd be a fool caper," Dolly said. "Don't get mixed up in the case at all. They might try some rough stuff on you. And besides, it could take you a hell of a while to talk your way out of it. You've got your exams coming up and everything. Of course the crucial thing is what chance there is the damn things can be traced to you."

"Well, as I said, I know the prescription is a very common one. The doc told me so. And how are they going to know what oculist they come from? They'd have to go through the records of every oculist in town and then check on a couple of thousand people."

"Hell, let it go. You don't know your glasses are gone. Make 'em come to you. Then, if worse comes to worst, you can be so surprised that the glasses are yours. Then's the time to tell your story about losing 'em birding."

"But officer," Will said, suddenly shifting into her pedantic student voice. "I felt it was my civic responsibility to at least come by and offer my assistance. You see I'm an ornithologist, and I frequent those very woods with my students a couple of times a week. When I saw the story in the paper I thought ..."

"And where were you, Missy, on the evening of Wednesday May twenty-first?" Dolly asked in her best dumb cop brogue.

"Why I was with my friend, Dorothy Raab. She's also a student at Barnard."

"Oh, dat's dat hoity toity school for women?"

"It's a Seven Sisters school. It only accepts young ladies of good breeding, officer."

Dolly smiled. That was a good one. Maybe Willsie had some finesse, after all.

"Ok, so where were you two that day?"

"Well, let me see. That was a Wednesday. We had our literature class in the morning, then philosophy."

"Whaddaya need that for—just to learn how to cook and clean for your husbands?"

"Well, officer. Philosophy really is just the study of *man*, you know."

Jeez Louise, Dolly thought. She's actually flirting, but just a tiny bit. She's got perfect pitch!

"So, what'd you do *after* school?"

"Well, we took a ride in my car—it's a Stutz Bearcat. We had dinner at Le Bistro on the East Side and then we wandered around Central Park a bit. Near the boathouse we ran into a couple of boys—who started a little rap with us. We ended up going to a jazz club in Harlem with them."

"You mean that jungle music?"

"It's the cat's meow, officer!"

"And what were the names of these two laddies?"

"Pete and Charlie– but I don't think those were their real names. And frankly officer, we didn't give them our real names either. It was sort of a wild night."

"Heavy petting?"

"Not heavy. When the boys tried to get randy, we hauled ourselves out to the old jalopy—heh, hch—and left 'em in the dust."

"So you teased the boys, huh?"

"We didn't mean to, officer."

"Not strong enough," Dolly said. "We need a real reason why we'd be so shamefaced."

Dolly bit her cuticles then slapped Will on the shoulder.

"I got it," Dolly said. "They're negroes!"

They both laughed. It was perfect!

Chapter Twenty-Five
Will

The girls drove to a newsstand about twenty blocks south of campus. It seemed as if the whole city was ablaze over this terrible crime. Will felt detached from the facts, as if she were merely a research student, puzzling over the different aspects of the story.

KIDNAPPED BOY KILLED;
RANSOM WAS DEMANDED

Son of Wealthy Watch Company Head Slain
as Father was Sending $10,000 Ransom

Body of Youth Left in Swamp

Clues leading both to high culture and to degeneracy mystified the police today in solving the kidnapping, murder, and attempted ransom of Edward Diller, fourteen, son of Bernard Diller, a wealthy manufacturer. A stocking identified as worn by the boy and a pair of horn-rimmed eyeglasses were found on the bank. The father said the boy had never worn glasses.

GLASSES NEAR BODY
NOT SUCH AS MAN WEARS

Small Lenses and Frame Opticians Say

A woman probably owned the pair of horn-rimmed spectacles picked up near the culvert in Spuyten-Duyvil where the deceased body of Edward Diller was discovered on Thursday. This theory, voiced yesterday by three expert opticians, injected a new and puzzling element into the murder case.

The opticians shook their heads when Lieutenant Charles Downing said that no trace of a woman associated with the crime had been found, and the opticians must be mistaken.

Lenses Are Small

"It would be a strange kind of man, a little bit of a wizened-face fellow, who could wear these," said one of the opticians, fingering the thick lenses of the glasses.

Not only are the circumferences of the glasses extraordinarily small for a man's glasses but the ear supports are far too short for the masculine head, it was pointed out. Illustrating his point, one of the opticians attempted to fit the glasses on a detective. The effect was grotesque. The supports scarcely reached the officer's ears.

EXPERT FIXES ON KIND OF MACHINE KIDNAPPER USED

Writer a Novice on the Typewriter

The man who wrote the letter in the Diller kidnapping and murder was a novice at typewriting, or at least someone who never learned the touch system. The letter was written on an Underwood portable typewriter purchased less than three years ago, a machine with a defective lower case "t" and "f."

These clues were furnished to Assistant State's Attorney Henry Dawfield, by J.S. Sutphin of the Royal Typewriter Company, an authority on typed documents. For twenty-six years Mr. Sutphin has made a study of the different makes of typewriters.

Never Learned Touch System

"The person who wrote this letter never had learned the touch system," Mr. Sutphin said. "A person using the touch system strikes

the keys pretty evenly, with an even pressure on the keys. The man who wrote this was either a novice at typing or used two fingers. Some of the letters were punched so hard they were almost driven through the paper, while others were struck lightly or tentatively."

"We've got to get rid of that machine," Will said. "It's hot."

Dolly glared at her. "Oh you think so? You and your nervous typing—you think you're so smart but ..."

"So what? I can't touch type. Neither can you."

"You were the one who had to swipe that lousy typewriter!"

"It was never reported missing. Those sorority girls kept their mouths shut just like we knew they would," Will said. "They didn't want their precious reputations blown to bits."

"Don't act all palsy-walsy with me," Dolly said. "Of all the bubble-headed ideas. Why'd you have to nab that rotten portable? The glasses would've been bad enough ..."

It was all unraveling. Dolly rolled up the paper and smacked Will across the face with it then let it fall to the ground. Why did she have to do that? Will was getting pretty damn sick of this foul treatment. She'd sacrificed everything for her, and it was time Dolly started treating her with some goddamn respect. It was just like this when they were in the car with Eddie Diller, when it was really happening. Dolly wasn't as in control as she thought she'd be. She liked to blame Will for everything, but wasn't it Dolly who panicked when strangling the boy hadn't been enough to make him pass out? When he kept fighting? Dolly liked to paint herself as the brave one—the master criminal—but sometimes she was a helpless little child who relied on Will to do all the dirty work.

Will retrieved the newspaper from the gutter and shoved it back in Dolly's face.

"What about this one, *Dorothy*?"

DILLER LETTER LIKE CURRENT STORY IN MAGAZINE

Police criminologists, detectives who have made names for them-selves solving difficult murders like the bewildering case of Edward Diller, keep coming back again and again to the letter received by the father of the boy by the "kidnappers." The letter with its faultless English, its scholarly diction, bore a striking resemblance to several such letters of fiction which appeared in a story, "The Kidnapping Syndicate," which appeared in the May 3rd issue of the "Detective Story" magazine.

"Look for the subject with the magazine in his possession and you'll pretty nearly have the man who killed Edward Diller," was the detectives' conclusion after hours of study.

Here are both letters—the one of fiction, and the one of fact as received by Mr. Diller—as Detectives studied their similarity after James Gorman, Secretary to Chief of Detectives O'Brien, laid them out side by side yesterday.

"Same denominations. Same warnings. It's practically word for word!"

"This means nothing," Dolly said. "These are called *popular* magazines for a reason, you idiot. Do you know how many people read these?"

"Well do you know how people wear horn-rimmed reading glasses?"

"Yeah, but not so many women I bet!"

"How many women read the crime pulps?"

Dolly ignored the question and barked back: "And I also bet if they tried those glasses on you it would fit on your big fat head."

"I believe the papers suggested my head was small," Will said, not wanting to fight with Dolly.

Dolly laughed and knocked her in the head but playfully.

"For a man, *milady*, for a man."

Will felt as if the sun was shining on her again. That's how she always felt when Dolly got over being mad at her, or even worse, bored with her. But now that Dolly had lightened up, she could smile too. Her lungs filled with fresh air.

"But listen, we've got to get rid of everything," Dolly said. "Ditch all the evidence, pronto."

She pulled the magazine with "The Kidnapping Syndicate" inside, set it on fire with a match, and dropped it in the wastebasket. They watched as the embers blackened into nothingness.

"Done," she said.

It was getting on toward dusk. They drove the rental car north through the Bronx till they reached the Lorillard Snuff Mill where the Bronx River had transformed into a natural sewer. Preserved in the Ground of the New York Botanical Garden, it was the recipient of manufacturing waste. Dolly hawked the chisel out the window and watched it get pulled downstream by the Bronx River current. They kept driving north till they hit Putnam County.

"Pull over up at the edge of that little footbridge," Dolly said.

Will knew it was the Mohegan Outlet. She'd gone birding there once in search of a rare white owl. She never found it, but tonight she was sure she could hear it hooting a warning.

"Someone could see us," she whispered to Dolly.

"So what if they do? We can say this is where I'm tossing my fella's class ring. My guy is a no-good cheat and I don't belong to him no more!"

Dolly laughed, but Will was not amused.

She felt a shiver as she read the sign posted at the foot of the Mohegan Trail:

We are the Wolf People, children of Mundo, a part of the Tree of Life.
Our ancestors form our roots, our living Tribe is the trunk, our grandchildren are the buds of our future.
We remember and teach the stories of our ancestors.
We watch. We listen. We learn.
We respect Mother Earth, our Elders, and all that comes from Mundo.
We are willing to break arrows of peace to heal old and new wounds. We acknowledge and learn from our mistakes.
We walk as a single spirit on the Trail of Life. We are guided by thirteen generations past and responsible to thirteen generations to come.
We survive as a nation guided by the wisdom of our past. Our circular trail returns us to wholeness as a people.

Next they took the typewriter, wrapped in a sheet and dug a small hole a few feet from the footbridge to bury it.

"Nothing should be found together," Will said.

"Nothing better be found, period."

Will let Dolly drive them back, figuring that would make her happy.

Like the Mohegans, Will felt an old wound healing as she realized they had to rely on each other, they were bound together forever. This is all she ever wanted. But at what cost? They weren't passing on wisdom. They'd taken a life. But hadn't Will taken the lives of birds merely to exhibit them or study them? Wasn't this but a study too?

She could see sweat drip down the side of Dolly's neck as she lit up a smoke. No. It wasn't a philosophical experiment. It was a study of how far she'd go for Dolly. Will couldn't help looking at the way Dolly's curls, now moist, stuck to her scalp and the back of her neck. Will wanted to feel what they felt like in her hands. She wanted to push Dolly against a tree and kiss her hard, rip her dress off. She wanted them to make plans for running away together, for starting anew, putting all of this behind them. The awful month of May would be over in a few days. They could pack to sail to Europe on June first, and they'd never come back.

It could all work.

Unless the police catch us, and the jury hangs us.

Will could almost laugh. She'd been so lonely before meeting Dolly. Her life lacked joy. Well, she certainly valued life now since hers was in danger of ending any day, any moment even. On the other hand, she considered, after that luxury liner ships off with us on it, their life together could just be beginning.

"Come on, let's go get soused," Dolly said with a wink.

They avoided Chum-Chums because Will did not want to risk seeing Maeve. She feared it would be too easy for such a sensitive girl to see into her.

"Come on, I know just the juke joint on Broadway," Dolly said, hitting the gas and heading to the parkway, following signs to New York City.

Will closed her eyes for a moment as Dolly drove. She imagined them off on an island together where no one knew them. With Sappho on the Isle of Lesbos they could write poetry to each other and bask in the glow of each other's love. If only they'd been born in a different time, a different place, or perhaps if Will had been born a man, things would be different.

Buddy spotted Will right away.

"Look at you," he said.

What was he trying to suggest?

"Well, look at *you*," she replied.

"I ... I mean, what a great surprise. I was just about to jam with the band. Was just grabbing a drink. You want one?"

"Hey where's your side man, Buddy-O?"

"Joe? He's home sick with a water bottle. Here," Buddy said, lifting two rickety wooden chairs over the heads of the crowd and placing them down at the foot of the "stage." "Make yourself at home."

He blew that cornet with eyes closed and full lung power. Afterwards the band slowed down, and Buddy asked Will to dance.

"Jazz Vampire" played and Will tried to find Dolly in the crowded room.

When she spotted her, she was flirting with some dapper Don. Loosening his bow tie, then fixing it up nice and natty for him.

It hit Will all of a sudden. They had failed. They hadn't gotten away with anything. And she wasn't bonded to Dolly for life. Dolly was exactly the same. Just as alluring, just as worthy of worship for her beauty and grace, her brilliance. But she would always seek out the attention of nobodies. She needed adulation not just from Will but from everyone. She would always have to raise the stakes. Together, they had done something unforgivable.

She had done something in the hopes of being with Dolly forever. But Dolly was just as unpredictable as ever, Will just as alone. And now, the boy just as dead. There was no beauty or perfection in the act itself. And they could be caught and imprisoned like animals at any time. The thought of prison terrified her. Not just the terror of the rough inmates and the humiliation of being locked up. No. It was the idea of being separated from Dolly—for life. The thoughts in her head were so unrelenting she wanted to scream.

Will must've stopped moving because Buddy tipped her chin up to look at her.

"What'sa matter, kid?"

"I ... can't ..."

"It's ok. You can tell me."

Will thought about running out but didn't want to panic Dolly, make her think she was cracking up.

"I just wish I could crawl into a hole and die."

Where had these words come from?

"I sound like a teenage girl." She laughed, allowing Buddy to wipe her tears with his handkerchief. "Which I am."

She laughed at herself.

"Blow," he said, putting the cloth to her nose.

"Oh, Buddy," she said.

"Shhhh ... it's all right, kid."

He placed her head against his chest and hummed as they danced, stroking her hair tenderly.

By the time the clock struck three they'd made a coffee date. Will was surprisingly happy about it. Maybe it wasn't too late to throw everyone off the trail. If she could get Buddy to make a move, that would make Dolly jealous. She knew it would. And it would keep her family happy and quiet. Will could create the illusion of just being a normal girl. This was the opportunity she'd been waiting for. Throw everyone off the scent. Besides, she liked Buddy. Being physical with him was neither here nor there to her. She could just relax with him. This could be the answer. The more average and banal she and Dolly appeared on the outside the safer they'd be. Fitting in—at least during this short interlude before the ship sailed—would be her key to escaping into a new life. A free life.

Chapter Twenty-Six

It seemed right to return to Etta Louise Sweet Shoppe, this time without Dolly or Joe. They ordered a couple of ice cream sodas and sat down with nothing to say. Will was not used to being with someone so quiet. Dolly chattered like teeth in a rainstorm.

"Wanna take a walk?" Buddy asked.

As they entered Morningside Park at West 110th, Will felt at peace. It was a relief to experience something akin to normal. She looked at Buddy. His mouth tended to hang open and his jaw needed a better shave. But hand in his, he seemed to be offering her protection. Buddy threw his suit jacket on the grass, and they sat on it, staring at the Bear and Faun Fountain.

"I'm not good at small talk," he said.

"Me neither."

"So, can I ask you something?"

"Sure," Will said, nerves vibrating.

"Would you be my girl?"

Will wanted to laugh, then wondered if this was some kind of joke.

"Did your friend Joe put you up to this? Did he pay you a couple of sawbucks so he'd have a better chance with Dolly?"

"No, of course not. Where did you get that from? That's the pits, Will."

"Are you sure I'm not just a little bit right?"

"I'm sure you're a thousand percent wrong."

"I just don't get it," Will said.

Buddy didn't say anything then. She waited. It wasn't like with Dolly. Silence beat out nervous chatter.

"You look like you can keep a secret," Buddy said.

"I can keep a secret," she said.

"I'm not like the other fellows," he said.

"What do you mean?"

He looked at her, raised his eyebrows, and lit a cigarette.

"You know what I mean. You're the same. I recognize it in you."

She was going to protest, but she couldn't work up the steam.

"Okay," she said.

He put his arm around her as they sat and stared out at the calm water. He seemed much manlier than his friend, Joe. Will would have never guessed Buddy to be queer. But, she supposed, things were not always as they seemed. She thought what it could be like, to have Buddy as a cover. Wasn't that how Dolly treated the boys anyway? Buddy placed his hand on the side of her head and started stroking her hair. It was soothing. But it hurt her heart, too. It reminded her of the tender moments she experienced with Dolly. How did everything get so jumbled up?

Buddy must've known she was crying before she did because he stroked a tear from her cheek with the back of his hand.

"Hey, it's ok," he cooed. "There's nothing to cry about."

"No, you're wrong. There is so much to cry about. If I were to really let myself I wouldn't be able to stop."

"So how about you let me take care of you a little."

"What do you mean?"

"Get you away from Dolly a bit. I know how you feel about her. I've been there, kid. But I know the toll it takes. Come play in my band. Let me take you out. Bring me home to meet the family. It'll get them off your back. You can still have your Dolly."

"So who is *your* Dolly?"

He lit another cigarette and she already missed his arm around her.

"I was fifteen and he was a year younger," Buddy said. "We were in the school band. One night after practice we took a walk in the park ..."

"Like this?"

"Yeah." He laughed. "But we just sort of fooled around until dark. Then his father came looking for him and found us and ... well, he got knocked around and so did I when he called my old man. And the solution my folks came up with was to send me to boarding school, then the Army. That's where I really got to spread my wings. What do you think it's like when you're a guy like me and you're surrounded by other guys all the time?"

She, of course, had read Havelock Ellis and Kraft-Ebbing, and recalled descriptions of female inverts as possessing a "masculine soul heaving within a female bosom." The opposite description was used for male inverts. Looking at Buddy, she would have never guessed such desires lived within him.

She wanted to ask him what about what happened between them in the car? She seemed to recall him looking at the back of Joe's neck. Is that what got him so excited? But she didn't want to know the truth. All she knew was he'd confided in her, and he'd intuited who she was. She had thought that Dolly's appearance in her life made her less lonely, but actually it filled her heart with pain. She never knew what mood Dolly was going to be in; nor could she predict what would send her into a rage or turn her indifferent to Will. The only thing that held them together now was the murder.

"What is it, Will?"

Buddy was a friend. That's what she needed right now. He'd said *you look like you can keep a secret*. He looked the same way to her. But confiding anything would be tantamount to confessing. No, she couldn't trust anyone.

"Take me home," she said. "Please. To my family's house."

"Sure," he said. "And if there's anything you want to tell me ..."

"There's nothing," she said. "Just take me to Sutton Place."

Will asked Buddy not to come in. She needed quiet. Lucille, the maid, opened the door and said Estelle was here with her fiancé. The word still galled Will. Why was it all right for Estelle to have love and not Will? The two of them could be celebrated, but the only way Will could get the same approval was by bringing Buddy home to fool them all. She went to her mother's sick room. Daddy hadn't touched it. There in the green club chair next to the bed, Will had read to Momma in all different languages. In the end she was comatose, and it didn't seem to matter what came out of Will's mouth.

"Miss Wilhelmina?"

The knock startled Will.

"Yes? Come in."

"There are two detectives here to see you."

"Detectives?" Will said, her heart rattling.

Within seconds she calmed her nerves and reminded herself she knew exactly how to act. Her family was extremely rich, and her parents had taught her how to treat authority figures with respect but not fear.

"Has there been a robbery?"

Lucille shrugged, and Will walked downstairs to greet the two who introduced themselves as Mott and Johnson. They were dressed in shabby suits instead of uniforms. Will asked for identification, which the detectives produced.

"Oh, thank you," she said. "When I heard the name 'Johnson' I thought this might be the person involved in the Diller case."

They didn't crack a smile, and Will instantly regretted the remark.

"We looked for you at school but couldn't find you," Johnson said.

"Do you wear glasses, Miss Reinhardt?" Mott asked.

Will could not believe they were here. The police. They'd joked about this possibility, but experiencing the reality was jarring. She told herself to speak very calmly.

She said yes, occasionally, but that she was not wearing them at that moment of course.

"Did you lose them?"

"No. But I'm sure they're around here someplace."

Estelle entered with her fiancé, Sanford.

"Is everything all right?" Sanford asked.

"Yes," Will said. "These officers were just hoping to take a look at my glasses. I thought I had them around here somewhere."

As Will went through the motions of searching, the detectives explained their instructions. They'd been told by Bertram Gaines, the State's Attorney, that if the glasses were not easily found, to bring Will downtown to meet with him. Will seemed put upon at first, saying she was just home at her family's to grab an old birding book but had to go meet a few students for an ornithology class at Adams High School on the West Side. But the two insisted.

"We'll go with you, Wilhelmina," Estelle said.

"It's all right," Will said, insisting she'd be fine on her own.

Whatever was going to happen would be worse having her family there.

Instead of taking Will to headquarters, the detectives escorted her to the Roosevelt Hotel. She stayed quiet in the car and forced herself to imagine a banal outcome. Uneventful, like a routine tooth extraction. It's not like they'd give the "third degree" to a girl!

They seated Will in a wing chair to wait for the man in charge. She looked around the suite, comparing it to The Ziegfried and The Savoy. She'd seen the inside of more hotels in these last six months than she'd seen her whole life.

Gaines was a short man, not much taller than Will—but beefy and surprisingly graceful on his feet. He rose from an easy chair to greet her and shook her hand gently while guiding her with a hand on her back to the very same chair.

"Please make yourself comfortable, Miss Reinhardt. Sorry to bring you here and interrupt your studies, but we're trying to avoid unnecessary publicity. This Edward Diller case, you know ..."

Will nodded, put at ease by his manner. When asked if she wanted water or a coffee, she declined politely.

Could Dolly be on the other side of the French Provincial wall-papered wall? What was she saying? It was up to Will to maintain a cool head. Dolly had nothing to do with the glasses. There was no point in asking for a lawyer. That would just make her seem guilty.

The State's Attorney pulled a pair of glasses from his breast pocket and asked if they belonged to her.

"They certainly look like mine. If I didn't know mine were at school I'd suspect they were."

"Yours are at school?"

"Yes."

"Do you recall the last time you wore them?"

"No, I can't say I do. I use them for reading on occasion, but I often forget about them altogether. They may be in my dorm room desk or in a pocketbook or jacket."

"But these *could* be yours?" Gaines pressed.

"I seriously do not believe so, sir, but yes, it's *possible*," Will said. "I do frequently go birding in that area, though."

"But you never reported them missing. Miss Reinhardt, I'm trying to dot all the i's and cross all the t's on this Eddie Diller case. You understand. These glasses were found at the scene of the crime. If you can prove these glasses aren't yours, we can cross this bit of business off our list, you see."

"Of course, sir," she said.

"Would you mind if we all took a ride to your dorm room and looked for them?"

"No, no, let's clear this up now. I don't want you to have to waste any more time when you could be searching for the real killers."

She kept going through the alibi in her mind and making it as real to herself as possible. There really was nothing to worry about. Will tried to emanate a still, peaceful calm, just as she did when she did not want to alert birds to her intrusive presence in the marsh.

Back at the dorm, Will made a show of looking through all her purses, jackets, and desk drawers, but she was unable to locate them.

"I'm sorry. I guess I haven't been much help, Mr. Gaines."

"Not at all, but I would like to ask you some more questions, and I don't think this is the right place," he said.

She wasn't sure if his awkward blush suggested that a girl's bedroom wasn't the right place or if he was being respectful of the privacy she was afforded as the daughter of one of the wealthiest men in the city.

They escorted Will by unmarked police car to the Roosevelt Hotel on East 45th, where Gaines awaited her.

"Getting close to summer," he said, loosening his brown tie. "Any plans for vacation?"

"Well, Europe awaits. Some more musical training."

"Not bad. You college girls live quite the life."

"I suppose," Will said.

She smiled and watched as his affable smirk disappeared. The small talk was over.

"*Now* are you ready to admit these are your glasses?"

"Well, I'd hate to say something I wasn't absolutely sure of. There must be thousands of reading glasses just like these in New York City."

"Four thousand ninety two to be exact," Gaines said. "But this pair isn't like all the others."

"Oh no?" Will asked.

She felt the need to swallow, but didn't want him to notice. She counted to five before slowly allowing the saliva to slip down her throat.

"Oh the glasses themselves are quite ordinary, it's true," Gaines said holding them up to the light. "But the hinge is quite modern and unique. The Almer Coe Company reported selling only three pairs of glasses like these in New York City, glasses with this unusual hinge."

Gaines demonstrated the way it bent with more flexibility than an average hinge on a pair of spectacles.

"One pair was sold to a frail older lady in the Bronx. She can't get around at all but for the help of her family and a nurse. The other was sold to an attorney who has been traveling abroad for the last two months. And the third ... to you."

Will nodded. She could no longer deny ownership, but she could furnish a reasonable explanation.

"Well, let me see them," she said.

"Sure—try them on."

She put them on her face and immediately regretted it. She could see the look of victory in the State's Attorney's eyes.

"But you see I think I know what happened."

"Go on, Miss Reinhardt."

"You see, I go birding—I'm an ornithologist—in those very woods, and I believe I was out there last Sunday. I wear an old blazer like this one when I go out there. I have a few of them. And I may have left my glasses inside the pocket of the coat and tripped and lost them out there."

It sounded clunky coming out of her mouth, but at the same time believable. If she were feeding them a line, she'd sound more polished wouldn't she?

"I'm terribly embarrassed."

"So you admit that these are your glasses?"

"Yes. I believe they are. And I'm sorry they've caused you so much trouble."

Stop apologizing, Will commanded herself. You're not dealing with Dolly. He's a grown man, and reasonable. But this did prove Dolly was right. She *had* made a mistake. Yet even in her embarrassment and anxiety she remained calm, and *believable*. She wished Dolly could see her performance!

"So let me see if I understand. You were out birding last Sunday … by yourself?"

"I sometimes take students, but yes on that particular day I was by myself, and I must have tripped and fallen—I was wearing rubber hip boots—it's quite a look, heh-heh," she laughed. "And the glasses must have fallen out of my pocket."

"I see," Gaines said, placing the glasses inside his breast pocket and then walking towards the detectives and Will.

After a few steps, he fell forward and braced himself on the carpeted floor with his hands.

"Sir, are you all right?" Detective Mott asked.

"Yes, yes. Thank you," he said, standing up straight. "And so are the glasses, it appears. They didn't fall out of *my* jacket."

It took Will a couple of seconds before she realized.

"Oh, Mr. Gaines. That performance was worthy of a jury," she said but smiled with special warmth to show she was being a good sport.

"Well, I guess we litigators are all performers at heart. But... would *you* care to show me how it happened?"

He handed the frames to her and she placed them in her jacket pocket. Ever the eager student, she was about to do as directed by the elder Gaines. Then thought better of it.

"You know this is a carpeted hotel floor."

"Yes, I'm aware of that."

"Well, it's just I don't think this is ..."

"You can refuse, of course," he said, challenging her.

It would be unwise, she knew, to appear resistant. She didn't want to arouse suspicion so said good-naturedly, "Okay, here goes nothing."

Will walked a few steps and then fell forward catching herself with her hands. She peered down and saw the glasses had slid forward slightly, but had not fallen out or even come close. When rising she made a slight show of having hurt her wrist. She rubbed it and waited for a sympathetic response, but none came. If a more typically alluring girl like Dolly had done the falling she bet they would've gushed all over her.

"Here, let me try again," she said.

"Be my guest."

This time she tried to fall much harder, but still no dice.

"You know," Will said. "It's very hard to *make* yourself fall. It's not the same as actually tripping. And the ground out there is rather rough and uneven. I could have tripped over a root and really gone flying."

"Sounds like you're speaking hypothetically. I imagine you'd remember a spill like that quite vividly. That's a rather rough incident—especially for a girl, isn't it?"

She knew what he was thinking. She'd experienced this kind of attitude before. He didn't think she was a normal girl. He could sense something different about her. Perhaps she was overreacting.

She had to keep her composure. Everything was riding on this. Be still, Will told herself, like you don't want to disturb a chick in the nest.

"Yes, I suppose so. I wish I could say for sure *when* or *how* I lost them, but the point is, I *do* go to that area frequently with my students *and* by myself, and I guess they must've fallen out without me realizing."

It was a reasonable explanation. There was no need to say more. Let him play his next move.

"So where were you on the evening of May twenty-first?" Gaines asked.

"The day of the murder?" she asked.

"That's right."

"The twenty-first? Today's Thursday—that was last Wednesday— over a week ago. Let me see ..."

She and Dolly had agreed to use the alibi for one week. It might be best to just remember as little as possible. One week. She needed time to assess whether it was best to use the alibi or not. They had picked her up just on the borderline. She really didn't want to bring Dolly into it if she didn't have to.

"Well, if it was a Wednesday, I was in classes ..."

"I'm interested in where you were *after* class, Miss Reinhardt."

"Please, call me Will."

"Will."

"I believe I was studying that night in the library."

"Did anyone see you?"

"I'm not sure."

"Did you take out any books on that date?"

"I don't think so."

"I see."

Gaines took out a cigar and said he'd return in a bit. He told Will that his men would stay with her.

For the next four hours they grilled her about why she couldn't remember any details of that date. She wished she could protest, but she wanted to stay strong. The toughest line she could come up with was:

"Honestly, do you remember what *you* were doing a week ago last Wednesday?"

They were polite but unrelenting. Just as soon as one got tired, the other would step in newly energized. And just like in the picture shows, one would come on strong then pace off in a huff, only to have another one come on like a loving parent. Will was tired and hungry by the time Gaines returned.

"You see the predicament I'm in, don't you? Your glasses are found at the scene of the child's murder."

It seemed too complicated to *avoid* the alibi. If Will could account for her whereabouts this little interview would be over and done with. Dolly was a smart cookie—always three steps ahead. She'd corroborate.

Will sighed, then looked down and fidgeted with her hands—she knew she could perform this part with confidence.

"Yes, Will. What is it?" Gaines said.

"I was with a friend, but ...well, she'll never speak to me again if I tell you what we were up to."

"Will, I don't want you to get a friend in trouble," he said, softening. "But I'm sure she'll understand. This is serious business."

His tone had shifted to fatherly. Perhaps he did want to let her go.

"All right, sir. I guess I don't have much choice. I was with my roommate—my best friend—Dolly Raab. Dorothy. But we all call her Dolly."

"Dolly Raab?" Mott said. "She's friends with Kent Mishkin—the reporter. Kid from Columbia University."

"Yes," Will said.

"She's helped out with questions we've had about some of those teachers at The Collegiate School."

"She loves mysteries," Will said. "Anyway, after class we went out for dinner at the Grimes place on West 118th. And well, we were a little tight. Sometimes we drink in my car, sir."

Gaines gave an indulgent smile.

"And we took a ride up to one of the speakeasies on Broadway. We popped in; not much was going on, but outside a couple of fellows asked us if we wanted a smoke and we said sure."

"What were their names?"

"Pete and Charlie."

"Their last names?"

"I don't know, sir. We could see they weren't exactly—college boys—so we didn't give them our real names. I have to assume they may have made up their names too."

"I see."

"Let me explain something, sir. Dolly and I are musicians. I play clarinet and she plays piano. In fact, we'll be sailing for Europe next week to study at the Leipzig Conservatory."

"Next week, eh?"

"Yes. But you see, sir, there's something called jazz."

"Yes, I know about jazz," Gaines laughed. "I'm not one hundred years old."

"Yes, sir. Well, these boys liked jazz too, and I guess it was the gin we had in the car and the gin we had at the club ... but Dolly and I were pretty tight. We ended up getting back into my car. I've got a nifty little Stutz Bearcat my father gave to me. The boys wanted to see it ... and try some of the gin we had in the glove compartment."

"I see. So you and the boys got into your Stutz ..."

"Well, we drank some more with them, and I let Pete drive us to a quiet overlook on Riverside. We played some jazz on the radio. And let's just say they were all hands ..."

"What did you expect?" Gaines asked. "Were you just teasing them?"

"No. No. We did some necking, but we're nice girls, sir. We ..."

"You mean you're virgins?" Gaines asked bluntly.

"Yes, sir. Of course."

"All right so you necked with Pete and Charlie. What did they look like by the way? And who was with whom?"

"I was with Charlie. He was short and stocky ... and Dolly was with Pete. He was tall and lanky."

"Sounds like they could be anybody."

"Well," Will said, a little worried about the reaction she'd get. "They weren't like us."

"A little on the rough side?"

"No. They were nice fellows. Not so different from other boys. Except ..."

"Yes?"

Will waited a full minute, even shifting in her seat for effect. "They were negroes."

Will could see Gaines blink and blink. How could a man in his position be so astounded?

"Negroes? I see!"

"Please don't tell our folks. You see this is why I didn't want to tell you the truth."

"I can certainly understand that, Miss Reinhardt."

Will breathed, feeling the relief fill her lungs. Dolly had been right. This was just shocking enough to explain why they'd kept it to themselves.

"Let's bring in Miss Raab and see what she has to say."

Chapter Twenty-Seven
Dolly

The key was to keep cool. So they wanted to ask her a few questions. Well the week had passed, and the alibi was out. It was every man for himself. That was the deal.

"I don't remember, gentlemen," she repeated.

Dolly had read enough crime stories to know that criminals tripped themselves up by not learning how to keep their bloody mouths shut.

"I wish I could help, but I just don't remember," she insisted jovially. "Fellas, that was over a week ago."

The dummies were about to let her go when Gaines came back in and caucused with the underlings. As soon as she heard "Couple of negroes" she understood.

"Wait a minute," Dolly said. "Did *Will* tell you I was with her last Wednesday?"

"Were you?"

"That little squealer," Dolly said. "She *promised* she wouldn't tell."

Gaines waited.

"Yes, sir. I was with Will, and I guess she already spilled the beans about the ... uh ... mischief we got into. Oh heck, it was more than just mischief. If my parents find out, I'm dead—*dead!*"

"Well why don't you just tell me what happened."

Dolly went on to recite the same alibi, to which Gaines responded, "Well, you both could've saved us a lot of time if you'd just told me the truth right off the bat, Dolly."

Dolly nodded, chastised, right on cue.

"Now, I don't want to tell your parents anything they don't need to know."

Mott approached Gaines and pulled him aside, whispering something Dolly couldn't make out. Gaines excused himself and left Dolly under Mott's watch. She wondered what they had now? Was Will in the next room mucking up the plans some more?

"So Detective Mott, what's it like chasing criminals?"

He just shrugged.

"Don't think badly of me and Will because we played around with those negro fellows. It's the Jazz Age, you know? Have you heard of Jelly Roll Morton—he's got this riff—the King Porter Stomp—it moves, brother. When you hear it your fire is suddenly lit!"

"I'm not much for jazz," Mott said. "Or negroes."

"Yeah," Dolly said. "Neither are my folks. But you know jazz is not just improvisation. If you've got some background in classical music—as I do. You know I'm a piano prodigy. Been at the keys since I was three. Well, let me tell you, Mister, then you can really bang out a good stomp. You know the stomp is an eight-bar chord progression ... it hits hard on the *stomp* ... and you can play jazz versions of the classics too. Are you familiar with Dvorak's 'Humoresque'? Boy, play that baby ragtime and the joint will jump."

Gaines came back in with Will and Dolly burst out of her seat, thrilled to see her pal.

"Willsie!" she shouted. "Hey don't look glum, sister. All is forgiven. I know you had to tell the truth. And I did too. But I'm trusting Mr. Gaines and his men will find it in their hearts *not* to tell our folks what we were up to."

"Okay, Dolly. You don't have to panic. Come on. We've held you girls long enough. It's time to get you something to eat. We'll take you to dinner at the hotel restaurant."

Dolly wasn't sure if Gaines planned to let them go, but this certainly seemed like a friendly outing. It gave her a chance to work her charm, which was a big relief. Naturally Will had to show off by ordering for all of them in French, and then the real fun part, Gaines goading her about her philosophy of life.

"Well, I suppose at present I'm enamored with Oscar Wilde," Will said. "He believed that the artist sees beyond morality."

"We all know how he ended up," Gaines said, though Dolly could see that not all the men knew about the conviction for *gross indecency*.

"Yes, the end of Wilde's life was filled with degradation, but the body of work he left behind and his belief in the worship of beauty—these things live on. He was above other men despite being penalized for the prejudices of his time."

"So would Wilde fall under the label of Nietzschean superman?"

"In my estimation he would not," Will replied. "For Wilde was very undisciplined."

"And is self-discipline a characteristic of the superman?" Gaines prodded.

Dolly could see what they were doing. Trying to use Will's big intellectual ego to help her to hoist herself by her own petard. It was time to step in.

"Oh boy! Can't we talk about something we don't get to talk about all the time in school? Will, you're putting me to sleep."

"What would *you* like to discuss, Dolly?"

"How do you solve a crime? Give us the inside scoop!"

"So you read a lot of crime stories, Dolly?"

"I love 'em!" she replied. "Can't get enough."

The moment the words escaped her mouth Dolly wanted to punch herself in the head. *Idiot!* Then she turned it around in her mind. So what? Everybody knew what a joker she was. She loved silly detective yarns. Big deal!

205

It was about 11 p.m. when the cops dropped them off at their dorm, once again in an unmarked car. Once upstairs in their room, the first thing Dolly wanted to do was leave.

"I want to hit a newsstand, see what the papers are saying."

But Will told her to calm down. "They might have someone out front to keep an eye on us. Let's lay low."

"You weren't so cautious when you dragged me under with you, Reinhardt."

"What are you talking about?"

"A week had passed." Dolly said. "It was every man for himself, remember?"

Will gave Dolly that slack-jawed look, as if she were in shock. It made Dolly want to hit her over the head with a lead pipe, drag her body into an alley, and be done with her. There was no untangling from her spidery grip. She kept growing more legs. She just wouldn't let go.

And then she couldn't believe it, Will was pushing her down onto her bed.

Dolly shoved her back hard. "What are you doing, you perv?"

"I'm no perv," Will said. "And what if I were? We've done everything. Why stop now? You promised me."

Will pinned Dolly's arms down and kissed her. Dolly tried to resist, but Will was surprisingly strong. What was with her? Dolly looked at her and could see a different kind of desperation. Maybe Will was afraid they'd be caught and killed by the state and never have a chance to fool around again. Well too bad. She couldn't force Dolly to do anything. Even now.

"You'll never see me again. Get the hell off me."

"You owe me this. You owe me this," Will said.

"I don't owe you a damn thing."

"The contract, remember? Come on, Dolly. Come on, Dolly. Come on, Dolly."

Dolly imagined herself in front of a room full of reporters telling them all how she did it. SHE, a weak little girl. Well she fooled them all didn't she? She suddenly felt the heat of Will's desire, and it excited her. As Will pulled down Dolly's underwear, Dolly held

Will's head to her breast, pushing hard. She wanted to make Will mad, get her all mean.

Will wiggled upwards, biting into Dolly's neck. The roughness of the way she pressed her body into hers made Dolly forget the whole nerve-wracking ordeal with those flatfoots. Dolly felt a surge of excitement and ran her hands through Will's hair, moaning in her ear.

And then she saw the flash of him. The boy. The way he looked at her in the end, like she was a monster. She was no monster. They were all just a bunch of helpless vermin scavenging for food, fighting off predators to stay alive. So she had the power to survive, to be the last man standing. Did that make her evil? It just meant she had the wits to win! What was so wrong with that?

"What's the matter?" Will said.

"What?"

"You just got really still all of a sudden and stopped moving."

Dolly had no memory of such a thing. But Will was too blunt to lie. Dolly could feel her body split up into dozens of pieces and come apart, like the wheels and gears of an automobile flying over the railing during a crash. *Think fast.*

"Fooled ya, Willsie!" Dolly said. "But you know I am going to pass out cold if I don't get a shot of hooch and fast. Those coppers did give me the creeps."

Will rose, half-undressed, and pulled a flask out of her drawer. They sat on the bed and drank till it was dry, then lay back down together. She could feel Will's hand stroking her own.

Dolly felt sleepy, and in that space between wakefulness and slumber, she could hear herself saying "I love you" to Will. Whatever love was she must be feeling it because her heart ached and swung between pain and pleasure with every beat.

The knock came hard and fast.

Will yelled, "Just a minute."

They threw their nightgowns and robes on.

"Is the door locked?" Dolly whispered.

Will had another moronic look on her face, unsure of what was going on. Dolly sprayed a little toilet water on her hand, rubbed some on her hands and face, and did the same to Will.

She opened the door to find Gaines and his men back again.

"Gentlemen," Dolly said. "Back so soon?"

They weren't amused.

"Will, we'd like to see your typewriter."

Dolly felt her stomach turn as if she'd swallowed a bad oyster, but she kept smiling quizzically as if she hadn't the faintest idea why they were here. They weren't going to find that damn Underwood, that's for sure.

"It's right here, sir," Will said, showing them to her desk.

"No. This is a Smith Corona."

"That's right."

"We understand that you are the owner of an Underwood portable, which you've used in your Latin study group to write up study sheets. Where would that machine be?"

"I'm sorry, sir," Will said. "I have typed up the notes with our group, but I don't own any portable."

"Have you seen such a machine, Dolly?" Gaines asked.

"No, sir. Not that I can recall."

Gaines whispered into Johnson's ear, and Johnson pulled out a large mailing envelope which contained a series of typewritten notes.

"You see these notes, Will?" Johnson asked. "You recognize them?"

"Well they *look* like carbons of the study sheets to which you're referring."

"They are," Gaines said. "And here's a copy of the ransom note."

Will nodded.

"You see how the 'T' prints heavy at the top and light on the bottom. You see how the 'I' is somewhat twisted, and the 'M' somewhat slanted."

"I haven't had a chance to examine these two documents," Will said carefully.

"And you don't have your glasses on either," Mott said.

Dolly could feel the noose swinging. They had Will. And Will had handcuffed herself to Dolly.

"We've had an expert from the Royal Typewriting Company examine these documents for us—and he has sworn that they were written on the same machine. That's quite a coincidence, isn't it?"

"I suppose, except I don't own such a machine. I want to be of help to the authorities, but I am beginning to feel scapegoated," Will said.

Arrogant son of a bitch. If ever there was a time to play innocent and child-like this would be the time. But Will didn't have that arrow in her quiver, and Dolly didn't want to butt in and have them turn the bright lights on her.

"Oh you do, do you? Well, I'm sorry you feel that way, Will. But we have to pursue every clue, and this is a big one, even you must admit."

Will said nothing.

"Bring in the girls," Gaines directed, and Johnson went out into the hall and brought back the four Janes in Will's Latin group. One by one each said yes she'd been there when the notes were written—and remembered Will typing them—but each said she was not the owner of the portable. None of them would meet Will's eyes. Were they scared of her? Did they know what this was about? Did they think she was a murderer?

Will practically lunged forward, insisting to each of them, "Are you sure? Are you one hundred percent *certain*?"

"You had it over there," Betty Traison said, pointing to the tall dresser. "You took it down from there and put it on Dolly's desk to type."

"No, no. You can't be sure."

"*Are* you sure, Miss Traison?" Gaines asked.

"Yes, sir, I am."

"No, no. Now I remember, it was Heinbach's machine," Will said.

"Gloria Heinbach is in Europe," one of the other Janes said.

"Very convenient. All right, thank you girls," Gaines said and summarily dismissed them with the wave of a hand.

Mott escorted them out. Then Gaines waited a moment and announced it was time to go back to the hotel to answer more questions. *Both* of them. Dolly looked at Will.

Gaines took Will while Johnson politely chaperoned Dolly into a room.

"Water?"

"No. Do our parents know we're here?" Dolly asked.

"They're out in the hall," Johnson said. "They think you're innocent and will cooperate. The State's Attorney agreed to do the questioning here to keep your names out of the paper."

"I want to see my parents," Dolly said.

"You will. But first let's talk. Look, it's your friend who's in big trouble. But it's in your best interest to tell your side of the story, to clear your own name. Understand?"

Johnson asked about the negroes—their names, their heights, the instruments they said they played. Back and forth up and down and sideways. It was like keeping a tennis ball in the air, but Dolly just thought of the alibi as the truth, facts she'd memorized. It was best if she treated the interrogation like an exam at school.

But she was growing edgier and wearier. They could see that.

"Can I get up and stretch my legs a bit?" she asked, and they said okay.

Dolly tried to think of what she would do if they had her dead to rights. She peered outside through the open window, which looked out onto a rooftop. She imagined making a run for it.

When Gaines came back in, he had a smirk on his face that made Dolly's skin prickle.

"All right, Raab. It's over. We know you and Reinhardt did it, so you might as well confess."

"Ha! That's a good one Mr. Gaines. You should be in the picture shows."

"It's no joke, Raab. You two couldn't have been driving around with those negro jazz musicians in Reinhardt's car. The car was in the garage all day. Waldek the driver was working on the brakes."

This was bad. Bad, bad, bad, Teddy.

"Who told you that?"

"Waldek. He's right outside. He said he was oiling the brakes because your pal complained about them squeaking. He has proof that he had the car in the garage that day because his wife took his daughter to the doctor for a cold and got a prescription with the date on it—May twenty-first. The same day Eddie Diller was murdered. You two have no way out."

"Oh God," Dolly said.

She felt like she might pass out.

"May I have a cigarette and glass of water please?"

They hopped to it like a tag team and provided a cigarette, a light, and cold water as if they'd been waiting all along for this moment.

"So before we talk to your friend, would *you* like to tell us what happened, Dolly?"

She didn't have time to think, but her mouth started talking.

"Well, I wouldn't have gotten into any of this trouble if it weren't for Will. She kept wanting to try things—experiments, she called them—I didn't really think she wanted to go through with them. But she just kept upping the ante. She did it all, and I just went along for the ride. I drove the car when we picked up Eddie Diller and she sat in the back and smashed him over the head two or three times with a chisel. Then when he struggled, she pulled him from the front seat and put a cloth in his mouth till he was dead. She picked the burial spot. She typed the ransom note. I'm not saying I was innocent, but I was ... well ... hypnotized by her, and frightened too.

"I mean, look at me fellas. I'm just a regular girl. Gosh, I just ... I'm relieved that you're finally onto her and know the truth. This has all been too much for me to handle myself. I was afraid if I called the police she'd try and kill me. She's gone off the rails ..."

"Let's get a typist in here and start from the beginning, Dolly, all right?"

"All right, sir," Dolly said.

She imagined the rope swinging away from her neck and catching Will around the throat.

Chapter Twenty-Eight
Will

What did they really have? The glasses, yes, but what did that prove? Her explanation was reasonable, Will knew. She was an ornithologist and regularly spent time in those woods. The glasses could have easily gotten lost at any time. Gaines was just trying to unnerve her with his showmanship. Making her pretend to fall—on the carpeted floor of a hotel room. Come now! Surely he could do better than that.

And yes, the typewriter complicated matters. But again—what did that prove? The machine had been destroyed and discarded. It could not be connected to Will, despite their best efforts. There was no motive.

She was in the hot seat, but the bottom line was this would all be over within a matter of hours, and she could leave for her trip to Europe with Dolly. Dolly didn't know it yet, but their lives together would soon begin. They could spread their wings like a pair of glorious blue herons and fly away from this provincial world.

Gaines returned to the room. Will was still imagining the beautiful life that lay ahead of them. Europe would change everything. They'd meet people, they'd play jazz, maybe they'd find a couple of nice queer boys like Buddy to marry just to make everything look legit. They'd sunk to their lowest low; there was only one place to go—up.

"Mr. Gaines, I have a hypothetical question for you," Will said cheerily.

"Yes. What do you want to know?"

"Suppose," Will said, "that someone from a wealthy family, a family as rich as my own, had committed this murder—what chance would that person have of beating the murder charge?"

These philistines could smell fear. Let them smell confidence too.

"You're going to get a chance to find out," he said. "I intend to draw up a charge of first-degree murder against you for the killing of Eddie Diller."

Will smiled, seeing through the bluff. The State's Attorney was getting irritated and wanted to close the case and thought that a little bit of trickery might get him what he wanted.

"While you have a few pieces of circumstantial evidence that points to me, you haven't sufficient evidence to bring me to court ... and you won't."

Gaines pulled up a wooden chair and sat face to face with Will.

"Do you remember renting a Willys Automobile with which to commit the crime? And those frankfurters and root beer you purchased at The Dew Drop Inn after you killed Eddie? Do you recall those? And the difficulty you had concealing the body inside the drainage pipe?"

Will made sure her face showed nothing.

"Dolly has told us everything in detail and confessed to the kidnapping of Eddie Diller. Do you *still* think you can beat the murder charge?"

Will remained silent, stunned. It was still not possible. He was telling her the facts of the case and putting them in Dolly's mouth. It was still possible that he'd found evidence but not linked it to them.

"Did you enjoy dressing as a man?"

Will could feel her face redden. She never thought this moment would come and never imagined Dolly would be the one to break. How could she commit suicide? Will wondered. Would they leave her alone for a few minutes, perhaps to use the bathroom? It's not as if a straight razor would be there for her to slice her wrists with. She took a breath. She was incapable of dealing with blood, especially her own.

All right, fine. She knew from her work with birds that predators smell fear. She wouldn't give him the satisfaction.

"So she broke. I thought she was stronger than that. I guess that was my error in judgment."

Gaines looked at the policemen quizzically.

Will felt a change in the weather. There would be no sweet sailing to Europe. The waters were in deep tumult. They were caught. She thought she knew Dolly. She didn't know her at all. And then it dawned on her. Gaines said that Dolly had confessed to the *kidnapping*. Well now the traitor was most likely claiming the wielding of the weapon was Will's doing.

"So Dolly is talking now," she said, then paused for effect. "I will tell you the truth about the matter."

A male stenographer entered, and Gaines greeted him with a hearty handshake. He was followed by two more men in suits. Once everyone was settled in, the State's Attorney announced, "Now we may begin."

Part III
The Trial

Chapter Twenty-Nine
Dolly

A press conference! Dolly sat to the left of Gaines as the flash-bulbs snapped; Will flanked his other side. She couldn't help but be excited. She'd fool these wurps still. Dolly felt as if her brain were being split into three precise triangles. She'd seen such an image when she was eight years old. Daddy had taken her to see a picture called *Suspense*—full of camera tricks that fascinated Dolly. On the screen the audience could see a crusty burglar in one triangle of the frame at one point, in the center triangle a man calling home, and in the other triangle the innocent wife talking on the horn, about to become a victim.

"Do either of you believe in God?"

"I consider myself an atheist," Will said. "I have studied all of the world's great religions and consider the question of whether or not God exists to be a fruitless pursuit. It cannot be proven one way or the other so I have stopped thinking about it."

"And you, Dolly?"

"Well, I more or less always doubted the existence of God, and I found those doubts confirmed when I studied paleontology and evolution in college."

"So attending a women's college turned you against God, Dolly? Was this something that was taught in the classrooms?"

"Why do you point out it's a women's college," Will asked. "Shouldn't all colleges teach the sciences?"

"Why did you do it, girls?" an elder reporter asked. "For the money?"

"Well the money was part of it, yes," Will replied in that same know-it-all tone. "But, clearly it wasn't something we were desperate for."

"Then why?"

"All right, gentlemen, I'm calling a halt to this impromptu press conference."

A man walked in, rumpled in appearance, but forceful in presence. Dolly recognized him from the papers. Warren Clemmons, famed defense attorney, a staunch opponent of the death penalty. He approached Gaines who stood up to shake his hand.

"Hello old friend. I see you're hard at work."

"Once the truth came out, it's been smooth sailing, Warren."

"Well, batten down the hatches, Bertram, I'm afraid I have to call an end to this little show for the press right now."

He approached Dolly first.

"You're Miss Raab?"

"Dolly. Yes, sir."

"And you're Miss Reinhardt?"

"Will, please. And yes, I am," said Will. "It's a pleasure to meet you Mr. Clemmons. I greatly admire your work."

"You know who admired it too?" Gaines said. "Little Eddie Diller. He participated in a debate the month before his death. The subject was capital punishment. He argued against it. But I will be arguing for it, and I shall win."

"Take it easy, Bertram," Clemmons said. "And gentlemen, I must ask all of you to leave immediately and let me speak privately with my clients."

Dolly glanced at Will and they shared a perplexed but amused look. It appeared they were in this together. Much as ole Willsie had screwed things up, she still needed her, didn't want to play out the final act without her.

"Fine, Warren," Gaines said, signaling the reporters to make haste. "But you're a little late to the party. I've got two air-tight confessions from these girls. And reports from Dr. Bowler and Dr.

Aames—two of the most respected alienists in the field, who attest to the girls' sanity. They're guilty, they're sane, and they're going to hang. Good day, sir."

"Well, top of the morning to you too, sir," Clemmons said with a bow that showed a jam stain at the end of his tie. "Oh, but before you go, I humbly suggest you not be too overconfident. A little wisdom from the Greeks:

'Minerva did her best and the result was a marvel, but Arachne's work, finished at the same moment, was in no way inferior. The goddess in a fury of anger beat the girl around the head with her shuttle. Arachne, disgraced and mortified and furiously angry, hanged herself. Then a little repentance entered Minerva's heart ... Arachne was changed into a spider, and her skill in weaving was left to her.'"

Dolly giggled, recognizing the passage from their freshman mythology course. Once her laughter was released, Will couldn't help but join in. Gaines looked at them with contempt, then turned back to Clemmons.

"Well, if being turned into a spider is the price for making sure these deviants hang, then I will happily sprout six more legs and spend the rest of my days weaving webs."

Dolly and Will shared a laugh knowing their attorney had just taken down the almighty State's Attorney by comparing him to a *female* mythological figure. They met each other's eyes for a moment and were friends again.

"Girls, my name is Warren Clemmons, and your families have retained me as your counsel. From this moment forward I do not want you to speak to anyone. Much damage has already been done. Let's not court disaster any further. Just to make sure we're clear, I'll be representing both of you and your cases will be tried together, as one. Are we clear so far?"

Dolly and Will both nodded yes.

"Now, girls. It would help a great deal if you could come up with some character witnesses for the benefit of the jury. Who are your other friends?"

"Ask anybody at Barnard and they'll tell you. Helena Lances for instance ... she's a big woman on campus."

"What about boys?" Clemmons asked. "Anyone special?"

Dolly let out a girlish giggle, but before she could speak Will cut in, and stated in a sober voice.

"You can talk to Buddy about me."

"Buddy?" Dolly asked.

"Yes."

"Is he your fella?"

"Yes. Well, we were becoming close ... We *are* close."

"All right, I'll speak with him."

"I don't want to get him involved unnecessarily."

"I'll be discreet. I'll have my assistant take down his information."

"Well, well, well. How the tide has turned," Dolly said. "Okay, if you're going to talk to Buddy you can talk to my fella, Joe."

What game was Will playing?

"Girls, there's going to be one question and one question alone on the minds of the jurors. Why would you do such an awful thing? You've confessed to it and provided every last detail—allowing the State's Attorney to obtain every shred of physical evidence he needs to sign, seal, and deliver you both to the gallows. Now what can you tell me on your own behalf?"

"I have to tell you girls, the alienists who observed you and made light banter with you at the State's Attorney's behest believe you to be sane enough to understand the difference between right and wrong. You have to give me something."

The next morning, inside the courthouse, Mr. Clemmons hustled them into a small waiting room the size of a closet about twenty minutes before showtime. They wore skirts that covered their ankles and modest blouses, Will's with buttons, Dolly's with ruffles.

"Girls," said Mr. Clemmons. "We're going to ask you to do something that may strike you as most peculiar, but I want you to trust me. Your families and my staff have all gone through this every which way. So here it is: we are going to ask permission of the court to withdraw our plea of not guilty. We're going to plead you guilty.

"Let me explain my thinking, for I realize this might come as a shock. This trial is really about the punishment that fits the crime. You see, if we go before a jury of twelve men, it is going to be near impossible to find you not guilty of murder. Mr. Gaines has gathered all the evidence that he needs and more, plus your confessions. Now, let's say by some miracle you are found not guilty. What does he do? He tries you for the second charge of kidnapping. Tell me then, why should we give him two bites at the apple? The only way to deprive him of that chance is the element of surprise, and surprise depends upon strict silence.

"If we withdraw our plea of not guilty and enter our guilty plea to both charges he loses that chance. Then the case will be tried before a single judge. And honestly girls, we stand a much better chance pleading our case for life imprisonment with one reasonable judge, over twelve members of the jury, thirsty for blood.

"So as you see, I believe passionately in this strategy, but I also believe that I owe you both a sincere apology. You see, I know in my heart that I could have told you girls about this little plot before, and I am convinced you would not have breathed a word of it. But I couldn't take any chances. What if one of you talks in your sleep? What if you decided you had to discuss it with each other? After all, that's not unreasonable; it's a pretty important decision. And should someone have overheard you, oh wouldn't the press have loved to get a scoop like that! And so I bowed to the diktats of prudence. But I apologize for doing it. I am truly, heartily ashamed."

The girls looked at each other. Will squinched her face up a little and shook her head. Dolly knew what she was thinking and she felt the same way.

"Mr. Clemmons," Dolly said. "Will we get to speak before the judge?"

"No. That would be suicide. What we are trying to do here is to save your lives, girls. It is up to me to speak for you, to present the most sympathetic case possible on your behalf so that the judge, we pray, will show mercy and spare your lives."

"But what if we want to share our story. What it was all about. Our reasons ... What really led us to ..." Will said.

"What reasons could you possibly give?"

Dolly looked at Will, and she thought of her family's and Will's family's hypocrisy. They wanted to keep the girls in their place, just like they wanted to do with all the "inverts" and negroes and immigrants. But as the potency of Will's gaze, and her love, penetrated Dolly's heart, she realized something about herself. *Maybe I'm just as much of a hypocrite. I have a chance to tell the whole world how rigged the game is for anyone who isn't deemed normal by the simpering masses. Wasn't this the time to be fearless?*

"All right, girls. If you're sure you wish to speak on the record, would you like me to bring in a court stenographer?"

Dolly and Will both nodded, and Clemmons excused himself for a moment.

"They tried to keep us apart," Dolly said. "Our families, the university. They were embarrassed by us. But why? Do they think they're above *us*?"

"Yes," Will said. "That's what they must understand. If they hadn't tried to keep us apart ..."

"But it's more than that. How is it that a jury of men gets to decide our fate—white Christian, married men? That's hardly a jury of our peers! Or we are left to throw ourselves on the mercy of one old codger of the same breed who sees us as defectives, deviants, when we no doubt top his IQ by dozens of points."

Clemmons returned with a stenographer, who set up her machine in the corner of the room.

"All right, girls. We are just going to go over the basic information again about your names, addresses, birthdates etc. and then you may make your statement."

"Together?" Will asked.

"I'll let you both speak as you see fit and the stenographer will transcribe your statement," Clemmons said.

He directed the stenographer to label this document as evidence under the heading of "Motive for the Crime."

"I'll start," Will said. "We were being forced apart by our families and by the Barnard administration because they believed our relationship to be unnatural, immoral. In reality, the spectrum of the animal kingdom and of humanity includes a great deal of variety when it comes to sexual intimacy. Males and males. Females and females. Not just males and females. We did nothing wrong, but out of what we believe is an immoral *conditioning*, we had been trained to keep our mouths shut and to keep our relationship hidden."

"Which we did," Dolly said. "All to appease our families, the school, our provincial peers. But when we visited the Jazz clubs of Harlem just blocks away, it was obvious that there was another way of life that included true freedom. We could express ourselves openly and with abandon. The irony, however, is that most of the patrons of the clubs we went to were Black. The very same people who are being judged as 'inferior' by whites."

"We did not set out to commit such a violent act. But two things converged that lit the match for us, so to speak," Will said. "Number one, being kept apart by our families and the school, and threatened with never being able to see each other again. And even though we were able to be reunited and room together once more, we never knew when the ax might fall again."

"Yes, we knew we were living like criminals already, under constant surveillance, for what?"

"For loving each other, that's what!" Will said.

Dolly felt like she and Will really had a rhythm going. It was like they were finishing each other's thoughts. Just like a great jazz improv!

"And the second thing: my family decided to scapegoat a woman with whom I only shared a friendship, and for whom I held great esteem. Celia Sutherland. A jazz musician and cabaret performer of immense talent. They tried to set her up as the so-called 'reason' for my fall into debauchery. As if none of us have free will of our own. They even went so far as to arrest C.C. on some trumped-up charges, and here's the worst part: they took her kid away from her. A little kid."

"Now, we are not stating that what we did was right," Will said. "But how can the State jump to a conclusion so easily that we are the force of evil because we killed a while male when the State, and society as a whole, even our own families, are convinced that the life of a Black woman, her Black child, and the lives of two so-called 'inverts' such as ourselves have less value?"

Dolly looked at Will. Ok, so now they'd said it. And not so many words either. It wasn't that complicated. Hypocrisy was hypocrisy, and why should they cry crocodile over poor little Eddie Diller? What about poor C.C. and her poor orphaned child? And what about Dolly and Will?

It was all out in the open now, and Dolly could feel herself sighing in relief. She and Will smiled at each other. One thing was clear now, they'd tried to turn them against each other, and it almost worked. But they were a team and even if they ended up swinging from ropes at the end of it all, at least they would go down with dignity, and maybe they'd be remembered for the truths they told, not just the killing of one average kid.

"Okay, I think we've got it," Clemmons said.

A matron escorted Dolly into the courtroom and brought to the desk where Will already sat and where Clemmons paced about in a rumpled seersucker suit.

"All rise," the bailiff instructed. "The case of the People against Dorothy Raab and Wilhelmina Reinhardt."

The judge was a compact man, with small foxy eyes and close-cropped hair.

"Please proceed, gentlemen," he directed.

Clemmons looked down at his tie and then up at the judge, a man chagrined.

"We want to state frankly here that no one in this case believes that these defendants should be released. We believe they should be permanently isolated from society and, if we as lawyers thought differently, their families would not permit us to do otherwise.

"After long reflection and thorough discussion . . . we have determined to make a motion in this court for each of the defendants in each of the cases to withdraw our plea of not guilty and enter a plea of guilty.

"The statute provides that evidence may be offered in mitigation of the punishment and we shall ask at such time as the court may direct that we may be permitted to offer evidence as to the mental condition of these young women, to show the degree of responsibility they had and also to offer evidence as to the youth of these defendants and the fact of a plea of guilty as further mitigation of the penalties in this case. With that we throw ourselves upon the mercy of this court and this court alone."

It was as if a round of gunfire had blasted through the courtroom. Everybody jumped up, screaming and demanding explanations.

Gaines wasted not a moment smashing his hand on the table and objecting, demanding a meeting in judge's chambers, which the judge granted. The reporters cleared the courtroom, presumably to call their papers and announce the surprise change in plea.

"Girls," Clemmons said in a whisper. "You have to trust me. Your families have insisted, and I must agree, that your lives are worth saving and the only way to do that is to throw yourselves on the mercy of one judge, not a jury of twelve men."

"But we'd rather die and let what we believe be known!" Dolly said.

"Yes, and die together," Will said.

"What about the statement we just gave to your stenographer?" Dolly asked.

"I gave it to your Uncle David for safekeeping. I don't know what he plans to do with it, but I am quite sure none of your relatives want any of your thoughts shared in a court of law nor released to the newspapers."

"But that's not right!" Dolly yelled. "That's not what you promised us!"

She slammed her hand on the table just as the judge and Gaines came back into the courtroom.

"Mr. Clemmons, I am running out of patience already. Can these girls submit to the rules of the court or not?"

"Yes, sir," Clemmons said. "I apologize to the court. The girls are naturally quite emotional and prone to fits of hysterics, given all the pressure of this situation. But I assure you I have them thoroughly under my control. Just give us a moment, please."

Clemmons turned to the girls and moved his icy gaze from one to the other.

"It's the time of reckoning, girls. You must plead guilty or you will have no support whatsoever. If you do not play this my way, you will be left with only the counsel assigned by the court, and there will be nothing to stop a lynch mob from breaking into these proceedings one day and doing what they will with you. I'm here to protect you."

"No one's going to lynch a couple of white girls," Dolly said bitterly.

"Jewish girls," Clemmons corrected her.

But she knew the forces against them were too strong. One look into Will's defeated eyes and it was clear that they'd run out of options.

The attorneys then received the green light to decide whether psychiatric evidence could be introduced at a hearing to consider mitigation of the sentence.

"The ordinary hearing of insanity in criminal trials," Clemmons began, "is much in the nature of a vaudeville show. It looks like high-class arguments, bickerings, denials, one set of alienists say one thing, another set of alienists say another thing. It brings disrepute on everyone involved. Each set of psychiatrists impugns the honesty of the other; psychiatry is regarded by the public as a laughingstock, less a serious science than an exercise in charlatanism and buffoonery. And the attorneys—never reluctant to purchase testimony from expert witnesses to say whatever served their purpose—are damned in the public eye as corrupt and venal. We suggest before the hearing begins a joint conference of the alienists of the defendants and the State ..."

"Now, just a minute," Gaines cut in. "Is there a plea of guilty entered here by two sane women or is the defense entering a plea of guilty by two insane women?"

"I ask counsel not to interrupt until I finish ..."

"I know, but what I want to know is whether the contention here is the girls are sane or insane?"

"I am not to be sidetracked, sir," Clemmons said, digging in. "We ask counsel for the other side to assume that we are in good faith. What we desire to do is to determine the degree of mental responsibility of the defendants. When the court hears all of the evidence, it is his duty to fix the penalty. I think it comes with bad grace for the State's Attorney to try to shut me off at this time. The alienists we've talked to want to meet with the alienists of the State and talk it over with them and see if they can iron out whatever differences there may be among them. Maybe our alienists will be won over to their side; maybe it will be the other way, but at any rate they want to present a joint matter."

"Well," Judge Ellsworth said. "The court, of course has no power to require the State's Attorney to do that."

"The State's Attorney is in a position to prove by evidence beyond all reasonable doubt that these girls are not only guilty, but that they are absolutely sane under the law and should be hanged, and the State will introduce evidence beginning Wednesday morning to that effect."

"All right. We will suspend, gentlemen, then, until Wednesday morning at ten o'clock. All be here promptly at ten."

The judge banged his gavel, and Dolly and Will turned to each other. Now Dolly could see anger in Will's eyes. They both knew they'd been duped. Maybe they need to say something now. Was it too late to change the plea? Clemmons gave them a stern look, and soon the hands of the bailiffs were upon them.

Chapter Thirty
Will

They had placed her in a two-person cell, but she had no bunk-mate. Bunk-mate! Will was reminded of Sterry walking in on her and Dolly on that bunkbed up at the Rhinebeck estate. Will sat on the bottom bunk, forcing herself to think about something else. But all that came was the image of the first time she'd entered Dolly's bedroom on Sutton Place. The canopied bed. Quite a different style than the rusted coils of this monstrosity, topped with a urine-stained flat mattress.

Still, the jail cell was not as dreary for Will as she thought it would be. Knowing that she and Dolly had broken the ice with each other, she could relax a little. She wasn't going to panic over the outcome of the trial. They'd live or die together. It was as simple as that. But Will would not be on her own. She and Dolly were one. If she doubted it before, she had to believe it now. They only had each other.

The New York Daily Spectator included a front-page plea to none other than Dr. Sigmund Freud himself from the blustery publisher:

UNRAVEL THEIR MINDS FOR US, DR. FREUD

Dear Dr. Freud,

On behalf of the good citizens of the United States of America, I am writing to you to humbly request your services in the Reinhardt and

Raab case. I am prepared to offer you a never-before-paid sum for the psychoanalysis of the two demented individuals at the center of this case.

Sir, I must admit I am old fashioned and know little of the modern techniques of alienists. But speaking as a citizen, a patriot, and a father, I must tell you, I am chilled to the bone by the acts of these over-educated young fiends who took it upon themselves, without a hint of hesitation, or a second's showing of conscience, to plan and execute the murder of an innocent boy.

Are they simply the products of the immoral age we live in? If so, we, the people of America, come to you, a respected scientist of mental matters, to delineate for us what exactly went wrong in their psyches? For we must look to the future and assure the public that no such fiendish behavior can ever take place again—not if we can prevent it.

I am told that three years ago you became a grandfather to a healthy little lad. Forgive this ghastly addendum, but I implore you to think for a moment, just as all of us here stateside have thought, imagine if what happened to the grief-stricken Mr. and Mrs. Diller happened to the parents of that wee child you bounce upon your knee.

Sir, I assure you my proposition is serious and sincere. Should you agree to this offer it is my desire, as publisher of The New York Spectator, to run daily the fruits of your razor-sharp analysis of these demonic females.

Humbly,

Thomas Bradford Parks

Will was kept abreast of the news by the guards. Word spread quickly that TBP (as he was known) had offered Dr. Freud a million dollars. It was reported on page fourteen the next day that the already legendary doctor sent a telegram from Vienna that he was in ill health, and unable to travel.

Will lay on the hard, itchy bed. She kept flashing back to Dolly's confession. The lie.

They both knew who killed the boy.

That did not make Will innocent, but since the perfection of their plan had unraveled, Will felt sick at the thought of the world looking at her like a common murderer. And yet, this was her way to honor Dolly. To stop pointing the finger at her, and to allow the world to see them both as killers. After all, the boy wouldn't be dead if it were just Dolly on her own. Will played a part too. A very, very big part.

She would have given anything to talk to Dolly. Since their capture, they'd been kept apart, never given a moment along together to compare notes on the experience. At least today they would all be meeting together—she, Dolly, Clemmons, and both families.

The guard led Will in where Dolly and Clemmons already sat. Dolly tried to look away, but the moment they caught each other's eyes they smiled. Will sat next to Dolly. The door opened and the guard brought in the families. Dolly rose, clearly looking around for her precious Mumsie. Dolly's Uncle David walked in beside her father, followed by Pop, Estelle, and Sanford.

"Where is she?" Dolly asked.

"Not feeling well," David said.

Dolly's father didn't look at her.

"Hi Pop," Will said.

"How are you, Will?"

"I'm fine, Pop."

"Are they feeding you girls okay?" Pop asked

Will nodded.

"Yes, Dolly?"

"Yes, Mr. Reinhardt," Dolly said.

"Folks, let's sit down," Clemmons said. "We haven't too much time. You can squeeze around this table. I'm a little hefty and I like to pace anyway, so I'll stand."

Clemmons smiled and held a chair out for Estelle.

"So Mr. Clemmons, we're in your hands. Do you think the girls have a chance?" Pop asked.

"We don't want a chance," Dolly said.

"Stop this nonsense," Uncle David said. "We're trying to save your lives."

"We want to testify, tell *our* story," Will said.

"No, girls," Clemmons said. "The judge hears the evidence and rules on the penalty for the crime. And in this case, your fates rest greatly on the alienists' evaluations. Ultimately, however, it's all in the judge's hands. You remember we discussed this many times?"

"He's trying to make us look like imbeciles," Dolly said. "Of course we remember you *telling* us that's how it was going to be but not giving us the freedom to even make a choice."

"Simmer down, Dolly," David said. "Might I remind you that that boy—Eddie Diller—was given no choice about his fate. The two of you are in no position to make judgment calls.

"What is your strategy, Mr. Clemmons?" Sanford asked him. "I mean, I know you described it to the court, but perhaps you can put it in layman's terms."

He practically pointed to Estelle as if she were a child. Will did not think much of her brainpower as it were, but who was he to act as if she were too ignorant to understand this whole process? From Will's experience, Estelle was bull-headed, but she caught on quick.

"We need the judge to see that the girls' minds were all twisted up. That something had gone wrong in their brains. He must see that they are damaged and in need of mercy."

"Insanity?" Pop asked.

"No. Not legal insanity, but something akin to a *damaged* mind. And when two damaged minds like this get together ..."

Mr. Raab looked up for the first time and stared at Dolly, "Well they had to be to do something like this, didn't they? My God. They had everything. Money. Brilliant minds. And more money! Every luxury provided them, and that wasn't enough. More. More. Always more. Spoiled. Spoiled rotten. There's no point to hope anymore."

He turned away from Dolly to Mr. Clemmons.

"I'm sorry I lost my temper. My daughter has always been ... troubled. Her mind is prone to fantasy—extreme, wild fantasy— and well ... I just never thought it would come to this."

"That's all right, sir," Sanford said. "Perhaps we can focus on how to keep the press at bay."

"That train has already left the station," David said.

"Those letters ..." Sanford said. "Will they be part of the evidence?"

"Anything that speaks to the diseased minds of my clients may be in our favor. We are not looking to win a popularity contest ..."

"Aren't we?" Dolly said.

"Hush," David said. He looked nervously at his brother.

"I mean if we win over the judge, don't we ... well ... win the case?"

"Stop!" Pop said. "Dolly, Dolly. You're a beautiful girl, but you must be silent. My daughter is a brilliant student. She speaks a dozen languages. I'm told you are brilliant as well. But you speak as if you are an eight-year-old. Surely you recognize you are in the best hands with Mr. Clemmons. He will take care of you both."

"Mr. Reinhardt," Mr. Raab said. "We have one thing and one thing alone to be thankful for."

The room fell silent as Mr. Raab pursed his lips and nodded his head as if in prayer.

"At least the boy they chose was also Jewish."

So it had been said.

Chapter Thirty-One
Dolly

The alienist's name was Dr. Axel P. Quincy or something like that, but Dolly decided to call him Dr. Quack. Not to his face, of course, but it seemed sort of fun to test her wits by giving him answers with one side of her mouth and silently saying whatever the hell she really thought with the other. She'd practiced her whole life for this. Performing on the outside, writing a completely different play on the inside. He really did look like a Dr. Quack. His hair and beard were yellowy white like a duck's ass and he waddled as he led her to the couch. And the size of him! Boy he didn't miss a meal, that's for sure.

The feeling of him sitting behind Dolly made her uneasy. She half expected to turn around and see the Grim Reaper himself. As she answered his general questions she kept trying to see if there was some weapon in the room she could use to bash in his brains if needed. That made her think of the whole incident in the car. She snapped back into focus.

"Miss. Raab, what were your early studies like as a child?"

"Well, I guess I was bored in grammar school a lot. I felt like I knew the answers before they even asked the questions. I would end up practically falling asleep in class, even though I aced the tests. My father got it in his head that I should be some kind of a math and language whiz so he hired a governess to ride me hard, make me shape up."

232

The Quack didn't say anything, so she kept prattling on.

"I guess he wanted me to do well in those areas 'cause he's the Raab in Raab's Department Store and he thought maybe I'd be part of the business."

"That's unusual for a girl, isn't it?"

"Well, I used to tell him when I was little that I wanted to work at the store, and I guess I did some genius math in front of him and his accountants when I was maybe three or four, and from there on in he would say I'd be his bookkeeper and that he'd rather keep the books handled by the family anyway. Then I was there for a couple of ribbon cuttings for stores in Vienna and Paris and said I wanted to learn more languages so I could help him manage the goods across the world. I guess I did have a nose for travel even as a little runt—ha, ha."

"So it sounds like you were quite motivated and precocious as a very young girl."

"Well, I knew enough to be Daddy's little girl. Tell him what would make him happy and all. Things changed a bit when the other kid came along."

"Sheffield, your brother?"

"Yeah, then I become Mum's little girl I guess. Daddy decided a boy would be better at handling business. Still, he knew I had big brains—ha, ha—so he got me Frau Eva to make sure I cracked the books."

"You said she rode you very hard."

"Yeah. She just wouldn't let up. I never had a minute to myself with that one hovering over me—*did you do this—do that?*" Just remembering that fat cow irked the bejesus out of Dolly. The way she would say "Sei nicht so blod!" as if Dolly was the stupid one. The problem was the wench had no sense of humor.

The doc was blathering, and she tried to answer his last question without letting him catch her not listening.

"When I was alone—which was rare!—I guess I didn't like to do all that much that was so special. I mean I would read a lot of magazines about the criminal underworld. That was fun. And then I'd just sort of lie on my bed and imagine myself in some of the scenes. You know shooting it out with the coppers. Just kid stuff!"

Dolly realized that this could sound strange to someone outside of her family. These old guys were not so wild about girls who acted like boys. She wished she'd really thought about how to play this with him. She could certainly make herself more into a little girl for him, innocent and worshipful. Make it seem like Willsie was the heavy, the invert, the one who thought she was a man. That could play well for Dolly. But it was too late for that. They were being tried together and they'd live or hang together. Besides, she just didn't want to make this guy feel good. Why should she?

"Did you know any negro children growing up?"

"No. The family wouldn't allow that. Just the servants. We never met their kids."

"Could you tell me a little about Celia? How did you two become acquainted?"

Okay, here we go.

"I like to play jazz, and all the best musicians play in Harlem. That's where I met C.C."

"Did you ever engage in any physical contact with her?"

"You're going to have to be more specific."

"Any forms of sex play?"

"No," Dolly said. "But I wished we had."

A sizzle of a thrill began to catch fire in her chest. Maybe the most seditious thing she could do would be the least expected: to tell the truth.

"C.C.'s the best," Dolly said. "She's got delicate moves on the dance floor and a deep bassy voice that fills the room. You should go up to Harlem and check her out when she gets out of the pokey. She'll be out before I am, that's for sure."

"I suppose you haven't heard," he said.

"What are you talking about?"

"I think we should stop here."

"No tell me, tell me what you know!" she said jumping up and slamming her hands on his desk.

"Lie back down," he said. "Lie back down or I'm afraid you will have to be shackled. If you want my help you must lie back down."

Dolly complied and it was just as well because she could feel her knees shaking.

"This is most unusual," he said, pulling a newspaper from his desk drawer. "But I want you to know you can trust me. So you may read the item in the paper yourself."

She sat up to read, but he made a sharp sound, advising her to lay down fully. In a prone position she couldn't focus on the words.

"I shall read it to you then," he said.

"Lynching in Lancaster ... En route to Lancaster jail, the Philadelphia-born negro was led to her death in the woods of Pennsylvania Dutch Country ... News of her criminal attacks on one half of the college girls killers ..."

Dolly's eyes started to roll in their sockets and her vision doubled. Nausea in her belly and palpitations in her heart convinced her that she had met her end. And when she thought of C.C. hanging from a tree because of a lie, thinking that Dolly had sold her down the river to gain sympathy for her case ... the shame felt so inescapable her body had no choice but to collapse.

Chapter Thirty-Two
Will

Clemmons called Dr. Haley to the witness chair for the defense. A small cap of white hair covered his head; his leg shook a bit when he crossed it. It was so easy to judge others, Will noted, but what if the microscope was trained back on these psychiatric professionals? The disgusting thoughts in their minds would be revealed. Will's thoughts drifted back to her studies of quantum mechanics and the theory that the observer affects the experiment. It helped Will to think of the courtroom like a classroom. She could simply watch the proceedings as if she were in a lecture hall. Having Dolly beside her helped, though Dolly was beginning to look frayed as alienist after alienist reported on the states of the girls' brains.

Will thought of that night when Dolly was out with Jane Sterry. She'd been studying and waiting up for Dolly, and Dolly pushed her off, complaining about Will being too clingy. Yet she pretended to be drunk and allowed Will to undress her and put her to bed. Dolly had moaned in response to Will's soft kisses along her spine. It had been perfect. So perfect Will hadn't wanted to risk rolling Dolly over to try and kiss her on the mouth. She had treated Dolly like a delicate bird who might fly away. Will had once believed they had all the time in the world to let their romance unfold. And now a teenage boy was dead, and they were on trial for their lives.

"What did you learn about the relationship between Miss Rein-hardt and Miss Raab?" Clemmons asked.

"It is very clear from the study of the girls separately that each came with peculiarities in their mental life. Each arrived at these peculiarities by different routes; each supplemented the other's already constituted abnormal needs in a most unique way. There seems to have been so little normal motivation, the matter was so long-planned, so unfeelingly carried out, that it represents nothing that I have ever seen or heard of before.

"In the matter of the association, I have the girls' story, told sepa-rately, about an incredibly absurd childish compact that bound them. For Raab, she says the association gave her the opportu-nity of getting someone to carry out her criminalistic imaginings and conscious ideas. In the case of Reinhardt, the direct cause of her entering into criminalistic acts was this particularly childish compact.

"You are talking about a compact that you characterize as childish. Kindly tell us what that compact was."

"I am perfectly willing to tell it in chambers, but it is not a matter that I think should be told here."

"I insist that we know what that compact is," Gaines replied, "so that we can form some opinion about it. Tell it in court. The trial must be public, Your Honor. I am not insisting that he talk loud enough for everybody to hear, but it ought to be told in the same way that we put the other evidence in."

Judge Ellsworth, after a discussion with the attorneys at the bench, told Dr. Haley to whisper his answers so that only the judge, the attorneys, and the stenographers could hear his words.

But Will's hearing was sharp. Most people didn't realize that a skilled ornithologist relies most on her sense of hearing, less on her sense of sight. Birds after all, identify themselves with their calls.

"This compact, as was told to me separately by each of the girls, consisted of an agreement between them that Reinhardt who has very definite homosexual tendencies was to have the privilege of— do you want me to be very specific?"

"Absolutely, because this is important."

"... Was to have the privilege of inserting her fingers, sometimes her entire fist inside Raab's vagina at special rates; at one time it was to be three times in two months, if they continued their criminalistic activities together ... then they had some of their quarrels, and then it was once for each criminalistic deed."

"I do not suppose this should be taken in the presence of newspapermen, your Honor," Clemmons said. "And certainly not newspaperwomen."

"Gentlemen, will you go and sit down. You newspapermen. Take your seats. This should not be published. And I must insist now that the courtroom be cleared of all ladies, including newspaper reporters."

The room was cleared with military efficiency.

"What other acts, if any, did they tell you about?" Gaines asked.

"They experimented with mouth perversions. Reinhardt has had for many years a great deal of fantasy life surrounding sexual activity. She has fantasies of being with a woman and usually with Raab herself. She says she gets a thrill out of anticipating it. Raab would pretend to be drunk, then Reinhardt would undress her, almost rape her, and would be furiously passionate. With men she does not get that same thrill and passion."

"That is what she tells you?" Gaines asked. "Rape? How is this anatomically possible?"

"Surely that is what she tells me. As to what she means by 'rape,' despite her linguistic skills she seems to have no better word to describe the hand and mouth perversions she cares to indulge in with Raab. Raab tells me herself how she sometimes feigns to be drunk in order to have her aid in carrying out her criminalistic ideas. That is what Reinhardt gets out of it, and that is what Raab gets out of it. When Reinhardt had this first experience with her hand inside Raab's vagina she found it gave her more pleasure than anything else she had ever done. Even in jail here, a look at Raab's body or her touch upon her shoulder thrills her so, she says, immeasurably ..."

"Doctor, you are an expert on female sexuality; have you ever heard of cases such as the one before you today?"

"Well, in *Sex in Education: or, a Fair Chance for the Girls*, published in the latter part of the last century, Harvard professor Edward Clarke predicted that if women went to college, their brains would grow bigger and heavier, and their wombs would atrophy. Dr. Clarke asserts that the pursuit of an academic career will cause a woman's body to shunt blood away from the uterus toward the brain, rendering that woman 'irritable and infertile.'"

Will wanted to render this imbecile silent by strangling the life out of him. How dare this pompous ass claim to be an expert on female sexuality?

"He writes, and I quote, 'There have been instances, and I have seen such, of females, in whom the special mechanism we are speaking of remained germinal—undeveloped. It seemed to have been aborted. They graduated from school or college excellent scholars, but with undeveloped ovaries. Later they married, and were sterile.'"

"What conclusion do you draw from your studies, Doctor?" Clemmons asked.

Here the doctor turned to the judge and replied in earnest:

"Perhaps if these girls had merely had a simple procedure, Your Honor, had spent but a few minutes in a doctor's office when signs of their abnormalities first appeared—well, then Eddie Diller might still be playing baseball, getting into school-yard tussles with his fellow boys, and soon chasing girls like any red-blooded American male.

"According to Freud—the complete elimination of the stimulation of a sensitive outer area of the female body is a necessary precondition for the development of femininity since it is immature and masculine in nature. Female infibulation—the removal of the inner and outer labia and the suturing of the vulva—is a simple procedure, easily done in a doctor's office.

"Had these girls spent but a few minutes submitting to an established medical procedure, one that is performed with the highest hygienic standards, a procedure that both Drs. Sims and Freud passionately advocate—they would then have the adult pleasure of through climax the normal way with their husbands to look forward to, the bigger pleasure of childbirth to which every normal girls aspires from the time she can pick up a doll or say 'Mama.'

"Now I believe, of course, a woman has the right to an education, but perhaps in colleges such as these so-called 'Seven Sisters' schools, we have made a tragic mistake in allowing girls to co-habit and to experiment with each other.

"We've heard testimony of how 'smashed on' Reinhardt was for Raab, how she would do anything, even kill for her. Surely, we have now exited any age of innocence in which we can say that girls getting these 'crushes' on each other, and exercising their proclivities towards excess emotion or physical excitement with each other is 'harmless.'

"Of course women should be educated if they choose, but in certain subjects, and by men. And colleges can now no longer turn a blind eye towards the dangers of abnormal females entering their ranks. Girls, along with adult women who are plagued by a draw towards masturbation, hysteria, nymphomania and excess sexual desire, lesbianism, lack of female orgasm during traditional intercourse, and a number of other conditions considered abnormal or immoral are not without hope.

"Perhaps if these two girls had been recognized as deviants to be treated and cured through a simple medical procedure, a female circumcision they call it—the male version which is an honorable ritual in their shared religion of the Old Testament—then they would be doing what all normal girls do along with their studies in college, they'd be husband-hunting! Instead, these poor diseased souls hunted a young boy and killed him for the thought of adult maleness terrified them so."

"Thank you, Doctor."

Will wished she could be sucked into the Salt Marsh and left to die, where the birds would remain her only companions through eternity. She could see the disgust on Gaines's face. She was a woman and she loved Dolly, another woman. She could tell by the way Dolly responded when Will first put her fingers inside her that she wanted more. Like the Salt Marsh, Dolly's body was pulling in Will, but not toward death, towards life! At least that's how it felt to Will. But these sour-smelling old men were treating it like a form of depravity. Hating them or pitying them. No one in the world could know what it felt like for the two of them when they were together.

The tenor of scientific curiosity changed considerably when Donald Horwitz, expert witness for the prosecution, took the stand.

"In my opinion, Dorothy Raab was not suffering from any mental disease, either functional or structural, on May 21, 1924, or on the date I examined her. The stream of thought flowed without any interruption or any break from within. There was not a single remark made that was beside the point. The answer to every question was responsive. There was abundant evidence that the girl was perfectly oriented as to time, as to place, and as to her social relations. Not only that, there was excellence of attention. There was not a single evidence of any defect, any disorder, any lack of development, or any disease, and by disease I mean functional as well as structural.

"As to Wilhelmina Reinhardt, there was no evidence of any organic disease of the brain, as would have been revealed by the Argyll-Robertson pupils—a highly reliable indicator of neurosyphilis. There was no evidence of any toxic mental condition resulting from any toxicity of the body because the pulse and the tremors that would have been incidental thereto were absent at this examination. She showed remarkably close, detailed attention; she showed that she was perfectly oriented socially as well as with reference to time and space. There were none of the modifications of movements that come with certain mental disorders."

"And do you have an opinion as to which girl struck the fatal blow?" Gaines asked.

"They both accuse each other."

Voices rose up throughout the courtroom into an unintelligible roar.

"Objection!" Clemmons said. "They are being tried together. Irrelevant."

The judge looked at Dolly, took his glasses off, and wiped them clean with a handkerchief. When he placed his glasses back on he looked over at Will. She recognized that look. She'd seen it in the eyes of those teenagers on the subway when she'd come back from birding. She'd seen it in Estelle's eyes. It said, "You're not a girl. You're not a human. What are you?" Everyone thought she was the real monster. There'd be no point in arguing for the truth.

Chapter Thirty-Three

The day of closing arguments, they were allowed to read the day's papers. Will and Dolly sat in a stuffy room outside the courtroom with Clemmons.

THE DAILY SPECTATOR

THEY WANT TO LIVE LIKE MEN? LET THEM DIE LIKE MEN.

EDITORIAL BY THOMAS BRADFORD PARKS

It is not, as Defense Attorney Warren Clemmons would have you believe, with a thirst for blood that I write these words, but with a hunger for justice. Not only justice in the criminal courts, but a return to a just society where girls are raised to be wives and mothers, and boys to be men who protect their family, their country, and all who abide by the laws of the Bible.

On this day, I declare: THE JAZZ AGE IS DEAD! It is a deep sorrow that an innocent lad had to die to make this apparent, but perhaps this will make it so his death does not have to be in vain. The combination of jungle music, bootleg liquor and education for women has mixed to form a deadly poison. Our youth are growing up without morals, and it is time to turn back the clock, to a time when the greatness of this country's ideals, and the Puritan wisdom upon which it was built is returned to.

Some, like the philosophical Mr. Clemmons, blame the War, and say that it showed our youth that life is cheap. But I beg to differ. There have always been wars and the fighting of great battles makes heroes of our boys, and turns them to men. The Great War that must stop and stop this instant is the War against Women.

The convergence of flapper degeneracy and the poisoning of female minds through education and vigorous exercise has turned our decent young ladies into evil temptresses. But for the love of God, even in the Bible the lowest a woman could sink was to the level of harlot, who used her powers of seduction to undo great men.

What Reinhardt and Raab have done is dismiss the need for men altogether! They have decided through the so-called progress of college education for women, that they are men. That they want to be "Supermen," and would rather pervert the sex roles by pretending to be men than to live on the pedestal of femininity and motherhood for which they were born.

Good citizens, none of us mere mortals created the human anatomy. God created man and woman as He did in all His great wisdom for a purpose. And that purpose is Procreation. These dirty girls have spit in the face of motherhood, and not only have they done things that will now prevent them biologically from ever bearing children, but they have taken the life of a child. A male child!

They have renounced their femininity, and they have sunk to the depths of the most savage violent urges that exist in the darkest hearts of men. So I say, if they want to live like men, and kill like men—on an imagined battlefield in which the war they fight is against the virtues of womanhood itself—then let them die like men!

This was outrageous. Will had to talk to Dolly. Why do men hate women so much? When it came down to it they were not being tried for what they did, but because of who they were.

"Mr. Clemmons," Will said. "May Dolly and I speak in private please?"

"I'm sorry. It's time, Will," Clemmons said, rising.

Will felt tears fill her eyes. *Just for a minute,* she wanted to say, but feared that she would break. She followed the guard, Clemmons and Dolly to the courtroom. Scanning the auditorium, Will saw the Dillers. The father's head hung low and his wife rested her head on his shoulder. They looked, even from behind, like they loved each other.

She then noticed Mrs. Raab in the front row, seated beside Mr. Raab and Dolly's Uncle David. What was she doing here? Why today did she have to make her grand appearance at last? Had Clemmons told her to show her face? Why didn't he warn Dolly? Wasn't he supposed to be protecting Dolly and her? Will knew that the surprise presence of Dolly's mother, after being absent from the proceedings for so long, would throw Dolly off. Oh how she wished she could talk to her, comfort her.

"I think it is fair to say that it was an act of God, an act of Providence, that was responsible for the unraveling of this terrible crime," State's Attorney Gaines began. "When the glasses that Reinhardt had not worn for months dropped from her pocket that night, the hand of God was at work in this case. She may not have believed in a God, but, if she has listened and paid attention and thought, as the evidence was unfolded, she must begin to believe there is a God now.

"We have been traveling considerably since this trial began. We have been through dreamland; we have been through the nursery. We have been in psychopathic laboratories, we have been in hospitals, we have been before legislature, and we have been addressing meetings of communists and expounding a doctrine I consider as dangerous as the crime itself. I think it about time we got back into the criminal court ... You have a right, and I know you do forgive those who trespass against Judge Ellsworth, but sitting here as the Chief Justice of this great Court, you have no right to forgive anybody who violates the law. You have got to deal with him or *her* as the law prescribes."

"If the defense alienists were paid by the job instead of by the day, I think they could have answered all the questions here in the three or four hours that our alienists employed.

When it was time for Clemmons to give his closing arguments, Will looked over at Dolly. Dolly no longer appeared alive. Her body, tall and graceful, seemed to have shrunk into itself. She turned her attention back to Clemmons as he moved about the courtroom, shifting his weight from foot to foot as if he himself were weighing the scales of justice. She listened to the rhythm of his words but disregarded their content.

"The easy thing and the popular thing to do would be to hang my clients. I know it. Men and women who do not think will applaud. The cruel and the thoughtless will approve. It will be easy today; but in New York City, and reaching out over the length and breadth of the land, more and more fathers and mothers, the humane, the kind, and the hopeful, who are gaining an understanding and asking questions not only about these poor girls but about their own, these will join in no acclaim at the death of my clients. But, Your Honor, what they shall ask may not count. I know the easy way. I know Your Honor stands between the future and the past. I know the future is with me, and what I stand for here; not merely for the lives of these two unfortunate girls, but for all boys and all girls; for all of the young, and as far as possible, for all of the old.

"I am pleading for life, understanding, charity, kindness, and the infinite mercy that considers all."

"And isn't love, the heartbeat that sustains a child in the womb, the one thing that will allow our civilization to go forward? Your Honor, the State's Attorney has consistently portrayed my clients as aberrations of nature and he has scoffed at the testimony of a host of the defenses' alienists who have noted that the overstimulation of a college education in the case of these two particular girls triggered a temporary hysteria. For the sake of future generations, can't we at least *try* to learn something from the distorted brains and internal physiologies of these girls? Can't we study them? Isn't that reason enough to keep them alive?"

Will felt a hopeless love for Dolly, like she'd do anything to protect her. She *was* her loyal servant. It was not a choice. But never in her life could she have imagined things would turn out this way. Was this the grand plan of these so-called experts? To preach that women should only be taught by men, to suggest they should not co-habitate in dormitories together and to insist upon an operation that would take away the feeling of ecstasy they were capable of experiencing, a feeling that she and Dolly felt with each other so many times ... No, Will would rather be hanged.

Chapter Thirty-Four

The day of reckoning had finally arrived. Will looked behind her at the faces in the packed courtroom, but it was Maeve's that caught her eye. Will felt her mouth open as if to say I'm sorry, but Maeve looked away. Will and Dolly were directed to stand before the judge.

"In view of the profound and unusual interest that this case has aroused not only in this community but in the entire country and even beyond its. boundaries," Judge Ellsworth began, "the court feels it his duty to state the reasons which have led him to the determination he has reached. It is not an uncommon thing that pleas of guilty are entered in criminal cases, but almost without exception such pleas have been the result of a virtual agreement between the defendants and the State's Attorney whereby in consideration of the plea, the State's Attorney consents to recommend to the court a sentence deemed appropriate by him, and in the absence of special reasons to the contrary, it is the practice of the court to follow such recommendations.

"In the present case, the situation is a different one. A plea of guilty has been entered by the defense without a previous understanding with the prosecution and without any knowledge whatever on its part. Here the State was in possession not only of the essential substantiating fact, but also of voluntary confessions on the part of the defendants. The plea of guilty, therefore, does not make a special case in favor of the defendant.

"By pleading guilty, the defendants have admitted legal responsibility for their acts; the testimony has satisfied the court that the case is not one in which it would have been possible to set up successfully the defense of insanity as insanity is defined and understood by the established law of this state for the purpose of the administration of criminal justice.

"The court, however, feels compelled to dwell briefly on the mass of data produced as to the physical, mental, and moral condition of the two defendants. The court is willing to recognize that the careful analysis made of the life history of the defendants and of their present mental, emotional, and ethical condition has been of extreme interest and is a valuable contribution to criminology. And yet the court feels strongly that similar analyses made of other persons accused of crime will probably reveal similar or different abnormalities. The value of such tests seems to lie in their applicability to crime and criminals in general."

A cottony sensation filled Will's mouth; she felt herself swallowing repeatedly yet still unable to satiate her thirst. So the alienists and all of their humiliating testimony was for naught? The judge found it of little significance?

"Under the pleas of guilty, the duty of determining the punishment devolves upon the court, and the law indicates no rule or policy for the guidance of his discretion. In reaching its decision, the court would have welcomed the counsel and support of others. In some states the legislature, in its wisdom, has provided for a bench of three judges to determine the penalty in cases such as this. Nevertheless, the court is willing to meet its responsibilities. It would have been the task of least resistance to impose the extreme penalty of the law. In choosing imprisonment instead of death, the court is moved chiefly by the consideration of the age of the defendants."

We are going to live.

"It is not for the court to say that it will not, in any case, enforce capital punishment as an alternative, but the court believes it is within its province to decline to impose the sentence of death on persons who are not of full age. This determination appears to be in accordance with the progress of criminal law all over the world and with the diktats of enlightened humanity. More than that, it seems to be in accordance with the precedents hitherto observed in this State.

"The records of New York show only two cases of minors who were put to death by legal process to which number the court does not feel inclined to make an addition. Life imprisonment, at the moment, strikes the public imagination as forcibly as would death by hanging, but to the offenders, particularly of the type they are, the prolonged suffering of years of confinement may well be the severest form of retribution and expiation."

He thinks we are too young to hang.

"And so for the indictment for murder, the sentence of the court is that you, Wilhelmina Reinhardt, be confined in the penitentiary at Bedford Hills for the term of your natural life.

"In the indictment for murder, the sentence of the court is that you, Dorothy Raab, be confined in the penitentiary at Bedford Hills for the term of your natural life.

"For the crime of kidnapping for ransom, it is the sentence of the court that you, Wilhelmina Reinhardt be confined in the penitentiary at Bedford Hills for the term of 99 years.

"For the crime of kidnapping for ransom, the sentence of the court is that you, Dorothy Raab, be confined in the penitentiary at Bedford Hills for the term of 99 years."

As soon as the gavel clacked, Will shook Mr. Clemmons's hand and thanked him. She realized with a sigh that she still wanted to live. There had to be a way she and Dolly would be together again. Dolly threw her head back, and all the lawyers up front looked at her appalled, believing she was about to laugh. Instead, she rose in a loopy fashion, put one foot in front of the other, and toppled to the ground. Will instinctively moved towards Dolly to reach down and help her, but the bailiff held her back.

Part IV
Jazz Vampires

Chapter Thirty-Five
Dolly

Spring, 1925
Harlem Valley State Mental Hospital

S he had to ride in the back of the van, arms crossed and shackled to the seat's metal arms. Dolly watched the Hudson Valley rumble past through the grimy window. Cattle stood still like statues on dairy farms, and she wished she could be out there with them. Even the rank, rustic smell refreshed her senses.

They'd had this meeting planned for months. Practically since they'd slipped a striped dress on Dolly after the verdict. Prison wasn't so bad, really. Spending her days talking the criminal lingo with the other inmates. It was sort of fun! Dolly had dreamed about this so long and now it was real. And she had a plan. She tried to use as much physical energy as possible during the day— jumping up and down like a kangaroo to wear herself out. Then at night she'd lay awake in bed outlining the plans for her escape. It entailed making good friends with certain high-level inmates. The ones who had the guards under their thumbs.

Sure, she felt restless and lonely some of the time. But she was proud of herself, the way she handled it. She would compose and play jazz songs in her head and use her fingers, plunking out riffs on her thighs. She saw herself hopping a boat to Europe and getting connected to a criminal gang there upon release, changing her identity. Playing jazz, drinking gin, stealing jewels. Her imagination kept her alive. Of course the reality of the tiny cell, the lousy food, and the lack of freedom took her down, sometimes real down, and on those days she had to find a quiet corner and punch herself in the head to stop from crying. But the mental discipline she was developing made her feel tough and strong.

The only thing that really put her on edge was what she kept hearing from Mumsie. A visit to the psychiatric hospital. She'd heard what they did to Will. Money bought information here, and the news was not good. They made sure she'd be one of those girls in *Herland*, the kind not fit for having babies. Sterilized her. She was the State's property now, so they didn't even have to pull one of those Mississippi appendectomies on her, the kind where they tell the patient—you're going to die, sign off on this emergency procedure. And really it's just a hustle to make sure the breeding stops with them.

Dolly wouldn't have minded that at all. In fact, they'd be doing her a favor. Once she escaped this hole she could have a good time with whoever she wanted, girls, men. Everybody. And as for the fellas, she wouldn't have to worry about being tied down with a brat. She was more worried about the other thing they might do to her. That doctor's office procedure Clemmons talked about during the trial. She knew what it was and it scared her. The boy flashed through her mind, the fear in his eyes when it happened, the culvert after. But she had the mental discipline to push thoughts of him down.

It was harder to get Will out of her head. The whole time they'd been in league together, she'd felt thrilled to have a witness to all her brilliance, thrilled to be worshipped on such an animal level. And Will was an animal. Despite being so awkward in public, and such a nervous Nellie, so insecure in spite of her brains, she was a beast when it came to Dolly. It didn't matter how many times Dolly closed her eyes and tried to think of her prison break and all the glorious jokes she'd play on the law once free, she could not shake Will from her mind.

Sometimes she'd torture herself by letting the images come. She'd see the way Will looked at her, like she was going to eat her alive. And yeah, she knew it was more than just *that* she wanted. She knew Will loved her completely, unconditionally, and would lay down her life for her. Remembering that made Dolly feel worth something, not like the faded ghost she saw in the mirror, glamour gone without the fancy clothes and sweet perfume. Will had seen something in Dolly that Dolly couldn't see in herself, not anymore. It's not like there weren't bulldaggers here willing to play that role with her. And sure, there was even one she'd already played around with. Same dark, brooding type as Will. But this one just didn't have the same hunger, the same ability to see into Dolly so deeply that it frightened her. It just didn't go that deep. But she was nice enough to pass the time with, and Dolly could always find distractions when she needed them!

Still, even if they'd done things differently and hadn't ended up in jail, Dolly would always hold something back from Will. She knew she had to. It was the only way to maintain power, to keep Will coming back for more, trying to sniff out more and more of Dolly's soul. And the way she did it was through her eyes, her hands, her mouth, her moves, and most of all how she took charge of Dolly's body like nobody else could.

It was Jazz. She and Will together. They were Jazz. When they physically came together that's what happened. The rhythm, the riffing, the melody. Just like Duke Ellington working the descending tri-tone, using the third bar of a nifty bridge to show what loving could feel like, she and Will found ways to move together—to connect—that no one ever had, nor ever would. They could find others to play with till kingdom come, but it wouldn't matter. They belonged to each other. If she could get a hold of a piano. Goddammit. A real piano. She could get close to it again. That thing. That thing between them.

254

Mumsie sat waiting in the office along with a white-bearded old man and four other old geezers. They sat behind a white conference table, all in white doctor coats except for one, all in some variation of shoddy wingtips. Mumsie looked so fresh and pretty it was hard to look at her. She wore a light spring dress, with thick graphic stripes crossing her body in diagonal lines. Dolly wanted to go home.

The guard unshackled her and walked her to a seat across from the table, with Mumsie to the left, a few feet away.

"Hello Mumsie."

Mumsie started to cry and then apologized, wiping her eyes with a lace handkerchief. She wasn't so upset that she couldn't blot perfectly. When she took the hankie away there was no mark of makeup to be seen.

"Good morning, Dolly," the youngest of the men said. "As you can see this is very upsetting for your mother. Your father remains incapacitated since his most recent heart attack and with you ... well, it's a heavy burden for a lady to bear. But I believe we have reason for her spirits to rise. First off, welcome to Harlem Valley State Hospital, formerly Wingdale."

She knew about this place. The new bughouse they called it, opened a year ago. Dolly had learned in these last months that it's best to listen before talking. You really had to get a feel for your audience, and this one made her skin shiver.

"This is Dr. Steinach, Dolly. He has come here all the way from Vienna to meet with you."

The old man nodded at her. With his white Santa beard and salt-and-pepper handlebar mustache he looked like Freud himself. Maybe since he came from the same place he was just going to ask her a bunch of questions and try and get inside her head. Dolly smiled, sensing it would do her no harm, and perhaps much good to get on the old codger's sweet side.

"Thank you," she said.

He nodded back with a genuinely warm look in his eyes. Maybe she'd found an ally! These Americans were a little too energetic and rough for her taste, the way they treated her. Bossing her around, telling her what was wrong with her. So many diagnoses even though she was deemed "sane." She couldn't take them seriously. Maybe this guy would be a bit smarter and a bit friendlier towards Dolly.

"Dr. Steinach is Director of Vienna's Biological Institute for the Academy of Sciences."

"We call it the 'Vivarium,'" Dr. Steinach said.

Like she was supposed to know what his slang meant! In Latin, "vivus" meant "alive," and "arium" usually referred to some kind of phony environment. Dolly felt a jolt in her heart as she flashed back to the Congolese boy on display in a cage at the Bronx Zoo. What the hell was this "vivarium" anyway?

"Dr. Steinach has been nominated several times for the Nobel Prize in physiology. We'll leave you to talk privately with him. Gentlemen, Mrs. Raab ..."

Once alone with *Herr Doctor*, she wished Will were here.

"Miss Raab," Dr. Steinach said, approaching her chair and leaning over her. "I'm told you've adjusted rather well to prison life, yah?"

"I'm getting along."

"But certainly if you could turn back the clock, you would not want to find yourself here, correct?"

"Yes," she said. "Yes of course. I wish I could make it all a bad dream. I can't believe ... Eddie ... what we did ..."

"Miss Raab, that we know what happened. It was Wilhelmina. Your friend. She cast a spell upon you, overpowered you, confused you, made you her puppet, yah?"

"Yes."

Sorry Willsie. I'm doing this for us. Means to an end.

Dolly knew the only way to really stay connected to Will was through music. Dolly needed that piano.

"Good. I have had great success with my colleague, Dr. Lichtenstein, in performing sexual organ transplantation on homosexual men. I speak frankly to you because in Vienna we want our patients to feel completely at ease, so we do not use euphemistic language. I want you to be just as frank with me, for I am your doctor now."

"You mean they're moving me here permanently?"

"Well, permanently, I don't know. You will be residing here for a while. But let me tell you what I do know. It is my research that has brought me to international fame, but I am not so good with my hands."

He laughed, so she laughed too. Improvise! Just mirror his moves and stay in tune with him.

"Hands are not hard to find, Miss Raab. Good ones though—not so easy. But I found them attached to a kindred spirit, Dr. Robert Lichtenstein. A surgeon of God-like talents. He has brought my research to fruition in ways I could have never have imagined! With the use of *his* hands, my theories have been proven beyond a shadow of a doubt. We have seen enormous success in taking homosexual men and *biologically* transforming them into normal, heterosexual men.

"My research has taken years, but now the procedure has been perfected. We have documented hundreds of cases in which the perverted man becomes the recipient, through medical transplant, of the undescended third testes from a normal man who has proven beyond doubt to be heterosexual.

"And now, and now! We are just beginning to see the same hope in the female of the species. We need human subjects, and here you are. You are the perfect specimen upon which to prove what I know to be true: we can achieve the same success with girls that we have with men."

"Look, I like fellas, okay?" Dolly said. "There was Joe and a bunch of sweethearts before that. Ask anybody!"

"Yes, yes. We know it was Wilhelmina, your friend, who converted you. I am succeeding where others have failed because I am fully committed to my purpose, and I know that you will be my prize patient. You, Dorothy Raab, I will convert *back* to heterosexuality completely. The trick of it is so simple! We do not need to induce an attraction to males in you. We need only completely remove all attraction to females. It is much easier to cut something out than to graft something in. You are a heterosexual biologically. That is a fact. Your friend, she confused you with her masculine appearance and behavior. You felt so guilty after allowing her to perform unnatural acts on you, yah? You felt an overwhelming need to eject the masculine from your body. Your mind had become so twisted that you performed a masculine act of violence upon a member of the masculine sex. In a way, you are her victim. And unfortunately, before you could be cured you took a male victim. We want to convert you back completely.

"You want your women's colleges to continue don't you? You want to make them safe, yah? You don't want other girls to be victims of the vampiric likes of your Wilhelmina, do you?"

"What are you going to do to me?"

"Simple. We do what the courts are demanding, in return for allowing my team to perform the surgery. Dr. Lichtenstein will do a small procedure on your outer sex organs so that you no longer will be prone to any stimulation there. We sterilize you as we did to your friend. We have an entire Eugenic Society here in America, and in Western Europe too, that believes in sterilizing the unfit. That is not my area, to be quite frank, but that is the part of the bargain I struck in order to be able to obtain rights to your body. But then we simply inject estrogen and a series of hormones into your bloodstream that will return you to your original feminine, heterosexual state. You will be cured."

"But what's the point if I'm locked away?"

"We all have to make sacrifices for science. For future generations. Yah?"

"Yah," Dolly said.

Chapter Thirty-Six

It was hard for Dolly to know how many days it had been since the operation. She felt no physical pain, just a bit lethargic. It was when the nurse with the light tap of the shoes helped her get out of bed that she realized how weak she was. She almost slid to the floor, but the nurse caught her.

"It's all right now. Let's get you a wheelchair," she said. "You're just shaky from the injection."

"Where are you taking me?"

"Dr. Steinach wants to see you."

"What for?"

The purr of the wheelchair and the tappety tap of the nurse's shoes were soothing to Dolly's senses. She could make out a II-V-I jazz progression and it gave her a little more energy. It was funny how a variation on a familiar riff could sound new when it was given a twist. In this case the instruments were shoes and a wheelchair. Dolly felt a little cheery. They had promised her a piano. They didn't have to, but she'd been such a compliant patient that they came around right before she went under.

"Yah, yah," the big doc said, hovering over her in the operating theater.

And then she began to count backwards and disappeared out of time and space. She was glad to leave this place for a while.

An attendant wheeled her into what looked like the art history lecture hall at Barnard, just smaller. A brawny male nurse said he'd watch her from there. No sign of Dr. Steinach. Dolly felt sleepy, and her mind soon returned to Barnard. Professor Lakey stood beside the triunial—the triple-lens projector she'd scored to show slides of works of art. Will was the one who told Dolly that old Lakey was in tight with one of the school's fattest patrons. Good for her. A tall drink of water with tiny eyes to match her tiny wire frame glasses, but this professor had a certain spark. She probably asked for what she wanted in the sack! Like a thousand bucks for a piece of German machinery for Modern Art I!

"What we have here is Picasso's 1896 'Autorretrat' sketched with charcoal on paper in Barcelona."

"He was still working in a realistic manner," Will noted. "It's interesting how he continues to use his face—to mark the physical change in his corporeal self and in his style as an artist. What we see here is quite realistic, but soon enough he will break through tradition to look at the world, and himself, from a multitude of viewpoints."

Yeah, yeah, no surprise Willsie always had a commentary. But as Dolly sat in the dark staring at the sepia-toned drawing, she shuddered. The dark thick hair. The serious yet mischievous arch to the eyebrows, the distinct nose, and those penetrating brown peepers. It was like looking at ole Willsie as a man. Well, wasn't that what they'd been toying with?

"Miss Reinhardt, you're fluent in Spanish. This is a statement Picasso made in May to Marius de Zayas in *The Arts*. Could you translate for the class?"

"Claro, Profesora," Will said. "'Picasso says: 'I can hardly understand the importance given to the word research in connection with modern painting. In my opinion to search means nothing in painting. To find is the thing. Nobody is interested in following a man who, with his eyes fixed on the ground, spends his life looking for the pocketbook that fortune should put in his path. The one who finds something no matter what it might be even if his intention were not to search for it, at least arouses our curiosity, if not our admiration.'"

"Thank you, Miss Reinhardt. Here is this next slide," Professor Lakey said. "Look closely at this 1907 work—'Les Demoiselles d'Avignon.' What do you observe?"

"Looks like a sorority house on Sunday morning!" Dolly said.

Everyone laughed, and the girls in class began sharing their proper little answers.

"This was his first foray into Cubism ..."

"He created a new form ..."

"Some say it was a response to Henri Matisse ..."

They'd been taking notes all semester and giving the right answers like good little girls. The dim bulbs didn't even get what Picasso was saying. None of these dishrags had found an original thought in her life.

"Now, let us look at this next slide of Picasso's wife, Olga, the French ballerina."

Dolly heard the click of the magic lantern, and a wild and modern depiction of nude women dissolved into a photograph.

"Here is an image of Olga when she danced for Nijinksky in 'Afternoon of the Faun.'"

"Debussy wrote the symphony," Dolly said. "Miss Reinhardt and I can hum a few bars if you like."

"Perhaps after class," Professor Lakey said with a wink. "And Mr. Nijinsky played the role of the Nymph."

"Well Mrs. Picasso looks like quite a nymphette," Dolly said. "A real flapper!"

The class tittered.

"Actually," Will corrected in her stodgy way. "She didn't become Mrs. Picasso until 1918."

"Why thank you, Miss Reinhardt," Professor Lakey said and clicked off another slide.

This time they looked at a painting of Olga reclining on an armchair holding a fan. She appeared less playful in the photo, but she was still a looker.

"Here we have a 1917 portrait Picasso painted of Olga during their courtship," Professor Lakey said. "They married the following year."

Will leaned over and whispered, "She reminds me of you. Her long neck, her baby face, and womanly body."

"Can it, will ya?" Dolly said.

Of course, she was pleased. Nobody could make her feel as wanted as ole Willsie. And nothing seemed to douse that flame.

"Picasso continues to paint Olga," Professor Lakey said with another click. "This one is from 1923, two years after the birth of their child."

Dolly suddenly felt a queasiness bubble inside her. All Dolly could see was a woman disappearing. It was as if she was peering at the face and bust of Olga through a key hole. A light yellow surrounded her. Soon her image would grow smaller and smaller and smaller till she disappeared. Faded into nothing.

"Wake up now, Miss Raab," Dr. Steinach said.

"What's going on?"

"It is the final step," he said. "We must scientifically prove that you have been cured."

"How are you going to do that?"

"Hmmm? You like jazz music your mother tells me, yah? We'll put some on. Set the mood. You're going to view some slides, that's all. Some pictures. All you have to do is look at the screen."

The needle dropped on the record as the male nurse strapped her arms and legs to the wheelchair and turned her head to the blank screen. The tune rolled out with sentimental piano chords. The center key moved around a major third. She would have to try that riff.

The click of the projector brought images to the screen that took Dolly back in time. She looked at the images of nude women doing things to each other, just as she and Will did. The first night back together in their old room after they'd been separated, Will and Dolly played a few hands of gin rummy with some dirty cards of Will's. Soon they played with real gin. Dolly began to slur her words, just to make Will unsure if she was playing drunk or not.

Dolly won the last hand and with a smile, she threw all the cards on the floor and kicked Will lightly in the face with her bare foot. Will squawked a few curses and grabbed Dolly's foot, pulling her close. Dolly lay on her back and clocked Will on the head with her other foot. Will managed to grab both of her legs, laughing and guffawing the whole time, and pulled Dolly closer. Dolly grabbed a pillow from behind her, smacked Will on the head, and then tried to crawl off the bed. Will pulled her back up, rolled her onto her stomach then sat on her rear, and pushed her arms down with all her strength.

"Say you're sorry!" Will yelled, laughing and panting.

"Never! Make me."

"Oh, I'll make you all right."

Dolly was still laughing, but Will's voice had dropped an octave to a rough growl. Will lay on top of her then pressed all of her weight down. She pressed her breasts into Dolly's back and lifted up Dolly's hips slightly, just enough so she could reach down and pull up her skirt. Dolly was still laughing and crying out protestations which only made her body more excited. Will slipped a hand inside the back of Dolly's bloomers and squeezed her ass hard. Dolly loved the feeling of force. The rhythm of the tune melted, hot wax hot into Will's touch. The rhythm of the music, a complex improvisation with a loose, straight eighth-note feel, inspired the movement in Dolly's body. Dolly yelled out, "I'm going to kill you!" still giggling and wiggling and feeling a surge of power.

Will slipped a hand between her legs and whispered, "I can feel how wet you are."

Without thinking, as if lyrics to a song were writing themselves, Dolly said, "For you. Always for you."

Will pulled Dolly up on all fours, and Dolly could feel Will on her knees behind her as she slipped what felt like almost her whole hand inside. Dolly reached back to unbutton the side buttons of Will's trousers. She could feel Will slipping out of them and kicking them to the floor. Will took Dolly's hand then placed it inside her underwear. She rocked against Dolly and pulled up her blouse with her teeth. The feeling of Will kissing and licking her back and the excitement building with the music was too much for Dolly. She had never felt what happened next, but cards flew everywhere and they both moaned with release and relief. Sinking down flat onto the mattress together, Dolly saw a half dozen or so cards staring up at her. Aces, deuces, and jacks all with dirty pictures of naked ladies looking up at her from the floor of the dormitory room, with knowing smiles.

The pain in her gut began with a rumble, something like hunger pangs but deeper. Dolly tried to move around, but they had her strapped in so tightly she could not. What she looked at brought a sharp metallic pang to her heart, as if she was being stabbed. Like a cow in a slaughterhouse she could do nothing to resist. Her body felt paralyzed. But the worst part was inside her head. It was if the music had the power to wrap her in filth and send a burning sting up her nostrils, making her sure she would vomit, yet the vomit wouldn't come.

"I'm going to be sick!" she called out.

"Good, good." Dr. Steinbach said. "The treatment is working."

Part V
Jazz

Chapter Thirty-Seven
Will

Summer, 1969
Greenwich Village, NYC

Will folded the map and slipped it inside the breast pocket of her tweed blazer. 62 Charles Street. "Sevilla." This was the place. She took a long drag from her cigarette and entered, being careful not to get in the way of the waiters in starched white shirts and their heavy silver trays, held high above their heads.

There didn't seem to be a hostess, so she walked to the bar. The smell of prawns and lobster intoxicated Will so, she almost didn't want to drink. Actually, she desperately craved a strong drink, but thought she'd best wait in case she was stood up. Will didn't have but a few dollars in her pocket. She saw him enter then and smiled.

Buddy walked straight over to her and held open his arms. They hugged for a long time, and then she took a good look at him. Could it be they were both in their sixties? Buddy had a paunch that pushed the buttons of his silky shirt forward, his hair looked lighter than she remembered from his last visit, years ago. Had he dyed it? His sideburns took up most of his face, framing his smile.

"Table, Señor?"

When they were seated, Buddy ordered for both of them.

"Two gin rickeys," he told the waiter, then turned to face Will. "We'll have wine after, before we order food. How are you, old friend?"

Will shrugged. "You look happy."

"I'm in love," he said.

"I'm intrigued."

"His name is Tomás. We met on the band's last tour."

Buddy had had another boyfriend—the word still sounded strange to Will—up until a couple of years ago when he died of a drug overdose. It kept Buddy from visiting Bedford. She was worried that Buddy might not survive the loss. She grew to count on Jane Sterry more, who became a regular visitor in the end, and they became even closer after Will's release. Turns out Sterry was in love with Dolly too.

Will had spent many lonely nights up late reading and smoking in the halfway house on East 24th Street, near The Armory. The only social life she'd had so far was with her parole officer and Sterry. She worked as a psychiatric social worker a few blocks east at Bellevue. She'd said that Will and Dolly's case was what first sparked her interest in the field.

"Here's his picture," Buddy said. "That's Tomás on the left. He's a musician too."

"Uh-oh! What does he play?"

Buddy hesitated. "Piano."

Will thought of Dolly.

The picture was actually a news clipping from *The New York Post*. The young man—no older than Buddy was when she first met him —was photographed with band members in a live music review.

"Two gin rickeys," the waiter announced.

They lifted their glasses, and Buddy said, "To freedom."

"To freedom."

"How does it feel to be free?"

"Lonely. I don't recognize the world, and the world has no place for me."

The drink went down hard and warmed her so deeply. She drank too fast and could feel herself getting more maudlin as they opened their first bottle of wine.

"I wanted to tell you everything," Will said. "But I just don't have the energy."

He put his hand on hers and nodded.

By the time her ceviche arrived, she'd lost her appetite. She forced a few bites but started to feel weepy and didn't know why.

"Hey, let's take a walk," Buddy said. "I want to show you something."

He paid the check, took her by the hand, and they walked north on Sixth Avenue. She remembered the walk they took to Faun Fountain all those years ago. In November, she'd turn sixty-five. Her gait had grown unsteady and her legs bloated. At Christopher Street, they turned left and headed west. Young boys in eye makeup and leather shorts licked their lips at Buddy as they walked by and called, "Hey Daddy." Will shivered. They couldn't have been more than fourteen or fifteen. She wondered if Eddie Diller had been a queer like them? Is that why they were unconsciously drawn to him?

Buddy stopped in front of a bar. The vertical sign read *Stonewall Inn*. She approached and read the sign posted inside the window: *"We homosexuals plead with our people to please maintain peaceful and quiet conduct on the streets of the Village—Mattachine."* Curious, she thought. The *mattachin* comes from the Arabic word *mutawajjihin* which translates to "mask-wearers."

"There was a riot here a few days ago. The police raided, and we couldn't take it anymore. We fought back—finally. We're demanding our rights."

"We? You were in this fight?"

"No, I wasn't actually here when it happened. When I say 'we' I mean all of us—gays."

"I don't think I'm part of that 'we.' That word strikes me as sorely lacking in irony."

"Okay, Will. Don't sweat it. So what are you doing with yourself?"

"I go to the library. I've gone to Central Park to watch birds, but walking in the woods ... it isn't quite the same."

"Does it make you remember?"

"I guess. You know I did a terrible thing, Buddy. A boy would be alive if it weren't for me. And now I'm free, but my life is over."

"Will, you've paid your debt. Forty-five years behind bars. Let yourself enjoy some quiet pleasures. A drink with friends. A walk through the park, even if you're not ready to watch birds again. You can begin a simple life, starting today. And to be honest, Will, I wasn't expecting this. All those visits to prison. You never once spoke of the crime and how you felt about it."

"I couldn't. I had to be tough."

"I just wish you hadn't dropped those damn glasses." He laughed.

"The spectacles. *My* reading spectacles," she laughed too. "You know there was someone else who maybe they could've pinned the rap on."

"Who?"

"Jerome Frank. He had the same pair with the special hinge. But he was in Europe at the time of the crime."

"Mmmm," Buddy said.

"I bring it up because he turned out to be another Jew who killed a Jew—just like us. Dolly and I. He was a judge on the Rosenbergs' appeal. He did nothing to stop them from going to the electric chair."

Will had had this crazy fantasy that Ethel Rosenberg would end up in Bedford Hills with her. She saw a kindred spirit in her. Something about her reminded her of Momma. Will was convinced they wouldn't die. After all, she and Dolly had been spared. Even when the papers reported that Judge Frank had sided with the lower court's conviction verdict, somehow Will believed they'd escape death. But they didn't. So why did she? Why did Dolly?

"That's awful," Buddy said. "He should have done something. I believe they were innocent.

"Well, I did nothing to stop Dolly. And Eddie Diller was a helluva lot more innocent than the Rosenbergs."

Buddy put his hand on Will's. The warmth made her pull away. It was too painful.

269

"I still think about her all the time," Will said. "But I can't go see her. It's part of the terms of my parole."

"Honey, even if they allowed you to see her, it wouldn't be *her*, you know. They destroyed her in that place. She can't play music anymore."

"The thought of her there. All alone. She hated to be alone. They killed her, Buddy. She may be alive, but … you know … they gave her one of those early lobotomies. They're probably still experimenting on her."

"If she's lucky she'll just pass away in her sleep. I agree: this can't be called life. But we're alive. Let's be gay—in the happy sense!" Buddy laughed. "While we still can."

"Havelock Ellis wrote about our kind, in the early days, before they started calling it 'gay.'" Will said. "He noted that in the studies of Edmund Selous, the British ornithologist, found that the ruff, the male of the Machetes pugnax, is more likely to court another male than a female."

"It's just their nature, I suppose," Buddy said. "Like music. A musician is born to play. There's no changing his nature."

"You know something," Will said. "I could really use another drink."

"I gather you're not a fan of the young hustlers and drag queens?"

"I … just try and remember the last time I went bar hopping, it was speakeasies with the college kids."

"Well," Buddy said. "There is a place around the corner that they call 'Princeton on the Weekends.'"

"Let's go."

They ducked down Waverly Place to West 10th Street. The bar looked like a simple tavern. To Will's surprise, you could see in through the windows. There was no shame. Men chatted with men, but it didn't look so scandalous. Inside, the atmosphere made Will comfortable. Barrels for tables, sawdust on the floor. The patrons were young men who did look collegiate and didn't seem too bothered by an old schoolmarm like her showing up. Will also knew how mannish looking she'd become in her older age. Maybe that helped.

Buddy ordered them a round.

"So what's this place called?"

Buddy held up his hands as if to say, "don't hit me."

"It's called 'Julius.'"

"Damn Rosenbergs!" Will said.

She drank fast and laughed. Maybe Dolly had it right all along. Maybe life was just a big joke.

"I have an idea. This one you are going to like."

Still trusting Buddy, all these many years later, she followed him. Walking alongside the river, what they called "the piers," she saw so many young men, some girls too, screwing and screaming and dancing and moaning. The smell of the dirty river mixed with marijuana and summer heat felt foreign. It was like she was one of the astronauts who landed in "Herland," someplace completely foreign. Instead of tensing when someone caught her eye she'd take a breath and try to think of what Dolly would do. She'd see this as an adventure. She wouldn't try to analyze it or figure out how to act. She'd just be. They turned left onto a street that smelled distinctly of urine.

The walk-up on 14th Street felt seedy and ominous. A rat crossed their path, dashing from a trash pile to under a Volkswagen. But when Buddy's friends rang them up, it was like coming home. She'd sold her clarinet and had no desire to ever play one again. But the standup piano seemed to glow under the lamplight, and Will asked if she could sit down and play.

Chapter Thirty-Eight

I t was a loft-like space with splintery pillars upon which symbols of all kinds marked the wood. She recognized the male and female symbols, a few Chinese characters, a cross, and a symbol for poison. They were playing jazz, but it was unlike any she'd heard before. It seemed more mature; she didn't hear the winks and gags that the old-timers played. There was less bounce and more experimentation. The musicians were all Black and dressed not in the tuxedos of Will's day, but in bright caftan shirts and ripped dungarees. Most wore sandals. Everything was different.

"They get together to jam. They're not a formal ensemble. Just individual players having some fun," Buddy said.

"Pharoah. Master Plan," the tenor sax player called.

He then blew a sound out of his horn that Will had never encountered before. The band circled wagons around him, making the notes rise high and slip low as if finding the perfect balance on a tightrope. A flute player kept playing a riff, a simple "da-do-da-dooooo" with blowing a twill on the last beat. The whole sound of this new jazz was slower, a few chords followed by a lot of space. Not so speedy and frenetic or slow and lowdown. A completely different frequency. But still … jazz.

"What is this they're playing?"

Buddy slipped in next to her. "They're improvising but riffing off of a song by Pharoah Sanders; he's one of Coltrane's men."

"Coltrane?"

"The closest thing to God the jazz world has ever seen. Sanders played on a bunch of his records, but some say this song is a kind of response to one of the most famous ones, 'A Love Supreme.'"

"It sounds very cerebral," Will said. "And more serious like ..."

"Art?" Buddy said. "Yeah, jazz is considered art now. It was art back then too. But I guess because Black people played it—invented it—the white world couldn't see it that way."

"I don't hear any swing."

"Nah. That's not popular anymore. Jazz has become something more explosive, and yet contained, controlled, a reflection of what's going on in this country—social upheaval, chaos, but much deeper conversations too. It's a lot to take in."

A young woman with tight braids approached. She wore cut-off shorts and a t-shirt with a black fist on it.

"Let me take over, Professor," she said.

"Sure. Will this is Celeste. Celeste, Will."

Celeste looked at her with a knowing smirk.

"You the killer?"

Will must have flinched because Celeste immediately placed a hand on her knee and said, "Hey, I'm sorry. It's okay. Nobody judges anybody here. It's all music. Besides, there's a war going on that we shouldn't be a part of and they're killing people every day."

"It's not the same," Will said.

"It's all relative. This is all an illusion, don't you know? Some call it 'Maya.' It's not real.

A heavy, bearded young man shaking maracas sang the refrain about the creator and a master plan a few times as the tune cooled to a low flame.

"I didn't do it, you know. It was Dolly—my friend—who killed him. I'm not saying that makes me innocent. We were tried together as one under the law, but I just ... I just want you to know. I don't know why I'm telling you this ..."

"Maybe so I won't shun you? I won't. I'm you and you're me. We're all one here. Not just here in this room, but everywhere. We're all just energy responding to the vibration of the music, of the universe."

She felt what Celeste was talking about, and her voice soothed and resonated with its throaty and deep timbre and resonance. Will thought of Pop, long dead, and how he would sit in his study sometimes when she was very young, before Momma got sick. He would write out the letters of the Hebrew alphabet and then look through the Torah, searching for clues as to the meaning in each. She thought of Dolly's father then and how he kept clippings of all the things happening in the world.

Celeste pulled out a marijuana cigarette from her pocket, lit it with the last match in a pack, and passed it to Will after a luxurious inhale.

Will shook her head no.

"Worried about your parole?"

Will smiled, but that wasn't it. She just felt out of place, and there was only so much newness she could take in at her age. Sixty-four! Celeste couldn't have even been twenty-four. Will would have preferred a drink but didn't want to interrupt the flow of the conversation.

"One day all communication will be through sound and light," Celeste said. "The whole world is on the verge of ascension. But first the old world has to completely die ..."

Will must've looked at her funny because Celeste started to laugh.

"I'm sorry," she said. "I know you just got out recently. I don't mean to blow your mind!"

"That's okay." Will laughed. "Is this all about religion? This music?"

"No, no. Not religion. Oneness. Music. It's the primal connection. The primordial drumbeat like Mother Earth's heartbeat. Hey, why don't you just pick up with these guys on the piano? Words are not so important. Music is the universal language."

"Are you going to play too?"

"In a little bit. You do your thing with the boys."

Will put her hands on the keyboard. She could play piano well enough, but was no Dolly. She followed the tenor sax up, up, up into a fast, brainy riff that sounded familiar. She picked up on the chord tone and tried to complement it, but with a twist. She recognized the thread of it running through the whole jam session. This was jazz now. Improvisation with a cool touch. It was like each movement was built on a classical structure, the repetitions were so familiar; but then someone would change them up in a clever way and another would find a way to keep the song afloat invisibly. Her hands moved naturally in a loose way they never had before. Only on Dolly's body. For a moment she felt a squeezing sensation in her chest, like her heart just couldn't take remembering Dolly, remembering the two of them that way. But then the lightness of Dolly started dancing in her fingers, bringing the sneakiest twitch of swing and bebop play to a grown-up exploration of sonic cosmology.

She closed her eyes and allowed a picture in her mind to appear and to lead her to the next image and the next image and the next. Her hands moved as the visuals swirled. She saw the letters of the Hebrew alphabet, notes and chord progressions on sheet music in her mind, colors and lights and patterns in elegant motion. As long as she didn't try to control what would happen next, every moment created a new now. And each moment contained within it a multitude of choices. A flash of Eddie appeared, and she saw the choice she'd made.

Yet she also saw in the darkness of her mind that she still had a brightness to explore, a life force that wasn't dependent on Dolly. She was free in body now with no idea how to liberate herself from the torment of her mind. But no. That wasn't true. Or at least it wasn't a permanent, immutable truth. Will was just beginning to understand jazz and the way it contained everything that exists in the universe and allowed a musician to continually rearrange the notes into new forms, new moments creating a brand new elegant symmetry every time. This was a new world, and Will felt connected to it in this moment. The power of jazz worked like a galvanizing force, bringing her back to life and connecting her to the vast universe in all its mystery, and connecting her to Dolly too, and all the love Will still had to give her.

Acknowledgements

I give thanks to my friends and family especially my beloved child Phoenix; and the following individuals and organizations for their generous help and support: Donna Brodie and The Writers Room; my agent Susan Golomb and Writers House; Jessica Bell, Alana King, Amie McCracken, my editor Melissa Slayton, and the entire Vine Leaves Press family; the Exiles; the PS 117 Gang; Wendy Jo Cohen, Marcy Dermansky, Chris Downey, Scott Duffy, Nanice Ellis, Veronica Gorodetskaya, Matt Howe, Philip Kain, Olga Katsnelson, Liz Kastor, Alice Kornhauser, Clarinda Mac Low, Melissa Marks, John McCaffrey, Carley Moore, Tim Murphy, Ed Pastorini, Steven Powell, Stanley Richardson, Judy Richter, Steven Rosen, Shakti Smith, Mariah Stovall, Claudia Valentino, and Lauren Yaffe. In memory of Anne, always.

CPSIA information can be obtained
at www.ICGtesting.com
Printed in the USA
BVHW071449240622
640596BV00014B/395